DEATH
WITH
HONORS

Forge Books by Ron Nessen and Johanna Neuman

KNIGHT & DAY MYSTERIES

Knight & Day
Press Corpse
Death with Honors

DEATH
WITH
HONORS

A KNIGHT & DAY MYSTERY

RON
NESSEN

AND

JOHANNA
NEUMAN

A TOM DOHERTY
ASSOCIATES BOOK
NEW YORK

DEATH WITH HONORS

This book is printed on acid-free paper.

A Forge Book
Published by Tom Doherty Associates, Inc.
175 Fifth Avenue
New York, NY 10010

Forge® is a registered trademark of Tom Doherty Associates, Inc.

Library of Congress Cataloging-in-Publication Data

Nessen, Ron, date
    Death with honors: a Knight & Day mystery / Ron Nessen and
Johanna Neuman. —1st ed.
        p.   cm.
    "A Tom Doherty Associates Book."
    ISBN 0–312–85594–X (acid-free paper)
    I. Neuman, Johanna. II. Title.
PS3564.E82D43 1998
813' .54—dc21   97–37099

First Edition: April 1998

Printed in the United States of America

0   9   8   7   6   5   4   3   2   1

A NOTE TO THE READER

This is a work of fiction. All of the characters and events portrayed in this novel are either products of the authors' imagination or are used fictitiously.

To Smokey, we miss you

DEATH
WITH
HONORS

CHAPTER ONE

Hollywood!" JERRY KNIGHT shouted when Jane Day delivered her news.

"Hollywood!" the star of the *Night Talker* radio show repeated loudly. "The most corrupting influence in America today, and you're leaving Washington to write screenplays in Hollywood?"

Jane kept her green eyes focused on Jerry, knowing that if she looked around she'd find most of the other diners in the Xing Kuba restaurant staring at them.

She'd deliberately chosen the trendy restaurant just north of Georgetown to tell Jerry about her Hollywood offer on the theory that he would want to avoid the embarrassment of a public argument.

Yet again she had overestimated Jerry's aversion to public embarrassment.

"So much for all the talk about your sacred duty as a reporter to—what is it?—'afflict the comfortable and comfort the afflicted,' " Jerry sneered, stabbing at his spring roll appetizer. "The first time a movie producer waves a little money at you, it's good-bye sacred duty, good-bye *Washington Post*, hello hot tubs in Malibu."

"That's not fair," Jane protested. She shoved her cup of black bean soup away.

Xing Kuba served a quirky combination of Asian and Latin food, advertised as the cuisine of the future. But Jerry's outburst had ruined her appetite.

"There are similarities between journalism and writing screenplays," she argued.

"Really?" Jerry was speaking in his full, orotund radio voice. Jane tried not to think about the restaurant full of people eavesdropping on their discussion. They had been given a table where everyone in the place could see them, right up front in the wide glass window overlooking Wisconsin Avenue.

"Am I missing something?" Jerry asked sarcastically. "Working for that liberal rag is about two steps up from hauling garbage, in my opinion. But covering the White House for the *Post* is at least a more elevated calling than writing screenplays that give Demi Moore an excuse to take off her clothes."

"I'm *not* writing a screenplay about Demi Moore taking off her clothes," Jane protested. "I'm writing a screenplay about a hard-core conservative congressman who develops compassion for the less fortunate after watching his daughter die of cancer because the Republicans cut off the money for research to find a cure."

"You know, maybe you *do* belong in Hollywood," Jerry told her. He signaled the waitress to bring him another bottle of Tsing Tao beer. "The entertainment industry demonizes anyone with conservative views and always makes liberals the heroes. You should feel right at home there."

"I'm glad we finally agree on something." It was her turn to be sarcastic.

They lapsed into sullen silence, pushing the food around their plates, not looking directly at each other. Jane made a pretense of studying the odd photo hanging above their table, two Chinese women tinted in garish 1930ish pastels.

She was not as committed to the Hollywood venture as Jerry assumed she was. At the Xing Kuba dinner, she'd intended to seek his views on the pros and cons of the offer. But when he reacted so derisively, she felt compelled to defend not only the screenplay opportunity but the entire Hollywood establishment.

The offer had come a week earlier in a letter from an independent film producer known for his sensitive treatment of difficult topics. He had offered her fifty thousand dollars to option a long profile she'd written for the Style section of the *Post*, "The Cancer Conversion," which traced the political metamorphosis of Congressman Revell Gates from conservative to liberal after watching his four-year-old daughter suffer and die from rare bone cancer.

And the producer had offered Jane another hundred thousand dollars to collaborate on the screenplay of her story.

Jane was uncertain about accepting.

On the one hand, she didn't want to appear to be cashing in on the congressman's tragedy. Jane had known Gates for years. She had dated him once or twice before he married, and she had used him as a news source. Their friendship was why Gates had been willing to open up to Jane about his child's death. He had trusted her to set down accurately both the public details and the family's private anguish, without making the story maudlin. So Jane worried that she would be exploiting a friend's private grief by turning it into an inevitably sensationalized Hollywood production.

On the other hand, Jane had grown bored covering the White House. The bland and pliant President Dale Hammond had become irrelevant. All the action was on Capitol Hill. The offer to move to L.A. caught her at a moment when she was receptive to a glamorous new career opportunity.

Besides, she felt Russ Williamson and the other editors at the *Post* had become particularly critical of her copy, as if screening it for a "Jerry bias." Ever since she and the conservative talk show host had become an item, she sensed she was being scrutinized closely at the paper. She imagined her colleagues whispering behind her back about whether she was being infected by Jerry's right-wing notions, whether she could objectively cover the White House when her significant other was a FOG, Friend of Grady, the president's outspoken and powerful wife.

Could a conservative and a liberal find happiness in Washington, where everything, even romance, was a political issue?

The waitress removed their appetizer dishes and delivered their main courses, crab cakes for Jerry, a vegetable-stuffed enchilada for Jane.

Was Jerry her significant other? Jane wondered. Was she *his?*

Where was this relationship going, anyhow? Two years of sporadic dating and even more sporadic sex. More time spent sparring over their opposing political viewpoints than making love.

Well, she thought, their modern two-career romance wasn't exactly conducive to long, passionate nights in bed.

Monday through Friday from midnight to dawn, while Jane slept, Jerry was in a radio studio expounding on the *Night Talker* show to the right-wing crazies who idolized him. Then, while he slept all day, she was at work covering the

White House for the *Post*. In the evening, when Jerry woke up, hungry for a meal and a nuzzle, Jane was often on deadline, writing her story for the next morning's newspaper. By the time she'd finished her story and was ready for the meal and the nuzzle, it was almost time for him to head to the studio to prepare for his program.

On weekends, Jerry was frequently away making speeches. And when Dale Hammond boarded *Air Force One* for a presidential trip, Jane followed in the White House press entourage.

The typical lifestyle of many Washington couples. When not otherwise occupied, they spent time with each other.

Jane tended to blame herself for their deficient relationship. Jerry had a reputation as a lech who came on to every woman who crossed his path. So what was wrong with her? Why wasn't he more interested in sex? Probably he didn't find her attractive, Jane fretted, unconsciously dragging her fingers through her tangled orange hair as if that would magically straighten it.

Well, he was no bargain either. Fifteen years older than Jane, fiftyish with thinning hair and a paunch, married and divorced three times. And he was probably the most politically incorrect man in America.

Still, she was attracted to him. She liked that he had convictions and defended them at every opportunity, even though she usually disagreed with his arguments. Jerry certainly was different from the usual mush-mouth Washington men she encountered. Jerry was funny and spilling over with life compared to the gray drones who occupied the city's law firms and Hill offices. The only thing they believed in was winning. Their opinions usually came from position papers written by image managers.

Jane's experience with men, such as it had been, was that

a romance either progressed or it died. There was no status quo in romance. With Jerry, the relationship *was* progressing, ever so slowly. And that was with both of them living in the same area code. If she moved three thousand miles away, Jane figured it would be all over for them.

No matter how alluring the Hollywood offer, she was reluctant to terminate this relationship, for the same reason she was unable to click off a lousy TV movie or stop reading a bad novel. She had to find out how it turned out.

Jerry, at once so maddening and so intriguing. Could Mr. Right Wing be Mr. Right? Shouldn't she stick around to find out?

If Jerry had declared right there in the restaurant that he would be brokenhearted if she moved to Hollywood, and would miss her terribly, she would have turned down the screenwriting job on the spot. Jane realized she'd provoked this discussion to test Jerry's intentions.

And just when she thought he'd flunked the test, Jerry tried to talk her out of leaving. In his own way, of course.

"Hollywood ruins good writers," he offered, shoving aside his empty plate and finishing off the glass of Chinese beer. "F. Scott Fitzgerald, Faulkner. Ben Hecht and Ring Lardner from journalism."

"Jerry, that's the nicest thing you ever said about my writing," Jane replied, genuinely pleased by the roundabout compliment. "But don't worry, I'm not going to be spoiled by Hollywood. I'm going to take the money and run."

"Don't get your hopes up about the pot of gold at the end of the rainbow," Jerry cautioned. "Ever hear of Hollywood accounting? Look at Winston Groom. The movie of his book *Forrest Gump* made millions, maybe hundreds of millions. But he didn't see any of it. Look at Art Buchwald. One of the studios stole his idea for an Eddie Murphy movie, and he had to sue to get any money. Screenwriters are at the bottom of the Hollywood pay scale. Stuntmen make more. Costume designers make more."

"Bottom of the Hollywood pay scale is still higher than the top of the Washington reporters' pay scale," Jane replied.

"Yeah, but in Washington your pay scale and the pay scale of the people you report on is roughly the same, comfortably upper-middle-class," Jerry elaborated. "You're equals. In Hollywood, the people you'll be working with live at a whole different level of wealth. You can't even imagine it. You'll just be one of the hired help, like the gardener or the dog walker."

Was Jerry, in his own curmudgeon's manner, letting her know he didn't want her to go?

"Twice a year my show originates in L.A. for a week," Jerry reminded her, "and I can't wait for the week to be over. Hollywood people give 'shallow' a whole new meaning. You'll hate them. They don't *read*. That producer probably didn't read your Style piece on Gates. He had some graduate English lit student read it for him and give him a twenty-five-word summary. You go to a Hollywood dinner party and their idea of an intellectual discussion is, 'What's really bothering Courtney Love?' Did you know some movie stars hire political consultants to tell them what to think about issues?"

"Which demonstrates how much Washington and Hollywood have in common," Jane opined, taking a sip of after-dinner espresso. "They're both one-industry company towns, populated by colossal egos and single-minded workaholics willing to do anything to climb to the top. Both places depend on perception rather than reality. In Hollywood, the prize is fame and money. In Washington, it's power. But the tactics are pretty much the same. I should feel right at home out there. Hollywood is just Washington with better-looking people."

Jerry laughed out loud at that, breaking the tension of the dinner.

He reached across the faux marble tabletop and took her hand. She didn't care if the others in the restaurant saw his gesture of affection.

"Washington and Hollywood are similar in other ways you're not going to like," Jerry warned her. "They're both full of low-level functionaries with a vastly inflated sense of their own importance. They both freely spend vast sums of other people's money. They're both totally out of touch with the everyday lives of real people. And there's no lasting loyalty in either place. One day you're on top. The next day you're Jane Who?"

They drank their thick coffee in silence for a while.

As she always did when they ate at Xing Kuba, Jane tried to decipher the eclectic ambience of the restaurant. Stools at the bar along the right wall were covered in soiled leopard-spotted shag, like some airport lounge. On the opposite wall, formal columns topped with urns rose up toward exposed heating ducts painted purple. Sixties music played loudly through hidden speakers. The weirdest touch to Jane was the hanging lights swathed in cones of thin white cloth like gauzy stalactites.

The place was eclectic, all right, Jane mused. Maybe the mismatched decor was meant to symbolize some Asian philosophy, yin and yang, opposites attract, something like that. The perfect metaphor for her relationship with Jerry!

"The Kennedy Center Honors ceremony is December sixth," Jerry interrupted her contemplation. "I'm one of the presenters. Want to go?"

"Of course!" she blurted.

Aside from White House state dinners, the annual black-tie Kennedy Center Honors event was the biggest night out of the year for Washington's movers and shakers and wanna-bes, even though ticket prices for the charity show ranged up to five thousand dollars. Staged in the opera house of the capital's massive white marble cultural temple beside the Potomac, each year the event honored five show business figures for their lifetime achievements.

"Great list of winners this year," Jane enthused.

Unlike the Academy Awards, winners of the Kennedy Center Honors were announced weeks in advance. The process for selecting them was never made public. But since most of the winners were in their seventies or eighties, longevity seemed to be the vital attribute. One theory was that a sure way to make the honorees list was to come down with a terminal disease. When composer Stephen Sondheim won the award a few years earlier, he grumped that he felt like construction had begun on his mausoleum.

Jane remembered the year there were complaints about the selection of Aretha Franklin because she was only in her fifties!

"Yeah, this year's winners are the usual triumph for diversity," Jerry proclaimed, reanimated by the opportunity to sound off about one of his pet peeves. "Two men, two women, one gender unknown—"

"Not true," Jane interrupted.

"—One African American, one Asian American, one white American, one white European, one Hispanic American, one actress, one jazz musician, one classical musician, one playwright, one dancer, one Jew, one Catholic, one Muslim, one New Age crystal worshiper, one atheist, one handicapped Native American opera singer—"

"You're exaggerating!" Jane protested. But not by much. Each year, the list of Kennedy Center honorees was relentlessly balanced, politically correct beyond cavil.

"Carla Caldwell, Ludwig Mersch, Aki Omaka, De-Wayne Robinson, Jose Sequeros," Jane enumerated the winners. "Which one are you presenting?"

"Jose."

Jane looked surprised. Jerry presenting the award to a Hispanic jazz innovator? Seemed unlikely.

"We became friends when I was still doing a local talk show in San Diego," Jerry explained. "He lived in Laguna when he wasn't touring. He's a hard-core conservative, you know. His family came to America from Mexico when he was three years old. They had nothing but the clothes on their backs. His father started selling tacos from a cart, saved his money, opened a restaurant, which became hugely popular. I used to eat in the place almost every night. The whole family worked there. Jose first started playing the guitar to entertain the customers. He believes America is the land of opportunity for those who work hard and don't rely on government hand-outs."

"And why were you chosen to present him at the Kennedy Center Honors?" Jane asked.

"I was chosen under an affirmative action quota to make sure that one token white male conservative appears on the program," Jerry replied. He said it with a straight face, so she wasn't sure for a moment whether he was kidding or serious.

"Just kidding," he laughed. "Jose requested that I present his award at the Honors ceremony."

Jerry continually surprised Jane. She fretted that his conservative bombast sometimes edged toward belittling minorities. And now she discovered that he had a close Hispanic friend.

"So, you'll go with me to the Honors ceremony?" Jerry asked.

"Sure." She was already worrying about what to wear. The big night was slightly more than two weeks away.

They lingered over a second round of espresso and a shared plate of fried plantains rolled in sugar. The conversation circled back to her Hollywood offer. They sparred in a desultory way. Jerry didn't ask her, in so many words, not to go. Jane didn't agreed to stay. But she didn't say, for sure, she was going, either.

Jerry looked at his watch.

"Got to go!" he announced. "My show is on the air in an hour. Don't want to disappoint my millions of loyal listeners."

"Your listeners are right-wing nutcases."

"So you say. I still don't want to disappoint them."

CHAPTER TWO

In THE RADIO studio, Jerry Knight hummed up and down the scale and sipped hot tea from a porcelain mug imprinted with his picture and the legend JERRY DOES IT ALL NIGHT. It was his preshow ritual, warming up his vocal cords.

"Testing, one, two, three. Testing. Testing. Stand by for God's gift to the airwaves. Testing. Testing. One, two, three."

On the other side of the glass wall, in the control room, Sammy, the Vietnamese technician, giggled at Jerry's egotistical boast, even though he'd heard it a thousand shows in a row. The technician gave the thumbs-up signal. The host's microphone volume checked out.

"Five minutes to air," Sammy informed Jerry through his headphones.

Next to Sammy, the diminutive K. T. Zorn hopped up on her high stool at the producer's console. She was dressed in her favorite color, black. Knee-high black leather boots, black leotard, short black skirt, black turtleneck, black beret atop her gray crew cut.

"Any friend of Zoro's is a friend of mine," Jerry commented through the control-room monitor.

Same line as always. Jerry's shtick was getting old. Maybe it was time to move on, K. T. thought. She'd worked for Donahue, Rush, Gumbel, and now Jerry. They were all the same. Boys with gigantic egos trapped inside grown men's bodies. They thought they were devastating conversationalists whose most insipid remarks were worthy of endless repetition. Maybe she'd try Oprah this time, or Rosie. Maybe Dennis Wholey on PBS. He seemed almost normal.

"Better get the bandages ready, K. T.," Jerry whispered into his microphone. "It's going to get bloody tonight."

The producer grinned despite herself. The Hollywood director fidgeting across the baize-covered table from Jerry in the studio was the kind of guest the host loved to cut up on the air. Ormandy Stern made popular docudramas that recounted recent history according to the prevailing Hollywood liberal canon. They usually involved convoluted conspiracies among conservative politicians, the CIA, the Pentagon, and Big Business to oppress the long-suffering poor.

Ormandy Stern was red meat to Jerry and his two million rabid right-wing listeners. It would be bloody, indeed.

"One minute to air," Sammy informed the host.

Jerry slugged back the remainder of his tea and hummed up and down the scale one last time.

The host didn't believe in chatting cozily with his guests before going on the air. He wasn't their friend. He was their inquisitor. He wanted them to worry about what was coming. That way, they were likely to nervously blurt out the most self-destructive remarks once the show began.

K. T. never understood why Jerry's guests, knowing what awaited them, agreed to subject themselves to his interrogations. Ego, no doubt. Despite the evidence heard Monday through Friday on the *Night Talker* show, each guest thought he was the one with the wit and adroitness to best Jerry Knight in verbal combat.

Ormandy Stern felt that way. He grinned smugly at the PR flunky who'd accompanied him to the studio. Stern was there to promote his new film. This right-wing troglodyte would be no match for an Academy Award–winning director with a social conscience.

"Fifteen seconds," Sammy warned.

Jerry sprang a gambit he sometimes used to disconcert his guests just before airtime.

"So, is it true that you faked a mental illness for three years so you wouldn't get drafted for Vietnam?" the host asked in a casual tone.

The director opened his mouth to protest. But it was too late.

"Quiet!" Sammy commanded. "Five seconds to air! Four, three, two, one."

The hands of the studio clock aligned at 12.

Midnight. Showtime!

The recorded theme music blared, a boisterous rock melody. After a few seconds, the technician lowered the volume and hit the button on a tape deck for the announcer's introduction.

"It's midnight, and ATN, the All Talk Network, presents radio's most popular all-night talkmeister, Jerry Knight, and the *Night Talker* show, live from Washington, D.C. For the next five hours, sit back and listen while Jerry entertains, informs, and sometimes enrages you. If you're working, studying, or just having trouble sleeping, you are not alone. Ladies and gentlemen, here to keep you company all night is Jerry Knight, the Night Talker!"

The theme music swelled to a raucous climax. The red ON AIR light on the studio wall flashed on.

"Hello! Hello, you night people! You lucky night people, I have come amongst you yet again, the greatest living talk show host in the world. No! The greatest talk show host in the *galaxy*. Here again to lead a mighty army of listeners against the forces of political correctness, against the whiners, the windbags, the femi-nuts, against the nagging national nannies who think normal people like us are too dumb to take care of ourselves, and against the *liberals.*"

Jerry nodded at Sammy. It was the cue to play a sound-effect tape of loud booing.

"We have a very special guest tonight," Jerry continued when the recorded booing had subsided. "The Hollywood director Ormandy Stern. What Leni Riefenstahl was to German Nazis, Ormandy Stern is to American liberals."

"Now, wait a minute—," Stern tried to interject.

"This is *my* show, Mr. Stern," Jerry informed the guest firmly. "I don't tell you how to direct your movies. You don't tell me how to introduce my guests."

The director subsided. Nobody in Hollywood ever treated him that way. He exchanged a troubled look with the PR flack.

"Topic one, how Hollywood promotes violence in America," Jerry announced. "Mr. Stern, in your latest picture, there's a scene—I haven't seen the movie, and I *won't*—but I understand there's a scene showing a gang of teenagers pouring lighter fluid on a homeless man and setting him on fire. Now, since the movie came out, police report three incidents of homeless people being set on fire. Copycat killings, they're called. Aren't you responsible for those deaths? Shouldn't you be put on trial for manslaughter, or contributing to a homicide?"

"That's ridiculous," Stern retorted. "That scene was meant as a symbolic indictment of you right-wing extremists for throwing millions of homeless people into the streets with your heartless budget cuts."

"Well, why don't you take some of those homeless people home?" Jerry asked with feigned reasonableness.

"What?" Stern sounded confused by the question.

"I understand you have a mansion in Beverly Hills with fifteen bedrooms and seventeen baths." Jerry sprang his rhetorical trap. "Sounds like you have plenty of room to give a home to some of those 'millions' of homeless people, instead of merely making a—what was it?—a 'symbolic indictment.' "

"You are worse than I expected you to be," Stern sputtered.

"I hope so," Jerry replied serenely.

K. T. Zorn put aside her ever-present clipboard.

All fifteen lines on her phone console were blinking already and the show hadn't been on the air five minutes.

Oh, yeah. After three hours at the mercy of the Night Talker and his fans, Ormandy Stern would need those bandages. It was going to be great radio, K. T. anticipated. She forgot all about leaving Jerry for Oprah or Rosie.

CHAPTER THREE

SOMETIMES HE'S WORSE than *I* expect him to be," Jane Day proclaimed to the radio in the tiny kitchen of her apartment in the Adams Morgan neighborhood of Washington.

She loved Stern's movies. They usually reflected her own view of society. And now that she was contemplating moving to L.A. to write a screenplay, Jane was eager to learn all she could about the movie business. So she'd been looking forward to Jerry's interview with Stern.

But after two hours of listening to Jerry put down Hollywood over dinner, she couldn't stand any more.

Jane hit the station-selector button on the radio, switching to the sixties music on Oldies 100. A Mamas and Papas song wafted through the cluttered apartment.

Her cat Bloomsbury yawned, stretched, hopped off the sofa, and ambled into the bedroom. He preferred classical music to oldies.

Jane needed to sleep. She was scheduled for an early-morning breakfast interview with the veteran actress Carla Caldwell, one of the winners of the Kennedy Center Honors.

Since the White House beat had become such a backwater for news under the vapid President Hammond, Jane often volunteered to write personality and entertainment pieces for the Style section. She had a talent for turning out illuminating, anecdote-filled profiles, like the Revell Gates article.

Since childhood, Jane had been a fan of Carla Caldwell—both her movie roles and her real-life political activism. Once, when she was young, Jane's parents took her to an anti–Vietnam War rally where Carla Caldwell spoke passionately against the war. In fact, Jane's mother and father had enthralled her over the years with tales of crossing paths with Carla Caldwell in various liberal causes going back to the forties. Caldwell had been a feminist before the feminist revolution, a stalwart defender of women's rights in an industry where women got ahead by behaving like sex kittens. She even dressed the part, wearing pants long before blue jeans became the common fashion statement of Rodeo Drive.

Jane turned the three dead-bolt locks on the apartment door and hooked up the two security chains. Above the sound of Credence Clearwater Revival on the radio, she heard a siren on Eighteenth Street. What was that scuttling noise in the hallway? A mugger? Or a rat?

Adams Morgan was a partly gentrified area of apartment buildings and town houses that had been elegant in the early decades of the twentieth century. Now it was the borderland between the run-down and foreboding Columbia Heights and Mount Pleasant neighborhoods to the east, and the expensive Kalorama section to the west, across Connecticut Avenue.

Jane picked up several days' worth of newspapers from the floor and tidied up the mismatched furniture in her minuscule living room. She fluffed up the flattened sofa cushion where Bloomsbury had been sleeping.

Switching off the lights, she wondered why she hadn't told her parents yet about the Hollywood offer. After all, they lived in L.A. They'd be thrilled to have her living nearby again instead of across the continent. Maybe that's why she hadn't told them. Maybe that was one reason she was ambivalent about accepting the offer.

From three thousand miles away, Mavis Day could only indirectly influence her daughter's life. With Jane in the same city, Mavis would want to reassert full control.

As long as Jane could remember, her mother had pressured her to pursue a career, to succeed, to excel. When Jane exceeded those expectations, Mavis changed her expectations. Now her mother was on her to get married.

Especially in the past five years, since Jane turned thirty, Mavis ever more insistently posed the question, "So, are you seeing anybody?" In every conversation, Mavis pointedly reported on the marital and parental status of Jane's cousins and friends in L.A.

Her mother's entreaties were hard enough to handle via long distance. They'd be a daily trauma to cope with in person.

Jane had lived on her own for more than fifteen years, counting college. If she moved back to L.A., it didn't mean her family would dominate her life again, did it? What if her mother suggested that she move back into the family house? Could she say no? Even if she got her own apartment in L.A., Jane was sure Mavis would drop in a lot, trying to fix her up with what her mother considered suitable men.

"Why is life so complicated?" Jane asked out loud.

In the bedroom, Bloomsbury raised his head. He didn't know the answer to that question, so he went back to sleep.

Jane stood in front of the mirror in the bathroom, wearing her sleeping outfit, a pair of cotton panties and a Run for the Cure T-shirt.

She studied her image in the mirror.

"Ugh."

Jane was feeling ugly.

She combed her fingers through her tangled orange curls.

"Fairy Godmother, please grant me one wish," Jane implored the mirror in a Cinderella voice. "While I'm sleeping tonight, bring me straight blond hair. Or is that two wishes? Anyhow . . ."

Anyhow, if her Fairy Godmother didn't come through—again!—she'd make an appointment with Turgot at George's hair salon in the Four Seasons Hotel.

Using her fingers like a pair of scissors, Jane pretended to snip off the end of her pointed nose.

"That would help," she said miserably.

At least her eyes were okay, big and green. Her best feature.

But her body! Yuck!

Jane pounded her fists on her hips, obvious even under the oversize T-shirt.

Okay, she was going on a diet, starting in the morning. No, wait, she had the breakfast with Carla Caldwell. Starting right after breakfast. She had to lose ten pounds before the Kennedy Center Honors event, or else her black knit dress wouldn't fit. Two weeks, ten pounds. She had to do it. Goodbye muffins, hello grapefruit.

After she washed her face and brushed her teeth, Jane considered phoning her parents and telling them about the screenwriting offer. It was only 9:30 P.M. on the West Coast. Of course, Mavis would ask her if she was seeing anyone. If Jane lied and said no, she would have to listen to a lecture about being too picky. If she told the truth and revealed that she was dating a thrice-divorced conservative closer to her mother's age than to her own, Jane ran the risk of sending Mavis into cardiac arrest.

She decided not to call.

Jane had known Jerry for almost two years. Their first meeting had been a typical Washington encounter, she the pursuing reporter, he the quarry. It was in the parking lot of the National Cathedral following the memorial service for the environmental activist Curtis Davies Davenport, a friend and source of Jane's, who had been bludgeoned to death after an appearance on Jerry's program.

Jane wanted to interview Jerry about what he might know about the murder. But he was uncooperative, to say the least. She ended up calling him a creep. He accused her newspaper of coddling criminals, and drove off in his obscenely large Cadillac without answering her questions.

Despite that antagonistic start, they eventually teamed up to solve Davenport's murder—with the timely intervention of D.C. Homicide Detective A. L. Jones—during a staged confrontation with all the suspects on Jerry's *Night Talker* show.

After that, they dated whenever their irregular schedules permitted. Their arguments over politics, ideology, and lifestyles gradually softened into a friendlier bantering. Jane was definitely attracted to this eccentric man, although she was often appalled by his exuberantly self-confident political incorrectness.

A year after they met, Jane and Jerry teamed up again with Detective Jones to solve the poisoning of CNN correspondent Dan McLean at the annual White House Correspondents Association banquet. The murderer was caught when he struck again during a ceremony at the Vietnam Memorial Wall.

When Jane returned to the memorial from filing her story on the killer's capture, she found Jerry leaning against the overpowering black marble wall of names, weeping for his colleagues lost in the war. It was the first time he'd allowed her to see his hurt and pain. She took him in her arms and comforted him.

That night, at his apartment, he cried again as he related to her his Vietnam experiences.

She kissed away the tears. Then she led him to the bedroom and comforted him in the most personal way she knew.

Jane shook away the memory of their first lovemaking. It would only make it harder for her to decide what to do about the Hollywood offer.

Bloomsbury hopped off the bed and walked stiffly back to his place on the couch. When she was in one of her moods, he waited for her to fall asleep, then curled up against her warm body.

Before switching off the bedside light, Jane clicked on her clock radio to see how Jerry's interview with Ormandy Stern was progressing. It was going pretty much as she'd expected.

". . . gives you the right to present a perverted view of history, an ultraliberal history of conspiracies and events that never occurred, to an impressionable generation of young people who have no firsthand memories of that period?"

"My view of history is *not* perverted," the director argued.

"Not perverted?" Jerry shouted. "Not perverted? J. Edgar Hoover as a drag queen? Henry Kissinger having an orgasm when he watches videotape of B52's bombing Hanoi? You don't call that . . ."

Jane clicked off the radio. She set the alarm for 6 A.M. and turned out the light.

Mom, I want you to meet the man I'm seeing, Jerry Knight.

She tried to imagine that scene. She couldn't.

CHAPTER FOUR

A HALF MILE away from Jane's apartment, D.C. Homicide Detective A. L. Jones signaled the morgue-wagon crew they could remove the body. The crime scene evidence team had finished its work.

Not that there was much evidence. The victim was a black male in his early twenties, dressed in nondescript khakis, a Hoyas T-shirt, and black-and-red basketball shoes. No ID in the pockets. Shot three times in the chest and shoulder.

Someone had called 911 anonymously and reported the shooting. When the call came in shortly before midnight to Homicide headquarters in the Municipal Center at Third and Indiana, A. L. was on the bubble, meaning he was the detective designated to investigate the next murder in the nation's capital.

Arriving at the scene in his vanilla white Ford detective's car, Jones had found the dead man sprawled on his back in the middle of Chapin Street a half block from Malcolm X Park. Despite the late hour, a dozen children, as young as four, stood at the curb solemnly staring at the body and at the rivulet of blood running into the gutter.

Probably wasn't the first murder victim they'd seen, A. L. thought. But such scenes didn't seem to provide a cautionary experience. Washington averaged more than a murder a day. Most of the victims were young black men. In fact, homicide was the leading cause of death among that group. A. L. and his fellow detectives rarely caught the perps.

"Oh, Lord," the detective groaned wearily, his stubby body sagging against the car. He was tired, as usual. He'd started the day in court, waiting to testify against two crew members, gangbangers, charged with busting an elderly Korean market owner who didn't respond fast enough to their demand for the cash in the register.

After A. L. had waited three hours for the case to be called, the public defender won a continuance for the crew members, their third.

Jones had spent the rest of the day staking out a basketball court off Minnesota Avenue hoping to catch a man suspected of throwing his girlfriend's newborn baby into a Dumpster. But the man never showed.

A. L. had been nearing the end of his shift when the call came in about the Chapin Street killing. He used to welcome extra work because it meant extra pay. But because of the city's financial problems, overtime pay had been suspended. There was still plenty of overtime work, just no overtime pay.

Abraham Lincoln Jones was a short, tubby, mahogany-colored man with a straggly gray mustache. His bald head glistened in the street lights. He wore a plaid sport jacket and gray slacks that had been neatly pressed for court that morning, but were now rumpled. A white stubble sprouted on his chin and cheeks.

It was hard to imagine anyone who looked less like his namesake. When he was young, Jones had hated his name. He regularly got into fistfights with other boys who taunted him. *Abraham! Abraham Lincoln!* But now, in middle age, Jones believed he had a special affinity with the Civil War president. Like Lincoln, A. L. was absorbed with the nation's divisions. Black and white. Rich and poor. North and South. Hell, Washington, D.C., was the capital of those divisions, and Jones was their daily witness.

The detective leaned against his car, craved coffee, and studied the sparse notations he'd made in his bent notebook. He had knocked on the doors of every house and apartment on both sides of Chapin Street. Half the residents pretended not to be home. The ones who did open their doors professed to have seen nothing and heard nothing.

Frustrating to Jones. But not surprising. Everyone knew that many of the victims in Washington's murder epidemic were witnesses to earlier crimes who were targeted by gang-bangers and drug boys so they couldn't testify. Dead witnesses or intimidated witnesses meant no convictions.

The detective watched the morgue team lift the bagged body onto their gurney. At this point he could only guess at a motive. Might be drug related. Possibly a mugging. Guy might have fooled with somebody's woman or dissed somebody. Or maybe there was no motive at all. Just a random, senseless thing. The shooter walking along or driving along Chapin Street didn't like the guy's looks, and popped him.

A. L. looked at his watch. Two A.M. He couldn't do much more until morning. He'd check up on LaTroy and sleep a couple of hours. Then he'd squeeze his snitches. And try again to persuade the fearful neighbors to tell him what they knew. A. L., like all cops, promised witnesses they would be protected. But Jones knew he sounded unconvincing.

The detective steered his white Ford south on Fourteenth and swung left onto U Street, toward his apartment in LeDroit Park. He needed sleep. But first, he needed coffee.

Jones turned right onto a side street and pulled to the curb in front of an all-night convenience store. A sign above the barred front windows announced that the place was called the Eleven Store. Not 7-Eleven, just Eleven. Every time the detective stopped there, he wondered whether it had once been a 7-Eleven that had been downgraded. Or maybe it was in a probationary period on its way to becoming a full 7-Eleven. A. L. never asked.

He pushed against the security grill covering the front door, went in, and poured hot black coffee into a cardboard cup.

Oh, man! He needed that.

A. L. chatted with the clerk awhile, learning that a man who had been sent to Lorton for seven years for stabbing a kid to death for his Redskins jacket was back on the streets and up to his old tricks. Jones made a note to check him out. The clerk was reluctant for the detective to leave. A cop in the convenience store meant a few minutes of respite from the ever-present danger.

But A. L. needed sleep.

Back in the car, Jones flipped on the radio. That clown Jerry Knight was giving some Hollywood dude a hard time.

The detective had crossed paths with Knight twice. Two years ago when he was investigating the murder of a guest after an appearance on Knight's program. And last year, when he was trying to find out who poisoned a CNN reporter at the White House Correspondents dinner. Knight and that weird orange-haired girlfriend of his, the newsie from the *Post,* had gotten in his way in both cases by trying to play amateur detectives.

"Well, Mr. Stern, if you're so interested in violence in American society," Knight said to his guest on the car radio, "you should bring your cameras to the streets of Washington. You'll find plenty of violence here. And your fellow liberals who run this city, and the cops and judges they hire, aren't doing a damn thing to stop it."

"Oh, bullshit!" Jones shouted at the radio. He switched to WHUR. Soothing soul music filled the car.

At Eighth, U Street bent off at an angle to the right and became Florida Avenue. The night streets here seemed menacing even to an armed detective who had seen most of the cruelties humans could inflict on each other. Hostile eyes glared from doorways and alleys. Here and there human forms lay on the sidewalk. Were they dead? Overdosed? Just drunk and homeless? Two men hassling a third turned and ran at the approach of the detective's headlights.

Jones turned left on Third Street and left again on Elm. He pulled the white car into a spot at the curb. Howard University Hospital loomed at the end of the street, built on the site of the old Griffith Stadium, where his father had taken him to watch Negro League baseball games when he was a boy. Just north of the hospital was the university itself. Many of A. L.'s neighbors in LeDroit Park were students and professors.

Jones had attended the university for a year, hoping to become an architect. But when his father lost his job with Amtrak, there wasn't enough money for tuition and A. L. had been forced to drop out. Still, A. L. considered himself to be a knowledgeable amateur architectural historian of Washington's neighborhoods and buildings.

For instance, he knew that LeDroit Park's Victorian mansions and tidy town houses had been built after the Civil War as a white suburb of a much smaller national capital. In the early decades of the twentieth century, LeDroit Park became the dwelling place of middle-class and prosperous blacks. It still was, although decaying neighborhoods lapped at its edges, on the south side of Florida Avenue and to the east, near North Capitol Street.

A. L.'s apartment was the middle floor of a three-story, turreted town house. He let himself in quietly so as not to awaken LaTroy.

The detective pulled off his scuffed brown loafers and tiptoed to the bedroom door. He listened to the boy's breathing. The bedsprings creaked as LaTroy turned. The boy moaned in his sleep.

Jones had met the fifteen-year-old more than a year ago, when the detective was assigned to investigate the killing of LaTroy's mother. Returning from her all-night job cleaning offices, the woman had accidentally stumbled into a crew of drug boys popping a rival. The next day, the drug boys knocked at the door of her apartment. When she opened the door, they smoked her.

Ignoring the detective's pleas to be cool, LaTroy bought a piece and went after the drug boys. They hit him first.

He took two bullets, one in the left thigh, one in the left shoulder. As a result, LaTroy walked with a limp. A stubborn infection persisted in the wound in his shoulder. A. L. Jones had visited him in the hospital almost every day of his long recovery. Now, the detective drove him to Children's Hospital every Thursday afternoon for treatment.

LaTroy had only one relative in Washington, a sister who was a cokehead and worse. After their mother's murder, the boy had lived with the sister for a while in her disgusting hovel of an apartment on Fifteenth Street in the Kingman Park section.

After LaTroy's shoot-out with the drug boys, Jones insisted the boy move in with him. LaTroy didn't resist.

Something about the boy suggested to A. L. that LaTroy had the adroitness to escape the killing streets and make something of himself if encouraged and helped. In some way, LaTroy reminded Jones of himself.

A. L. had hung with a bad crowd for a while after he dropped out of Howard, got into trouble, saw his own brother wasted while trying to hold up a liquor store. The draft and service in Vietnam had saved Jones.

Back from the war, he'd joined the police department. In those days, his goal had been to save his city from the rising tide of drugs and crime. A quarter century on the streets had deflated his ambition to a more realistic size. Now all he wanted to do was stay alive long enough to retire. And, if he could, save this one boy.

LaTroy turned again on the bed.

A. L. Jones draped his jacket, slacks, and shirt over a chair. He washed up in the dark and lay down on the couch in the living room in his underwear.

As he did almost every night, the detective played with different scenarios for escaping from the battlefields of Washington. Tonight he drifted into sleep imagining life in the little North Carolina town where his mother's family had come from and where he still had many relatives.

CHAPTER FIVE

JANE ARRIVED EARLY for her 8 A.M. breakfast with Carla Caldwell at the Aquarelle restaurant in the Watergate Hotel. Most of the medal winners and other participants in the Kennedy Center Honors ceremony were put up at the hotel for the two weeks of festivities and rehearsals leading up to the Sunday show.

The Aquarelle was one floor below the lobby, reached by a curving staircase. The actress had not yet arrived, so Jane requested a window table, ordered coffee from the attentive waiter in white jacket and black pants, and pulled from her oversize tapestry shoulder bag an envelope of clippings on Carla's life to review while she waited.

But the breathtaking view through the window next to the table distracted Jane from her preparation. The Potomac River, looking gray and frigid, flowed past placidly on the far side of Rock Creek Parkway. The mammoth white marble edifice of the Kennedy Center loomed next door. And in the distance, across the river, rising over the Roosevelt Island sanctuary, the twin towers of *USA Today*, nemesis of the *Post*.

Jane forced herself to refocus her attention on the envelope of clippings, provided by the *Post*'s librarian, Ravi Bahrami. She had to get ready for her interview with Carla Caldwell. The clips traced Carla's career, beginning with her role as Maud Jones, a ravishingly beautiful farm girl defiantly standing up to the town banker trying to repossess her family's Nebraska spread—and possess her lithe body—in the depression-era melodrama *A Child Shall Lead Them*. A yellowed 1934 gossip column reported rumors in Hollywood that the seventeen-year-old actress was living with the movie's director, three times her age.

Shuffling through the clippings, Jane jotted notes in her reporter's pad about Carla's parade of hits—she soon became known universally by her first name alone. An Academy Award for the World War II film *GI Josephine* in which she portrayed a woman who went to the front disguised as a man. An Academy Award nomination for *Strike!*, an early-fifties movie about South Carolina textile workers battling for fair wages and humane working conditions.

And then, for the next twenty-five years, no mention of movie roles. Instead, the clips were all about Carla's political activities. Carla leading a Save the Rosenbergs march. Carla testifying before Joe McCarthy. Carla arrested while taking part in a civil rights sit-in, and arrested again for chaining herself to the White House fence to protest the Vietnam War. Carla almost drowning while trying to block a whaling ship on the high seas.

Jane looked at her watch. Twenty minutes after eight. If the actress didn't show up in ten minutes, Jane would phone Carla's room. She worried that she might have misunderstood the time or date of the interview.

The clippings showed that in the late seventies, Carla's acting career was suddenly reborn in character roles. She won a second Academy Award for her portrayal of Dr. Geneva Harrington, a feisty frontier doctor battling racist and sexist ranchers to treat Indians in the post–Civil War West.

Jane scribbled a reminder to mention in her profile that the causes extolled by Carla Caldwell's screen characters were similar to the causes she championed in real life.

"Hello, I'm Carla," said a husky voice beside Jane.

The reporter looked up from her notebook.

Carla Caldwell stood beside the table, looking smaller than she did in her movies. The tuxedoed maître d' fussed at her side, as obsequious as if he were attending royalty.

Jane scrambled up and extended her hand. The actress shook it with a firm grip.

"Sorry you had to wait," Carla apologized as the maître d' arranged her in her chair. "I was on the phone with Nelson and I couldn't get him off the line."

Nelson who? Jane wondered.

"South Africa is—what?—six or seven hours later," Carla explained. "If I don't talk to him in the mornings, it's too late his time."

Nelson Mandela! Jane wrote it down.

The maître d' hovered nearby, waiting to take their orders himself, not trusting the celebrity to an ordinary waiter.

The actress requested a cup of hot water and a slice of melon. Jane had intended to order baguette French toast with pear compote and maple syrup. But in light of Carla's spartan meal, she settled instead for the low-fat zucchini-and-carrot muffin from the healthful "elective cuisine" section of the menu.

Jane knew from the clips that Carla was over eighty years old. She looked sixty. The actress wore no makeup, as far as the reporter could tell. The spidery lines encircling her brown eyes were much less pronounced than they appeared in caricatures of Carla's face. Her white hair was done in a no-nonsense bob.

She was dressed simply in brown corduroy pants, a taupe sweater, a creamy patterned silk scarf wound around her neck, and lug-soled hiking boots. Jane wondered whether she had selected her outfit because it blended nicely with the Aquarelle's mustard yellow walls. But Carla didn't seem to her to be the type who paid much attention to fashion.

Carla's look and apparel were plain, unadorned, proletarian. Except for the ring on her left pinkie finger, a large ruby encircled in diamonds on a band of white gold.

A gift from one of her many lovers, no doubt, Jane guessed. She'd ask about it later.

"So, you are from the *Post,*" the actress began when their breakfasts had been placed and the maître d' had been persuaded that they had everything they needed for the moment and he could withdraw.

"Katie Graham's letting her newspaper get too damn moderate for my taste," she pronounced, not waiting for Jane to respond. "I've told her so to her face. Editorials sound *Republican* sometimes."

She made the word sound like an obscenity.

"Of course, it's the only paper left in Washington, isn't it? Unless you count that piece of conservative garbage," referring to the *Washington Times.* "I can remember when there were a half dozen newspapers here. The Kauffmann family and the Noyes family with their *Evening Star.* Never could make up their mind what they stood for. The *Daily News.* There was a working person's paper, all right. And, of course, Colonel McCormack's *Times Herald.* Absolute fascist. Nazi stuff. McCormack had that niece of his, Cissy Patterson—

niece? or daughter?—had her running the paper. Truly the most awful person I ever met."

Carla Caldwell rambled in her throaty voice.

Holding her knife in her right hand and her fork in her left hand, European style, the actress sliced a generous chunk from the bright orange cantaloupe and popped it into her mouth.

Jane took advantage of Carla's momentary silence to formally introduce herself.

"I'm Jane Day, Ms. Caldwell. I normally cover the White House for the *Post*. But I'm such an admirer of yours that I talked the Style section into letting me write a profile in connection with your Kennedy Center Honors award—"

"I know who you are, child," the actress interrupted. "I read your stuff. How *do* you stand covering that spineless toad we have in the White House now? The wife is really pulling the strings, isn't she? Gertrude Hammond. Grady. Whatever she calls herself. She's the power behind the throne, isn't she?"

"That's the general consensus." Jane grinned, flattered to be treated like a confidante by such a famous star.

"It's bad enough having one Neanderthal in the White House," Carla declared. "With this bunch, we've got two."

She paused to cut another slice of cantaloupe.

"I hear you've sold your Revell Gates story to Sheldon Berman for a movie," the actress resumed.

Jane was surprised she knew.

"I have, but how'd you know that?"

"I make it my business to know *everything* that's going on in Hollywood," Carla whispered conspiratorially. "How do you think I've survived out there for so long? Are you going to accept Sheldon's offer to write the screenplay?"

Jane was surprised again.

"I'm thinking about it," she replied. "I can't decide. I'm

tempted. But I don't know anything about Hollywood. What's your advice? You know the movie business."

"I've survived in Hollywood for more than sixty years," the actress confided in her husky voice. "Follow Carla's four rules and you'll be fine. Take their money. Don't trust a damn one of them. Do only what you believe in. And keep your legs together. Well, three out of four ain't bad."

The actress laughed deep in her throat and Jane joined her.

Carla flagged the adoring maître d' for more hot water.

Jane wasn't sure how much time the actress had allotted her. So she was anxious to start her interview.

"Did you always want to be an actress?" she asked.

Jane need not have worried about time. For the next two hours, Carla Caldwell recalled her long and eventful life, seemingly reminiscing to herself, all but oblivious of Jane's presence.

Carla began at the beginning, telling Jane how she had been born in Oklahoma just ten years after it became a state, the daughter of a grain dealer. She won a local beauty contest at fourteen and would have won the state contest except she lost out to an older girl who was fooling around with one of the judges. Carla vowed then never again to allow her fate to be determined by the whim of a man.

She landed a bit part in a quickie Western being filmed in the hills near her home. When the movie company left town, Carla left with them.

Carla related her life in Hollywood, movie by movie, role by role, man by man. Her account was filled with vivid anecdotes from her life in the film colony. Jane became so mesmerized that twice she forgot to make notes. Intertwined with the movie stories were tales of Carla's political activities.

"I was called to testify by Joe McCarthy, that son of a bitch," the actress spat. "It was a nightmare, a circus. Hordes of photographers screeching at me, practically in my lap. TV lights shining in my eyes. And McCarthy, drunk, a fat, unshaven lout, demanding that I identify the 'communists' in Hollywood. I wouldn't tell him a goddamn thing. Nothing. I wouldn't even give him the satisfaction of taking the Fifth Amendment."

Jane knew that from reading the clips.

"I hoped he would cite me for contempt of Congress and send me to jail. That would have been a cause célèbre, wouldn't it? But I was too big a star then. He was afraid to touch me. He did intimidate some of my fellow actors, though. To save their own skins, they gave him the names of people they attended meetings with in the thirties and forties. I hate the goddamn squealers! I've never spoken one word to any of them all these years. And I never will. I've never spoken to Ronnie Reagan, either, since the day he took over the Screen Actors Guild. Even when he was in the White House. He was a third-rate actor and a fourth-rate president."

Jane scribbled frantically in her notebook, trying to get all the juicy quotes down, her eyes glued on Carla's face. Her miniature tape recorder was rolling, but Jane never quite trusted technology.

"Not all my experiences in Washington were bad," the actress murmured throatily, her face softening into a dreamy grin. "I met the great love of my life here. *The* great love of my life."

Jane searched her memory for some politician linked to Carla Caldwell. Of course, the actress had been photographed with all the liberal icons of the last half century: FDR, Henry Wallace, Truman, Kennedy, Nader, McGovern. But Jane couldn't recall reading anything in the clips about a great romance with a Washington figure.

"And we managed to keep it a secret," Carla explained. "No one knows."

"Who was he?" Jane asked reflexively.

"Child, are you deaf?" Carla retorted, but not harshly. "I said we kept it a secret. And we mean to keep it a secret."

"He's still alive?"

"Of course he's still alive," the actress laughed. "Still alive, still rich, and still handsome."

"Will you tell me his name off the record?"

Carla threw back her head and laughed.

"Jane Day, I may be an actress. But I'm not stupid. I've been giving interviews to reporters since before you were born—probably since before your *mother* was born. I'm not going to fall for that old trick."

"Will you ever reveal his name?"

"I might, in my memoirs," Carla replied teasingly.

"When are you going to write your memoirs?" Jane pursued.

"I *am* writing them."

Carla stopped. She looked like she'd said something she hadn't meant to say.

"That part's off the record, about writing my memoirs," she ordered. "*Really* off the record. It hasn't been announced yet."

"But you said it," Jane objected. "You can't put it off the record after—"

"It's off the record!" the actress snapped, her husky voice now tough and insistent. "Off the record or I call Katie Graham."

"Mrs. Graham isn't going to—"

"Off the record or I call her."

Jane was sure the *Post's* publisher would never interfere in the news content of her story. Still, these two matriarchs of the liberal establishment obviously were close friends. Why take a chance? Jane had plenty of other material for her profile. And she'd try to confirm the memoirs angle independently with a source in the publishing industry.

"All right," Jane agreed. "If you say you meant the memoirs thing to be off the record, it's off the record."

"Thank you, child," the actress smiled on Jane. But her manner didn't seem as warm and winning as it had been when the interview began.

"I've got to go," she announced. "I promised Teddy I'd stop by his Senate office at eleven."

Carla slid back her chair. The maître d' was beside her in an instant, helping her up.

"Wonderful meeting you, Jane. I hope your article will be kind to a frail old lady," the actress said, looking neither frail nor old. "And if you come to Hollywood to write the screenplay for Sheldon Berman, remember Carla's four rules. Three out of four ain't bad."

Chuckling huskily at her own joke, Carla Caldwell walked out on the arm of the beaming maître d'.

CHAPTER SIX

Every december, the Sunday night black-tie Kennedy Center Honors show was the finale of more than a week of celebratory lunches, banquets, cocktail parties, news conferences, and other assorted soirees.

A White House reception, where the President presented the honorees with their medals, had always been held immediately before the Kennedy Center bash. But that tradition, like many other traditions, had been changed at the insistence of the outspoken and independent First Lady, Grady Hammond. In Dale Hammond's first year as President, Grady had decreed that the reception be moved to another evening, because she couldn't stand so many hours at one stretch with insufferably liberal show-business types.

So, on the Wednesday evening before the big show, President Hammond and his wife, Gertrude—she preferred Grady, and her many detractors pronounced it Grate-y—were getting dressed in the family quarters of the White House for the presidential reception for the honorees and members of the entertainment and political communities.

"Dale, you're going to come down hard on them for the junk they're putting on TV and in the movies, right?" the First Lady nagged, zipping up the back of her black sleeveless Bill Blass dress with its high silver collar. She was late, because a meeting at the headquarters of her company, H-Drive Computer Services, near Dulles Airport, had run long.

"Now, Grady," the President said soothingly, in the tone he always used when he was trying to brush aside one of her ideas. "I'll make the point in my own way."

"Which means you won't make it at all!" she said in an exasperated tone. "This is the perfect occasion for you to confront Hollywood for polluting our popular culture and poisoning our children's minds with sex, violence, and disrespect for traditional values. Everybody who's anybody in show business is downstairs waiting to hear you tell them how great they are. Nail 'em! On camera. It'll be a great issue for your re-election campaign. You'll force the Democrats to defend the junk coming out of Hollywood because they can't afford to lose the campaign contributions from the entertainment industry."

"I'm going to say something about the values imparted by the movies and television, and by popular music," Dale assured her, slipping into his double-breasted formal jacket. "But not as strongly as you'd like."

"You should have heard Jerry Knight rake Ormandy Stern over the coals on his program the other night," the First Lady told her husband. "He doesn't pull *his* punches when he goes after the liberals. Why can't you be more like Jerry?"

"Well, maybe after I leave the White House, I'll become a radio talk show host," the President said with a straight face. "Gordon Liddy and Oliver North did it."

"Dale, Dale," Grady laughed resignedly, straightening his black silk bow tie. "You're too nice to be President."

"Probably."

Dale and Grady Hammond stood arm in arm, contemplating their reflection in a large mirror in their bedroom.

"Jack and Jackie we're not," the President commented.

"Thank God," the First Lady exclaimed.

They went out into the central corridor running the length of the third floor of the White House, turned right, and swept toward the wide marble staircase that curved down to the ceremonial rooms one floor below. A Secret Service agent stationed at the top of the stairs spoke into the microphone in his shirt cuff, alerting his colleagues below that Teddy Bear and Manhandler were on the way.

Halfway down the stairs, the First Lady paused momentarily to smile at the oil portrait of one of her predecessors, Nancy Reagan, hung there at Grady's insistence. Nancy had been fiercely protective of her husband and hadn't taken any crap from the Washington establishment. A role model.

As Dale and Grady reached the landing at the bottom of the staircase, the red-jacketed marine band, arrayed in the marble foyer just inside the North Portico, struck up three rousing ruffles and flourishes, then blared out "Hail to the Chief." The sound of the brass bounced off the vaulted ceiling.

Dale weakly saluted the band. Grady winked at one of the trumpet players, whose off-duty jazz group she sometimes hired to play at private parties for friends.

As soon as the musical salute ended, the President and First Lady descended the final three steps, turned left, and crossed the red-carpeted main hall to their places outside the Blue Room. On their right were an American flag, a bust of George Washington on a black marble column, and a phalanx of military aides, social secretaries, and Secret Service guards.

To their left were more aides, secretaries, and guards, a blue-and-gold presidential flag, and the bust of some obscure diplomat Grady could never remember.

The receiving line of several hundred people, snaking through the Red Room, the Green Room, the Blue Room, and the State Dining Room, inched forward to shake hands and exchange a few words with Dale and Grady. And, of course, to have a picture taken by the ever present White House photographer.

The guests were an odd assortment of politicians from the administration and Congress, corporate executives being repaid for their financial contributions to the arts and to the campaign, and show business luminaries honoring their own.

Grady hated receiving lines, especially their rigid protocol and numbing inanity. Husbands always preceded wives, even if he was a vacuous nonentity and she was a Noble Prize genius. A blue-uniformed military aide asked each person in line his or her name, then whispered it to the President and First Lady, as if translating some foreign language. By the time all the guests had filed past, Grady's back would hurt, her right hand would ache, and she would have exceeded her maximum toleration for meaningless small talk.

The First Lady had devised little strategies to survive receiving lines. For one thing, she purposely mispronounced the names of people she didn't like. And she refused to speak at all to anyone she *really* didn't like, such as the actress in the inappropriately low-cut gown who lingered too long and smiled too flirtatiously at Dale. The woman's nipples were practically showing!

Another of Grady's survival tactics was to hold up the line for minutes while she chatted amiably with low-level nobodies just to disconcert the self-important somebodies.

When the five Kennedy Center Honors winners came

through the line, Grady greeted them with cool formality, except for Jose Sequeros, whom she kissed. He had campaigned for Dale.

Carla Caldwell returned Grady's coolness by lowering the temperature another ten degrees.

When the receiving line had at last ended and all the guests had taken their places on the wobbly gold chairs in the East Room, Grady stepped out of her high heels and rested her feet for a moment on the cool marble floor of the hallway.

Back in her shoes, she and Dale strode into the East Room, to tepid applause.

The First Lady took her place in the front row while Dale mounted the low stage erected in front of the marble fireplace. The five elderly honorees were seated in gold straight-backed chairs lined up across the stage. The President slipped behind the podium set up on the left side of the riser and withdrew his typed remarks from the inside pocket of his tuxedo. He refused to read from a TelePrompTer for fear that the operator would scroll the words too fast and he wouldn't be able to keep up.

"Honorees, distinguished guests, friends," the President began. He read a citation for each award winner, traced their careers, talked about their places in the pantheon of American artistic expression. At the end of each citation, he draped around the neck of the honoree a multicolored ribbon from which hung a heavy gold medal.

Grady glanced around at the audience while Dale droned on in his flat speaking style.

It was easy to tell the political types from the show business types by their clothes.

All the Washington men wore identical uniforms of black tuxedos, white formal shirts, and black bow ties. The Hollywood/Broadway men were garbed in every hue of the rainbow and in every combination of formal, informal, grunge, and bizarre. One man she recognized as the star of a popular TV sitcom had on black satin trousers, sandals, and a T-shirt printed to look like a tuxedo jacket and tie.

The contrast between the women was even sharper. Female politicians and the wives of politicians were mostly decked out with unmemorable evening gowns in subdued colors. Some of the actresses and the girlfriends of actors, Grady noted disapprovingly, were arrayed in wisps of cloth that barely covered their tits and asses. The East Room looked like the dressing room for a Las Vegas chorus line!

The Washington types and the show business types eyed each other with curiosity and envy, the First Lady thought. The politicians were dazzled by Hollywood's glamour and money, but repelled by the trashy popular culture it produced. Hollywood was impressed by the politicians' power, but scornful of their philistinism. An old, unresolved love-hate relationship, Grady mused.

She picked out Jerry Knight several rows behind, and flashed him a smile. He grinned back. She'd met the talk show host when Dale appeared on his program several times during the campaign, one of the few media outlets where Dale's conservative views weren't treated with derision.

Grady suspected Jerry had a crush on her. He made room on his show for the First Lady whenever she felt the need to sound off about some outrage. Which was often.

Grady looked at the back of the room, where the press was penned. She imagined they were concocting negative stories that would make Dale sound like a jerk while falling all over themselves to flatter the show business types.

The President had finished his homages to the five Kennedy Center honorees. Grady turned her attention back to the podium. If he was going to denounce the movies and TV for purveying trash, it would be now.

"To paraphrase one of my predecessors, this is one of the greatest gatherings of talent in the White House since Thomas Jefferson dined alone," Dale read from his script. There was a polite titter of laughter.

"Or since one of your fellow actors *lived* here," the President delivered the topper.

A collective sound arose from the Hollywood contingent at the reference to Ronald Reagan, not quite a hiss.

Dale ignored their hostile reaction. But Grady shot a withering look in their direction.

"Your talent is to entertain, to delight, to amuse and amaze, to educate, to elevate the human spirit with the beauty and inspiration of your music, your dance steps, your writings, your plays and your movies and TV programs."

Hell, he wasn't going to chide them for their junk, Grady concluded.

"But sometimes some of you misuse your God-given talent to appeal to the baser parts of the human spirit," Dale pronounced blandly.

Wait a minute! Maybe he was!

"Too often, I'm afraid, your popular entertainments, your avant-garde creations, even your more traditional forms of creativity, are drenched in gratuitous violence, casual sex absent of love, every form of deviancy, and contempt for the values of others who do not share your views."

There was a rustling sound in the audience.

"I speak these words as a firm adherent to the First Amendment," the President continued. "Under our system, guaranteeing unfettered expression, you are free to create and perform whatever your talent and mind can conceive, short of outright obscenity. But I also speak these words as a believer in the adage that just because you *may* portray the brutish side of human behavior doesn't mean you *should*. I am particularly concerned about the effects of exposing our children and young people to a never-ending tidal wave of violence and smut and disrespect for traditional values in your movies and television programs and music."

Grady, beaming now, glanced at the audience. The show business people were exchanging frowns.

"Therefore," Dale droned on, "on this night when we honor the best, the very, very best that our culture has to offer the world, I challenge you to clean up—"

"You have no right to denigrate the performing arts and the creative arts in this manner," Carla Caldwell called out in her husky voice, rising from her gold chair on stage. "It is censorship you are proposing, sir. Censorship, plain and simple. Conservative censorship. *Fascist* censorship. It has been tried before, to silence the creative, to silence those of us who oppose your right-wing policies, to silence the people who look ahead to the future, not back to a Norman Rockwell past, a Dwight Eisenhower past that never existed. But we shall *not* be silenced!"

Carla whipped off her medal and flung it at the President's feet.

"In the name of the people," she proclaimed, "I will not accept an award from a man with such a small mind and such a cold heart."

The ancient actress flounced off the stage, up the center aisle, and out of the East Room.

The audience buzzed. In the press pen, Jane Day frantically scribbled in her reporter's pad and worried about missing the first edition.

"Carla Caldwell always was famous for her exit lines," Dale Hammond quipped gamely at his podium.

"Bitch!" Grady hissed in a whisper that could be heard four rows back.

CHAPTER SEVEN

Dale hammond quickly concluded the reception, making no further reference to Carla's outburst and early exit. He congratulated the four remaining awardees again and told them he looked forward to seeing them again on Sunday night at the gala show in the Kennedy Center Opera House honoring the winners.

But nobody was listening.

The East Room was in an uproar.

"Can you believe it?" people asked each other, rehashing the startling scene they'd just witnessed.

The reporters stampeded out of their pen and descended on the celebrities—political and show business luminaries alike—demanding quotes. The tradition that no one at a presidential event moved until the Chief Executive and First Lady had left was ignored in pursuit of the story. Network cameramen yanked their minicams free from their tripods, hefted them onto their shoulders, and swashbuckled about the room for sound bites, trampling on satin-encased toes, snagging the gold drapes.

The Secret Service cleared a path through the commotion for Dale and Grady to make their escape. When the First Lady spotted Jerry Knight, she stopped at his seat and placed her hand on the sleeve of his tuxedo.

"Carla Caldwell is *not* sitting in the presidential box Sunday," she confided to the sympathetic talk show host, referring to the customary seating arrangements for the Kennedy Center honorees at the annual gala. "The only way that woman gets into the box is over my dead body!"

"Don't let her in," Jerry gushed like a love-struck schoolboy. "She doesn't deserve it. She was disrespectful to the President."

Grady squeezed his arm, winked, and swept out of the East Room with Dale.

"I'm so damned proud of you!" she told her husband when they reached the hall. She kissed him wetly on his cheek.

"Uh . . . ahem . . . thank you," the President mumbled.

Jerry gave several TV interviews after Dale and Grady departed, denouncing Carla Caldwell, defending the President's remarks, and adding a few anti-Hollywood flourishes of his own.

He knew the way to break out of the background noise of Washington's endless chatter and make it onto the television news was to offer a short and pithy sound bite that producers would find irresistible, whether it made sense or not.

The sound bite Jerry offered to each interviewer was:

"We pay the sanitation department to pick up the garbage. We don't need the movies and television to deliver more of the stuff."

It would be aired by all three networks, CNN, and *Entertainment Tonight*.

Eventually, the ushers herded the remaining guests, reporters, and cameramen out.

Jerry looked around for Jane. She'd been there a few minutes before, scurrying about, interviewing, scribbling notes, nervously twisting a tangled orange curl around her finger. Now she was gone. Jerry guessed Jane had rushed to the *Post*'s cubicle in the White House pressroom to file her story about Carla Caldwell's outburst.

He went out through the North Portico, turned left, and followed the walkway toward the West Wing entrance to the White House pressroom. He was supposed to wear a security pass on a chain around his neck. But the guards recognized him and waved him by.

Jerry had guessed right. Jane was in her tiny booth pounding on the computer keyboard.

"I hope you're not going to portray Carla Caldwell as some kind of heroine," he announced, poking his head into her cubicle.

"Jerry, please!" Jane screeched, not taking her eyes off the screen. She was obviously uptight. "I haven't got time for this. I'm ten minutes from deadline. Go away!"

"It's nice to be wanted," he replied.

"I mean it, Jerry! Get out of here or I'm going to call a guard."

She typed at a furious clip.

"Okay," he sighed. "I'm gone. Do you know who's writing the story for the *New York Times*? Maybe *she'll* want to hear the quote I got from Grady."

He started walking away.

Jane stopped typing and looked at him for the first time.

She was on an adrenaline high, her green eyes jumping with excitement.

"Wait a minute!" she shouted after him. "What quote? What did she tell you?"

"She said she wasn't going to let Carla Caldwell sit in the presidential box at the Sunday night performance," Jerry reported. He felt a tinge of guilt for divulging the First Lady's private comment. But he thought it would make Grady look good, standing up to the actress who had publicly disparaged the President.

And the quote would give Jane an exclusive tidbit for her story. Maybe that would put her in a better mood for a while, make her less prickly toward him.

"Grady said the only way Carla would get into the box was over her dead body," Jerry continued. "That's a quote, 'over my dead body.' "

Jane jotted the quotes on a scrap of paper.

"What else?" the reporter demanded. "What else did she say?"

"That's it."

Jane scrolled to the top of her story on the computer screen.

"I've got to insert this high up," she said, talking more to herself than to Jerry. "It'll make Grady look petty and ungracious."

"Petty and ungracious?" Jerry repeated. "Is that your approach? Petty and ungracious because she refuses to offer hospitality to a woman who's publicly insulted her husband? Wouldn't you act the same way if someone insulted your husband?"

"I don't have a husband."

"Well, how would you react if somebody insulted me?"

"People insult you all the time," Jane replied, "and it

doesn't bother me at all. *I* insult you all the time, and it doesn't bother me."

She hit the ENTER key on her computer keyboard to make room between the second and third paragraphs of her story for the First Lady's juicy quotes.

"How can you defend—"

"Jerry," she cut him off, "I've got five minutes to write this insert, proof my piece, and transmit it to the paper if I'm going to make first edition. Sit down somewhere and wait."

Well, he thought, that was an improvement over "Get out of here or I'm going to call a guard."

"Don't identify me by name as the source of Grady's quote," Jerry instructed, concerned now that the First Lady might be displeased with his leak when she saw it turned against her in the *Post*. "Just attribute it to 'a source close to the First Lady.'"

Jane gave him a disgusted look, but nodded her agreement.

Jerry wandered out of the cubicle area and into the White House press briefing room, a messy miniature theater furnished with rows of shabby fold-down chairs. At the far end of the room, on a raised stage, stood the podium from which press secretary Garvin Dillon conducted his daily skirmish with the White House press corps.

Jerry sat in one of the fold-down chairs in the front row. The name tag said it was normally occupied by Helen Thomas.

Reporters and cameramen bustled around him, chattering about the astonishing scene in the East Room. Some congregated at the door to the left of the stage, which led to Garvin's office, clamoring for White House reaction to Carla Caldwell's denunciation of the President.

Jerry picked up a discarded newspaper and read yesterday's news while he waited for Jane.

She was on the phone in the *Post* cubicle, arguing with Russ Williamson, her editor.

"Well, if CNN had such great reaction from Richard Dreyfuss, insert some of his quotes into my piece," she snapped.

"How come *you* didn't get reaction from Dreyfuss?" Russ asked from the *Post* newsroom five blocks away.

"Because I was getting reaction from Kevin Costner and Jessica Lange," she replied tartly, "*and* I was writing you a goddamn story in time for the first edition."

"Where'd you get the Grady Hammond quote?" Russ asked. "It's dynamite, if she really said it."

"I got it from a source."

"Somebody you trust?"

"Yes."

"Who was it?"

"Somebody I trust!" The pressure was getting to her.

"We'll need a lot more for—"

"I'm coming back to the office," Jane interrupted. "I'll work the phones, gather more material, and I'll rewrite for the final."

"Okay, sounds like a plan," the editor concurred. "And when you're done, I'll buy you a nightcap."

"Sorry, Russ," she told the editor, who had amiably pursued her ever since she came to the paper. "I ran into Sean Penn at the reception and he invited me to spend the night with him. Maybe another time. Why don't you go home to your wife for a change?"

She hung up.

Jane found Jerry in the briefing room.

"I've got to go back to the paper," she advised him. "I'll try to call you before your show."

"Haven't you got time for a quick dinner?" he asked,

sounding disappointed. "I don't have to be at the studio until eleven P.M."

"I can't. This is a big story and Russ Williamson is pushing me for a lot more details."

"You're going to trash the President for speaking out against sex and violence on TV and in the movies, aren't you?" Jerry asked, knowing the answer.

"I sure am," Jane replied cheerily. "Why does he think he can impose *his* standards on everybody else?"

"You *approve* of—what is it?—six point two acts of violence per half hour on television? You *approve* of letting children watch scenes of graphic sex?"

"I approve of freedom of choice, letting people watch whatever they want to watch, letting them create whatever they want to create," Jane replied. "It's called freedom of speech. Ever hear of it?"

"This junk is debasing American society!"

"Please! Thank goodness for Carla Caldwell. She had the courage to stand up and tell the President to his face what she thinks of his right-wing diatribe."

"Her statement was a *left*-wing diatribe!"

"Her statement was a historic protest against censorship of free expression!"

"What she did was disreputable!" Jerry exploded.

"What she did was wonderful!" Jane retorted.

Jerry stared at this strange and maddening woman, whose politics he abhorred and whose affection he craved.

As he often did, he resolved the argument with a joke in an exaggerated radio voice.

"I'm just guessing, now, but I'd say we've still got a way to go before we reach consensus on this issue."

Jane laughed, kissed him on the cheek, and headed toward the door of the pressroom for a late night at the *Post*.

It was bad enough when they lived in the same city and their conflicting schedules prevented them from spending time together, Jerry brooded. If she moved to Hollywood, he would see her—what?—twice a year?

"Jane," he called.

She turned back.

"What is it now?"

"I'm sorry you're too busy for dinner. Maybe tomorrow?"

Jane saw that his eyes were trying to tell her something he couldn't say in words.

She came back to him, squeezed his hand, and kissed him again.

"Tomorrow for sure."

CHAPTER EIGHT

JERRY TOOK A cab to his penthouse apartment in Rosslyn, on the Virginia side of the Potomac River just across Key Bridge from Georgetown.

He changed out of his tuxedo, heated a frozen pizza in the microwave, and ate it in his underwear in front of the TV, watching CNN's coverage of the White House incident.

After consuming the pizza and a bottle of Anchor Steam beer, sent to him by a fan in San Francisco, Jerry dressed in corduroy slacks, sweater, loafers, and brown leather jacket. He called a Red Top cab to take him to the studios of the All Talk Network on M Street in the revived West End section of Washington.

His tiny producer, K. T. Zorn, was already at the studio when he arrived an hour before airtime. She was there when he left each morning and she was there when he came back each night.

When K. T. heard about Carla Caldwell's histrionics on

CNN, she had immediately canceled Jerry's scheduled guest, a foreign policy dork who wanted to plug his new book on the central role of France in twenty-first century Europe.

Consulting her overstuffed Rolodex, K. T. had booked a new guest. He was the Reverend Harlow Baskin, executive director of SOS—Stamp Out Smut—an organization dedicated to cleansing the movies, TV shows, and popular music of sex, violence, profanity, and any other prurient content.

The producer figured that five hours of Jerry, the crusading Reverend Baskin, and Jerry's rabid listeners all dumping on Carla Caldwell and defending Dale Hammond would be a lot more lively than a discussion of France's world role.

When Jerry arrived at the studio, he praised her for the substitution.

"You're a genius, K. T.," the host said, patting her gray crew cut, which was level with his chest.

"You say that as if it comes as a big surprise to you."

The first thing Jerry did each night when he arrived at the ATN studios was to sample the hate mail he received by the bagful.

"Listen to this one," he commanded K. T. and Sammy the technician. " 'You are a big, fat, lying, right-wing scumbag with the brains of baboon.' I don't think I'm so fat, do you?"

Sammy giggled. K. T. ignored Jerry's nightly recitation. She continued to go through the preshow checklist on her clipboard.

The host read next from a postcard.

" 'Compared to you, Rush Limbaugh is a voice of moderation.' Well, there's one I can agree with."

Jerry lifted another letter from his pile.

"Please crawl back under the rock from which you slithered and stop polluting the air with your hateful and cacophonous caterwauling.' Look at the letterhead. It's from a

Haaaavahd professor! 'Cacophonous caterwauling. It's the first time I've ever been accused of 'cacophonous caterwauling.' "

K. T. thought she might find out if the Rosie O'Donnell show had any openings for producers.

Jerry soon grew tired of the hate mail and dumped the whole stack into the trash can.

He wandered into his office and dialed Jane's apartment. Her answering machine was on. He hung up without leaving a message. She was probably still at the *Post* finishing up her Carla Caldwell rewrite. Jane didn't like him to phone her at the paper. She didn't want her colleagues to be reminded that she was friendly with America's most conservative talk show host.

Jerry leafed through that morning's edition of the *Washington Times,* the capital's other newspaper, whose conservative slant matched his own views.

"Jerry," K. T. shouted from the control room. "Pick up line four."

"Who is it?" Jerry avoided talking to his fans off the air. Some of them were so far out they made *him* uncomfortable.

"The Bitch."

Uh-oh. Jerry's latest ex-wife, Lila. A call from her at this hour could only mean she was drunk, and angry.

"You son of a bitch!" Lila greeted him.

"And a very pleasant good evening to you, too, Lila." Jerry spoke with excessive sweetness because he knew that would further enrage her.

"I saw you on TV spouting off at that thing at the White House!"

"Spouting off? You mean offering my keen analysis of the President's brilliant speech?"

"You were there with *her,* weren't you?"

"Who's *her?*"

"Jane Doe—Jane—whatever the hell your latest bimbo's name is. You took her to that Kennedy Center thing at the White House, didn't you?"

"You mean Jane Day? No, I didn't take her to the White House 'thing.' "

Which was strictly true. He hadn't taken her. She was there covering the story.

"Is she young enough for you?" Lila screamed. "Maybe you should try some high school girl."

"Lila, I'm not—"

"You never took *me* to the White House."

The longer the conversation went on, the louder Lila's voice grew. Jerry was holding the phone at arm's length and he could still hear her. He could picture her in their old house in Chevy Chase, a glass of bourbon in her hand, white spittle forming in the corners of her mouth as she grew more and more agitated. Her tirades had depressed him when they were married. Now he found them entertaining.

"Well, Lila, I would have taken you but they don't allow falling-down drunks into receptions at the White House."

"I'm not a falling-down drunk!" she screamed.

"Sorry, sorry," he said soothingly. "I meant they don't allow blind staggering drunks into the White House."

"You are a rotten son of—"

"Good night, Lila. I hope you and Mr. Jack Daniels have a very pleasant evening together."

He hung up.

"Fifteen minutes to air, Jerry," Sammy called from his technician's console.

Three marriages, three divorces, Jerry thought ruefully. Three strikes and you're out. He would never marry again. He couldn't afford it. Couldn't afford the cost in money, or in anguish, guilt, and remorse for his own mistakes.

But with Jane . . .

Jerry dialed her apartment one more time. Still no answer.

Damn. By the time he got off the air, she'd be asleep. And when her alarm went off, he'd be asleep. He wouldn't be able to talk to her until he woke up the next afternoon.

Jerry was going to miss Jane if she moved to Hollywood, he acknowledged to himself. He found their relationship comfortable. Although they argued frequently over politics, the repartee was not hostile or nasty. He found their discussions stimulating, energizing. And the sex was relaxed, undemanding. In bed, he didn't feel like he had to prove his acrobatic prowess or his endurance, as he did with the brainless bimbos he used to date.

He would miss Jane. What would he do if she took the screenwriting job? Probably go back to hustling the bimbos, as he had before he met Jane.

Jerry frowned at that unappealing prospect.

Maybe she'd pass on the Hollywood offer. Nah. Jane wouldn't be able to pass up the money, the opportunity to hang out with movie stars, the chance to dwell in the world capital of loony liberalism.

Jerry went into the studio, sat down at his green baize-covered table, and began his preshow routine. He sipped hot tea, hummed up and down the scale to warm up his vocal cords, and tested the microphone by making outrageous comments for the amusement of K. T. and Sammy.

The Reverend Harlow Baskin did not look at all like what K. T. had anticipated. She'd expected an oily-haired tub of a man in a cheap polyester suit, perhaps in neon blue, and cowboy boots.

Actually, he was a tall, distinguished-looking man wearing polished Italian loafers, a well-cut dark wool suit, monogrammed white shirt, and red silk tie that might have run him $125. Maybe the preacher wasn't spending all the contributions to SOS to fight smut, the producer guessed.

But once he opened his mouth, Baskin turned out to be an even more provocative guest than K. T. had hoped for. Egged on by the host, the antipornography crusader pressed all the hot buttons of both the Jerry-philes and Jerry-phobes out there in radioland. Before they hit the first commercial break, every one of the fifteen phone lines for listener calls was flashing.

"What did you think of the President's speech tonight, Reverend Baskin, challenging Hollywood to stop putting so much sex and violence in the movies and on TV?" Jerry served up a soft pitch right over the plate.

"It was a magnificent statement," Baskin replied, in the accent of his native Dothan, Alabama. "Magnificent, and long overdue. For too long, Hollywood has been poisoning our children's minds and debasing our cultural heritage. And the liberals in this country have been condoning it and defending it. Now, at last, we have a President who is willing to fight back against the left-wingers. What Dale Hammond did tonight was to stand up for the values that the real people of this country believe in."

"Carla Caldwell, the actress, didn't think the President was defending American values," Jerry set up another home run ball. "She accused him, right to his face, of trying to impose censorship. She called it 'fascist censorship.' What do you think of that?"

"Carla Caldwell was a communist in the 1930s and

1940s," the antismut crusader confided. "I've got proof of that right in my files. And I have reason to believe she still follows the communist ideology. That's why she defends the pornography that's put out by her friends in the movie business. It's a communist plot to weaken the moral fiber of this country."

"I was at that reception tonight, Reverend Baskin, when Carla Caldwell took off her Kennedy Center medal and threw it at the President," Jerry recounted. "I was horrified that someone could do a thing like that to our elected leader right in the White House, and get away with it."

"That woman insulted our President and she ought not be allowed to get away with it," Baskin proclaimed.

"So, you think they ought to take her Kennedy Center award away from her?"

"Of course they should take it away from her," the reverend declared. "But they should do more than that."

"Like what?"

"We must rid our society of this evil woman. The Bible tells us that God will punish 'the wicked for their iniquity.' Carla Caldwell is wicked and must be punished."

"How?" Jerry asked, hoping for a provocative answer.

"God will show us the way to punish this sinner, to remove her from the society of decent people."

"The Reverend Harlow Baskin of the Stamp Out Smut organization is our guest on the *Night Talker* program tonight, telling what he thinks of the outrageous behavior of actress Carla Caldwell toward the President of the United States at the White House just a few hours ago," Jerry announced. "I was there myself, friends, and I'll tell you, it was the most disgusting performance I've ever witnessed. We'll be back with your phone calls right after these messages."

The host signaled Sammy to trigger the recorded commercials.

K. T., at her producer's console in the control room, grinned. It was going to be another wild night.

Jerry's private phone line buzzed.

The producer alerted him in his earphones.

The host picked up the receiver in the studio.

"Give her hell, Jerry!"

It was Grady Hammond.

CHAPTER NINE

J<small>ANE DAY WAS</small> back in her Adams Morgan apartment, locked in for the night, after completing the rewrite of her story on the White House episode for the morning paper and brushing off one more invitation from her editor, Russ Williamson, for a midnight drink.

She listened to a few minutes of Jerry's *Night Talker* show. But when his guest started quoting the Bible about God punishing the wicked Carla Caldwell, she yelled "Shut up!" at the radio and switched stations to Oldies 100.

Her shout awakened Bloomsbury, the cat, who was sleeping against the pillows on her bed.

She's in one of her moods, he concluded.

Bloomsbury felt the urge for a midnight snack. But that would require getting up, leaving his warm spot on the bed, and walking across the cold floor a few feet to his food bowl. Maybe later.

Jane was too wired to sleep.

She poured a glass of Diet Pepsi and rummaged in the minuscule pantry for the box of chocolate chip cookies. She remembered her diet, and the need to squeeze into her gown for the Kennedy Center gala. She'd only lost three pounds so far and the event was just four nights away.

She left the cookies alone and removed an apple from the refrigerator instead.

She realized that a diet soda, an apple, music by Gordon Lightfoot, and a zonked-out cat weren't sufficient to help her unwind.

Staring at her image in the bathroom mirror only made her feel more forlorn.

She needed to talk to someone.

Jerry.

But he was on the air. He was *always* on the air when she needed someone to talk to, Jane thought irritably. And if she moved to L.A. it would be even worse. He'd always be on the air when she needed someone to talk to, *and* he'd be three time zones away. Let's see, when his program ended, it would be two o'clock in the morning on the West Coast. She'd be asleep. When he woke up in late afternoon in Washington, she'd be in the middle of her workday at the studio. It would be *much* worse than now.

"What am I going to do!" Jane wailed out loud.

Bloomsbury half opened one eye. Definitely one of her moods.

What a mess, Jane thought.

She was a thirty-five-year-old, never-married, less than dazzling journalist bored with daily reporting who had been offered the opportunity to move to sunny Southern California for twice the money she was making now to help write the script for a movie and get her foot in the door of the glamorous entertainment industry. And she was considering turning down that opportunity in order to stay in dirty and dangerous Washington, D.C., the hypocrisy capital of the world, living in a hellhole apartment in a hellhole neighborhood because she was half in love with the paunchy, balding national poster child for the right-wing kook movement who was almost old enough to be her father and had already been disastrously married to three other women.

Was that her dilemma?

Yes, exactly.

She didn't need someone to talk to, Jane concluded. She needed psychiatric help.

The closest thing available at that hour was a phone call to her mother in Los Angeles.

"Hi, honey," Mavis greeted Jane in her always-upbeat tone. "Your dad and I just got home from the movies. We heard about President Hammond announcing he's imposing censorship on the movies. Isn't that awful? Were you there?"

"I was there. I was covering it for the paper."

"Really? Did you see Carla Caldwell throw her Kennedy Center medal at him?"

"I sure did."

"It's about time somebody stood up to these conservatives. The next thing you know, Hammond will be announcing book burning. Carla's wonderful."

"I interviewed her last week for a profile for the Sunday paper," Jane informed her mother. "After what she did tonight, I'll have to do a major rewrite. It was scheduled for the Style section. But now it's such a hot story, maybe I'll make page one."

"Terrific, honey. Terrific. Do you remember when we took you to see Carla at the antiwar rally that time?"

"I remember."

"I adore Carla. She's been speaking out for good causes for as long as I can remember."

"Uh-huh."

"We were trying to get some news about her on the car radio on the way home from the movies," Mavis recounted, "and we picked up this *Night Talker* program. Have you ever heard of it? A man named Jerry Knight is the host. He's awful! He and some religious right preacher were just tearing Carla apart. That Jerry Knight is such a bigot. How can they let him on the radio?"

This conversation was not having the soothing effect Jane had hoped for.

"So, did you go with someone to the White House reception, honey?" Mavis asked.

"Mom! I was working."

"Can't you take a guest even if you're working?"

"No, you can't."

"So, are you seeing anyone?"

"Mom, please. Don't start."

"I'm not starting anything. Can't I ask? You know your cousin Iris is engaged. Just graduated from college. Twenty-two years old. To a lawyer. Already a partner."

"I'm thrilled for her."

"So, what did you wear to the White House, honey?"

"Mom, I've got to go to bed. I'm going to have a crazy day tomorrow updating my Carla profile."

"We're so proud of you, honey. If you'd only find some-one—"

"Good night, Mom. I'll call you over the weekend."

Jane hung up.

She went straight to the kitchen, yanked the box of chocolate chip cookies from the pantry, and ate every one.

All right, everybody goes off a diet once in a while, right? It was only Wednesday night. She'd eat only a salad on Thursday, Friday, Saturday, and Sunday. She'd still be able to fit into her gown for the gala. Really.

CHAPTER TEN

Detective A. L. Jones was in the all-night Adams Morgan 7-Eleven on Columbia Road, about a half mile from Jane's apartment, enjoying a late dinner. It consisted of a greasy half-smoke—an enormous spicy sausage served on an over-size hot-dog bun—a metallic bag of barbecue-flavored potato chips, and a can of root beer. The half-smoke was blackened from rotating for hours under the grill coils.

"Dining at its finest," Jones mumbled to the convenience store manager. The detective mopped grease from his straggly mustache with a white paper napkin.

It was the detective's first chance to eat since noon. That's when he'd received the radio call for a multiple homicide in an apartment on Monroe Street off Fourteenth in Columbia Heights. What a mess. A mother, father, son, and daughter, Hispanic-looking, hog-tied with tape, each shot in the back more than a dozen times. Three crazed dogs running around the apartment yapping and shitting all over the place. A baby in a crib, screaming her head off and shitting all over the place.

It had taken Jones hours to sort out that mess. None of the neighbors would acknowledge hearing or seeing anything, of course. A. L. figured it for a Hispanic drug thing.

"You, take one more."

The Asian manager of the 7-Eleven thrust another can of root beer at the detective. The manager provided free food and drinks to Jones and all other cops twenty-four hours a day. As a result, a couple of police cruisers were almost always parked outside, no matter what the hour. It deterred the street boys from holding up the place, and it gave the residents of the nearby apartment buildings a greater sense of security, too.

"You know that boy, goes by the street name Zip Face?" Jones asked the manager. "Got a big scar down his right cheek?"

"Yeah, I know. He come in sometime."

"Seen him lately?"

"No, not lately."

"You see him, you call me," A. L. instructed. "Got my number?"

"Yeah, I got." The manager fingered the detective's stained business card taped to the wall next to the cash register.

"What he did?" the manager inquired. "Something bad?"

"Yeah, real bad," Jones rumbled in a weary baritone. "I think he's the one cracked a kid at Bertie Backus Junior High School over there in Chillum 'cause he thought the kid was messin' with his girlfriend. Turns out it was the kid's older brother poking her. So Zip Face walks into Eastern High School and cracks the older brother."

"If I see, I call," the store manager promised.

"Appreciate your help," Jones told him.

Recounting the episode made A. L. think of LaTroy, the boy he was trying to rescue from a life on the streets and a likely early death on the streets.

The detective went behind the counter and used the manager's phone to dial his apartment.

No answer. Damn. Where was that boy? Maybe he'd gone to a friend's house to watch TV. After midnight? Not likely. He was out, and getting in trouble, Jones feared.

Please let him be okay, the detective prayed silently.

A. L. dialed again.

"Hello?" LaTroy answered groggily.

Thank God, Jones breathed.

"Where the hell were you?" the detective demanded.

"What do you mean where the hell was I? I was sleeping."

"How come you didn't answer the phone?"

"I did answer. I'm talking to you."

"I mean when I called the first time."

"I don't know. I was *sleeping.*"

"You okay?"

"Yeah, I'm okay."

"Do your homework?"

"Yeah."

"Write your report?"

"Yeah."

"Read it to me over the phone."

"A. L., come on! I want to go back to sleep."

"All right. Leave it out and I'll read it when I get off duty."

"Ah, it ain't nothing to read."

"Just leave it out. And *stay out of trouble* till I get home."

"Hey, A. L."

"Yeah?"

"You the one on the streets, man. *You* stay out of trouble."

"Yeah."

If he could.

CHAPTER ELEVEN

T HE DAY AFTER the Carla Caldwell episode at the White House turned out to be even crazier than Jane had bargained for.

No sooner had she reached her desk in the *Post's* vast fifth-floor newsroom than the newspaper's legendary and profane executive editor, Kirk Scoffield, descended on her.

"Hey, kid," he greeted her in his gruff voice. "Nice story. You really nailed that son of a bitch Hammond."

"Thanks," she replied. The frown on his leathery face suggested he hadn't made the trip to her desk solely to pat her on the back.

"One thing," he rasped. "The goddamn press secretary, Garvin Dillon, won't confirm your Grady quote, about keeping Carla out of the presidential box Sunday. You got a good source?"

"Yes."

"You got a second source?"

"No."

"Well, get one," Scoffield ordered. "I want to hang that pushy bitch out to dry."

The executive editor marched away.

Scoffield loved to expose the clay feet of the high and mighty, but not at the expense of his rigid commitment to accuracy.

Twenty-five years earlier, he had set the same standard for Woodward and Bernstein, two sources for every Watergate allegation. They'd done it. Could she? She'd better. The *Post* had splashed the "over my dead body" quote in bold type in a box on page one. If the White House denied Grady's quote, and Jane couldn't back it up, the reporter would be in trouble. Scoffield might bump her back to covering secondary environmental stories, where she'd started at the *Post*.

Jane needed coffee. She fetched a cup from the kitchen adjacent to the newsroom, accepting compliments along the way from her colleagues for her coverage of the Carla story.

She returned to her desk and dialed Jerry's apartment. Her call was diverted to the apartment-building switchboard operator, who explained that Mr. Knight was asleep and couldn't be disturbed.

Jane told the operator it was an emergency call from the White House and insisted that it be put through to Jerry. It wasn't a total lie, she rationalized. If she'd been in her cubicle in the pressroom, she *would* have been phoning from the White House. And this certainly qualified as an emergency.

"Yeah?" Jerry answered sleepily.

"It's Jane."

"What's the matter?" He sounded *very* grumpy.

"Are you sure Grady Hammond told you the only way Carla was going to sit in the presidential box for the Sunday night gala was over her dead body? Was that her exact quote?"

"Yeah, that's exactly what she told me. Why?"

"Dillon won't confirm the quote and the paper is getting antsy. Did anyone else hear her?"

"She stopped on her way out and said it to me."

"Was anyone else near you who might have overheard her?"

"Well, there was a woman sitting next to me who might have heard her."

"Who was she?"

"Hmm. Let's see, she said she was the wife of an assistant secretary of the treasury, I think—no, wait—assistant secretary of commerce."

"What's her name?"

"I don't remember."

Jane pulled down a directory of government officials from the shelf over her desk.

"Damn, there are a *dozen* assistant secretaries of commerce. Recognize any of these names? Cannon? Devonshire? Greenblatt? Murchison?"

"Jane! It's nine o'clock in the morning. I'm trying to sleep."

"Please help me with this," she pleaded.

His protest subsided.

"Evenrich? Duncan? Bierstock?"

"That's it," Jerry cut in. "Jennifer Bierstock."

"Oh, Jerry, thank you," she gushed. "How can I ever thank you?"

"I'll think of something."

"Good night. Or, am I supposed to say good day?"

It took her an hour to track down Jennifer Bierstock, a lawyer with Williams and Connally.

Jane had to stretch the truth a wee bit to persuade the woman's assistant to pull her out of a deposition to take the call.

Yes, Jennifer Bierstock had heard what Grady Hammond

said to Jerry on the way out of the East Room. Yes, his recollection of the quote was accurate.

Jane zapped a computer message to Kirk Scoffield, informing him that she'd confirmed the First Lady's quote with a second source.

"Good work, kid," he messaged back.

Jane slumped in her chair. An hour and a half—and a pint of stomach acid—to confirm one quote. Journalism wasn't *all* glamour and fame.

And her day was only going to get worse.

Jerry couldn't go back to sleep after Jane's near-hysterical phone call. He tried his usual sleeping potion—two warm beers. But it didn't work.

So he lay on his back in bed in the darkened apartment and thought about Jane. Actually, he thought about what he thought about Jane.

First of all, her looks were nothing special. That kinky orange hair. That nose. Little tits and heavy bottom. He'd slept with dozens of more beautiful girls. *Much* more beautiful girls. He'd slept with an Academy Award nominee for best supporting actress, for Christ's sake!

No, it wasn't Jane's looks that attracted him.

It was her . . . what?

Personality? Nah, her personality could get real shitty sometimes.

It was the intellectual challenge, Jerry decided. Jane was smart, smarter than almost any other woman he'd dated. Certainly smarter than any of his three wives. He could talk to her.

He and Jane disagreed on almost every topic. But he loved their arguments, the clash of wits. He even came on a little more far-out conservative than he really felt, just to goad her, to heat up their discussions.

She was okay in bed, too. Not the greatest he'd ever had, but good. With other women, that's all he'd thought about, getting them into bed. And once he'd screwed them a few times, he got bored and moved on to his next conquest.

He also found Jane's vulnerability appealing. She had so many self-doubts. Not like most of the hard-charging, ball-breaking career women he encountered in Washington. Jerry's reaction to her insecurity was to want to protect her from the cruelties and uncertainties of life.

But he wouldn't be there to protect her in Hollywood. And if there was anyplace where she needed protection even more than in Washington, it was in Hollywood. The liberal establishment out there was going to reinforce all her dumb liberal notions, and add a lot of new ones.

Damn it! Why was Jane leaving *him* for *them?*

Jerry punched his pillow in frustration. He had to get to sleep or he'd be dragging on the air that night. He tried a second dose of his sleeping potion—two more warm beers. And finally, he fell asleep.

Skimming the news wires on her computer, Jane saw that President Hammond's criticism of the movies and TV, and Carla Caldwell's public rebuke, was a story that had developed legs.

It seemed that everyone who was anyone in politics and show business had commented on the controversy with a sound bite, along with all the civil liberties organizations and all the antiporn groups.

Jack Valenti, chief lobbyist for the movie industry in Washington, had announced a news conference for noon. The heads of the three TV networks were holding a joint news conference in New York at 3 P.M.

CNN was running *Breaking News* special reports every

few hours titled "The President vs. the Actress—Battle over Censorship."

And the Reverend Harlow Baskin announced he would mass thousands of protesters outside the Kennedy Center Sunday night if Carla Caldwell wasn't disinvited.

Carla herself had disappeared from sight since stomping out of the White House reception.

The *Post's* morning news executives' meeting decided to assign someone else to cover that day's activities at the White House while Jane stayed at her desk, pulling together all the developments in the lead story for the Friday paper.

On top of that, she was directed to revise her profile of Carla Caldwell for the Sunday paper, expanding it from the standard puff piece on a Kennedy Center Honors winner into a detailed examination of the life, career, and beliefs of the actress who had publicly rebuked a President. Jane would need to extract information from as many people as she could find who had known Carla over the years, both friends and foes.

Jane's first stop was the *Post's* two-level library, established, like a hub, at the center of the newsroom. At the fifth-floor level, the unwalled library provided reporters and editors with ready access to routine reference materials, dictionaries, Who's Who, the *Congressional Record,* and so forth.

Jane needed more detailed and specific information from the past, so she descended a spiral staircase to the library's fourth-floor level, an oasis of quiet and calm compared to the constant hubbub of the newsroom.

One of the librarians, Ravi Bahrami, volunteered to help. He had done research for Jane before. She found him smart, competent, and fast. From his satiny cinnamon complexion and soft black eyes, Jane could never tell how old Ravi was. Since he had a master's degree in library science and a doctorate in history, she guessed he was closer to forty than to twenty.

Ravi had already assembled a more complete packet of clippings about Carla, anticipating Jane's needs. They agreed that while she read through the packet, he would compile a list of names and phone numbers of people who could provide information and anecdotes about Carla's long career as actress and activist.

Recalling Carla's intriguing reference to a Washington lover during the breakfast interview, Jane asked the librarian to be alert in his research for any clue about the identity of a secret romance the actress might have had in the capital sometime in the past.

For a sidebar story she was sure Russ would request, Jane asked Ravi to pull clips on Eartha Kitt, a sexy-voiced expatriate singer who had lectured LBJ about the evils of the Vietnam War back in the sixties at an East Room ceremony, and on any similar White House confrontations in the past.

The reporter's next stop was the office of the *Post's* gossip columnist, Jessie Bell.

In a building where the employees prided themselves on cluttered desks, Jessie won the Olympic gold medal in the messy desk event. Jane guessed that at the bottom of the mound of old newspapers, unanswered letters, torn-out clippings, pink phone-message slips, and dozens of PR handouts might be buried press releases dating back to the opening of *Gone with the Wind* or Marilyn Monroe's visit to the troops in Korea.

Jessie was a plump, fiftyish woman with mousy hair dyed flat black. She'd become a journalist in an era when many female reporters were consigned to feature articles and "women's" lifestyle stories.

When a gossip column called "The Ear" in the old *Washington Star* grabbed the fancy of readers, the *Post* reluctantly countered with its own gossip column, even though it didn't fit with the newspaper's serious image of itself. Jessie was assigned to gather and write the tidbits for the column. She was looked upon by the rest of the staff as a slightly disreputable aunt.

The gossip columnist was fond of Jane, frequently praising her for bringing gender equality to the prestigious White House beat.

And Jane liked Jessie for her irreverent attitude, her wicked laugh, and her treasure trove of Washington secrets.

"So, what do you know about Carla having a love affair with some man in Washington?" Jane asked the gossip columnist.

"Carla would like you to believe she's slept with *half* the men in Washington," Jessie snickered knowingly. "But I've always believed she cultivated that image as femme fatale just to gain publicity for herself. If you want my opinion, she was a lot more interested in pushing her causes than she was in fucking politicians."

Jane looked disappointed.

"Jessie, you're supposed to know everybody's secrets."

"I've heard rumors for years that Carla had a hot love affair in Washington a long time ago," Jessie continued. "One story is that the guy was a lot younger than her. But I don't know who he was."

Jane glanced at her watch. It was getting late. She'd have to put her pursuit of Carla's secret love life on the back burner for the time being.

"Got any ideas for other people I can call?" the reporter asked Jessie Bell. "People who knew Carla in the past?"

"You ought to try to track down Fran Turner," the gossip writer instructed.

Jane thought the name sounded vaguely familiar, but she couldn't place it.

"Her real name's Francis Anklum," Jessie explained. "She's from my hometown in Kentucky. That's how I know about her. She was a movie star in the thirties and forties. She and Carla were great friends then, but also rivals for title of queen of the silver screen."

Jane remembered the name now. She'd seen Fran Turner in an old movie at the Biograph in Georgetown, before it closed. What's his name had taken her there on their first, and only, date.

"I haven't heard much about Fran Turner lately," Jane said.

"Lately?" Jessie laughed. "You haven't heard much about her for *forty years*. She and Carla were both called before Joe McCarthy's committee in 1950-something and accused of belonging to communist front organizations. Somehow, it didn't hurt Carla's career. But Fran was blacklisted in Hollywood. She never got a role in a movie again. She eventually came back to Covington, Kentucky, and taught drama at the community college. She retired about ten years ago."

"Does she still live in Covington?" Jane asked, making notes.

"As far as I know. Get the number from directory assistance. Anklum is A-N-K-L-U-M. If she's not listed, call Terry Pike at the *Covington Weekly Gazette*. He might have her number."

Fran Anklum was not listed.

But Terry Pike turned out to be a rich source of information for Jane. He was just putting the finishing touches on an article about Fran for the next week's *Gazette*. Terry helpfully read the article over the phone while Jane scribbled notes.

One of Fran's former drama students at the community college, Traci Andrews, had gone on to become a minor TV actress, playing the part of a busty lifeguard on *Baywatch,* and later a brain surgeon on *ER.*

As a gesture of gratitude to her former teacher, Traci Andrews had bought Fran a ticket to the Kennedy Center Honors show, and had agreed to pay all her expenses, so Fran could be present when her old Hollywood friend Carla Caldwell received the award.

"Where's Fran staying in Washington?" Jane asked, excited by the prospect of interviewing someone who had known Carla in the early days.

But the small-town editor didn't know the name of Fran's hotel.

This was too good to drop. It took Jane just three phone calls to track down Fran Anklum's whereabouts in Washington.

From Jessie Bell she got the phone number of a gossip columnist in Hollywood. From the Hollywood columnist she got the name of Traci Andrews's publicist. And from the publicist, eager to see her client's good deed reported in the *Post,* she got the name of the hotel.

Traci hadn't cheaped out. She'd put up Fran at the Watergate Hotel, just a block from the Kennedy Center, the same posh hostelry where Carla and the other honorees were staying. Traci must be *very* grateful to her former drama coach, Jane thought.

The reporter's luck ran out with her fourth phone call. There was no answer in Fran's room.

Jane put the number aside. She had dozens of other sources to check in her quest for details on the life and loves of Carla Caldwell. She'd try Fran Anklum later.

CHAPTER TWELVE

F RAN TURNER ANKLUM ignored the ringing phone.

She only half heard it.

The birdlike old woman was preoccupied, watching the CNN coverage of her long-ago friend and rival, Carla Caldwell, and shuffling her old newspaper clippings. Over and over again Fran arranged and rearranged the yellowing stories on the stiff green spread of the king-size bed in her room at the Watergate Hotel.

Nicest room she'd had since the old days, the movie days, when the studio used to put her up at the Waldorf-Astoria when she was in New York promoting a film. And, of course, the studio had rented her the bungalow on the grounds of the Beverly Hills Hotel when she was shooting a picture, so she wouldn't have to drive back and forth from her place in Santa Barbara.

The best room she'd ever stayed in was the Lincoln Bedroom at the White House. Once Eleanor Roosevelt had invited her in appreciation for Fran's help in a war bond drive.

The last time Fran was in Washington she'd had a lovely suite, at the Willard, the old Willard, before they closed it down for so many years.

That was for the hearing.

"Miss Anklum, are you now or have you ever been a member of the Communist Party?" She could still hear the mean voice of Joe McCarthy. "Have you ever associated with members of the Communist Party?"

After the hearing, she'd never come back to Washington. Until now.

And she'd never made another movie, either.

Fran scrambled the clippings and started arranging them again on the bedspread.

It was thanks to Traci Andrews, a former student, that she was in this nice room with a ticket to watch Carla being honored at the Kennedy Center.

Traci was sweet and attractive. She'd phoned and written Fran faithfully over the years since she'd left Covington Community College to seek fame and fortune on television.

About all Fran had been able to teach her was to act natural, to be herself, to stop *over*acting.

It must have worked. Traci was a TV star now. She'd even had her picture on the cover of *People* magazine once. That issue had sold out in Covington.

Fran watched Traci on TV every week and was proud of her success. But she recognized that the girl was no threat to Meryl Streep. Now *there* was an actress!

Still, Fran was grateful to Traci for the hotel room and the ticket.

During her stay in Washington, Fran hoped for the opportunity to meet Carla again after all those years.

She rearranged her clippings again.

Some were from her movie days. The young star in the grainy photos, grinning at Douglas Fairbanks and John Barrymore, bore no resemblance to the white-haired old woman perched on the bed. A couple of the pictures showed Fran and Carla together in Hollywood, their rivalry showing through the smiles.

Fran stared at a torn photo of her and Carla posing on the red carpet outside the 1940 Academy Awards ceremony. They had both been nominated for best actress. Fran won. Her lips curled into a wintry smile at the memory.

Some of the clips were about the hearing.

"Actress Denies She's a Red," blared one headline.

"Senator Calls Turner 'Stalin's Favorite Star,'" read another.

The TV diverted Fran's attention from her clippings. The anchorwoman was introducing another report about Carla:

This is Wolf Blitzer at the White House, where the political fallout continues from last night's dramatic scene between President Hammond and veteran actress Carla Caldwell. The President used a ceremony honoring Miss Caldwell and four other performers for their lifetime achievements to deliver a blistering attack on television and the movies for, quote, gratuitous violence, casual sex, every form of deviancy, and contempt for the values of others, unquote. Obviously, the President's harsh attack was designed to appease the far right wing of his Republican Party. But before the President could complete his speech, Miss Caldwell interrupted him and denounced his remarks as, quote, fascist censorship, unquote. She then walked out of the White House ceremony in protest. Our sources tell us that the First Lady, Gertrude Hammond, is outraged at Miss Caldwell's actions and wants to ban the actress from the gala awards show at the Kennedy Center on Sunday night.

Just like the old days, Fran recalled. Carla was always

throwing a tantrum. About her lines or her billing. Or sometimes about her causes.

The White House reporter was replaced on the screen by the weatherman. Fran slid off the bed, hobbled to the TV set, and turned down the volume. She had never learned how to work one of those handheld zapper things.

The old actress wandered to the closet. Hanging there were two evening gowns, one black velvet, the other maroon satin. Fran had borrowed them from her friend Pete Fleming, the costume and property manager in the drama department at Covington Community College. She could still fit into a four, she'd told Pete pridefully.

She didn't own a gown. Once she'd had dozens, closets full. But she didn't need fancy gowns anymore.

Fran's lined face puckered into a frown.

What if she was denied her chance to talk to Carla again after all those years? The man on the TV had said President Hammond's wife didn't want Carla to come to the Sunday night show.

Fran smiled again, a chilly smile.

Carla would never allow herself to be kept out of the spotlight. She loved the big entrance scene too much. And the big exit scene. Carla would find a way to attend.

Fran debated which gown she should wear for her reunion with Carla. The maroon? Or the black?

The black, she decided. It was more appropriate.

CHAPTER THIRTEEN

Senator Oscar O'Malley also was watching CNN's relentless coverage of the Carla Caldwell controversy in his private hideaway office in the Capitol.

The high windows provided a spectacular view down the Mall to the Washington Monument and the Lincoln Memorial beyond and the gentle hills of Arlington Cemetery beyond that.

Arlington, where his beloved brother had been buried after the assassination.

Oscar O'Malley Jr., Double O to headline writers. Scion of a famous conservative family. In his third term as senator from Pennsylvania, the last O'Malley of his generation. The family's last chance to win the White House until the next generation of O'Malleys—now state legislators and junior bureaucrats—came of age.

One brother killed in Vietnam. One brother lost while sailing in the Caribbean. The only sister a suicide. And Danny, the baby, an assistant secretary of state, assassinated on a peace mission to the Middle East. Now entombed beneath the grass in Arlington Cemetery.

The assassin's bomb had claimed a second victim a year later, their mother, the blessed Mary. Dead of a broken heart, the senator believed.

The old man, Oscar senior, almost ninety, half-mad some said, brooded in his mansion near Scranton, staring out over the scarred hills from which he had gouged the coal that created the family fortune. Oscar junior believed the only thing keeping the old man alive was his burning dream to see his only surviving son elected President.

The senator bore the O'Malley family's distinctive physical traits, caricatured in a thousand political cartoons. The extremely wide jawline. Irish pug nose—*shanty Irish* nose, the old man called it. Rail-thin build. And thick ginger hair. *Washingtonian* magazine had once written that Double O had the best hair in the Senate, until John Warner was elected from Virginia.

Oscar junior focused on the TV screen. CNN was saying something about Carla.

It was just a rehash of what he'd heard previously, so the senator turned his attention to the invitation on his antique desk, his invitation to the Sunday night extravaganza at the Kennedy Center.

As a congressional member of the Kennedy Center's board of trustees, he normally attended, admiring the honorees for excelling at their art. He generally enjoyed the shows, although he sometimes dozed before the long program ended and dinner was served at 11 P.M. His wife, Anne, loved the annual gala. She always bought a new gown for the evening and kept up a running commentary on who'd had a face-lift recently and who was there with whom.

But this year the senator was not sure he would go.

It was because of Carla.

They ran into each other occasionally at conferences and other functions. The actress was invariably friendly, earnestly promoting her latest cause, lobbying him to vote for some pet piece of legislation, even though they were on opposite ends of the political spectrum.

He yearned for her to take him aside, to recall in private the summer of 1954, their summer of love.

But she never mentioned their affair. And that squeezed his heart every time he saw her.

He had been twenty, down from Princeton to spend the summer with his father, who was then commerce secretary in President Eisenhower's cabinet. Carla had been in her late thirties, a great movie star past her glamour-girl days but still captivating. They met at a Georgetown garden party.

Oscar junior was smitten. The day after the party, he delivered a dozen red roses to her suite at the Hay-Adams. She invited him in. An hour later they were in bed together.

Carla was in Washington for several months, promoting nuclear disarmament. He and the actress made tempestuous love in her suite every day, twice a day, three times a day, joyfully sweating in the Washington heat before reliable air-conditioning. In the languor of those steamy summer days, they clutched each other in sultry sensuality.

The senator remembered, and smiled.

On Labor Day, when he was preparing to return to Princeton, she smothered his face in kisses and promised to rendezvous with him again soon, in Washington or New York, or perhaps in Hollywood.

But when the summer ended, so did their affair.

The next time he met her was a dozen years later, when he was a lawyer with the Senate Foreign Relations Committee and she was part of a delegation protesting the Vietnam War.

Carla said she remembered him. But Oscar wondered if she really did.

Seeing her again at the Kennedy Center gala would be a painful reminder, not just of her inexplicable termination of their affair but of the passage of time since that unforgettable summer. Carla was an old woman now, honored for lifetime achievement. Lifetime achievement. It meant her life was almost over.

He was sixty-two. But he felt younger. He had a long life ahead of him. He had the presidency ahead of him if he didn't make any mistakes.

Oscar frowned.

They had kept their affair a secret. Unusual in this age when the media rejoiced in publicizing the most intimate secrets of politicians' lives.

What if their secret was exposed?

How would that play? Would it hurt his presidential prospects?

Voters too young to remember how beautiful Carla was in her younger days might think it kinky for a college boy to have made love to an actress they knew only as an old woman.

And now there was the controversy over her attack on Hammond for criticizing sex and violence in movies. The senator hadn't seen any polls yet on whether the public sided with Carla or the President.

He was worrying needlessly, Oscar assured himself.

How was anyone going to find out about their affair after all those years?

CHAPTER FOURTEEN

I DON'T WANT no damn coffee," LaTroy protested when A. L. Jones eased his detective's car into a loading zone in front of the Starbucks on Nineteenth just north of Pennsylvania Avenue. "Come on, man. Let's go to Mickey D's."

Jones ignored the boy's plea. He switched off the ignition and withdrew the key. The engine coughed a few times before dying.

The D.C. government had stopped providing maintenance for its police cars because it was out of money. A. L. sometimes spent his own money to change the oil in the white Ford. Once, when his battery died, he surreptitiously swapped it at 4 A.M. for the good battery in a lieutenant's car parked in the Municipal Center garage.

Hard times required ingenuity, A. L. rationalized. Yeah, but the times was getting so hard he didn't know how much longer he wanted to fight the system.

"You just coming here to see Shaneta, ain't you?" LaTroy taunted.

"Yeah, that's right," A. L. acknowledged, affectionately shoving the boy toward the door of the coffee shop. "You got something against seeing Shaneta? Maybe I give you a hard time next time you sneak off to see Jasmine. Yeah, Jasmine."

The detective drew out the name seductively.

"Man, get off my case."

A. L. had met Shaneta more than a year earlier, when he'd stumbled into the Starbucks in need of coffee after a meeting at the nearby Secret Service offices during the investigation of the Dan McLean murder. Usually the detective satisfied his caffeine craving at a 7-Eleven or a Dunkin' Donuts. But he'd been so desperate after the early-morning meeting that he'd stopped at the first coffee shop he spotted.

Starbucks had seemed yuppified and expensive to A. L. But, hey, he needed coffee. And he'd met Shaneta.

The pretty, light-skinned young woman behind the counter, with fat braids curled against her head and a saucy sense of humor, had flirted with A. L., attempting to ease his confusion about the many choices of coffee. She'd tried to entice him to buy a chocolate chip muffin.

A. L. had passed on the muffin but he sure was interested in Shaneta.

Because of the demands of the McLean case and the unremitting workload imposed by Washington's murder epidemic, the homicide detective had not gotten back to the Starbucks to see Shaneta for weeks.

But after that, things had gone pretty fast.

Of course, being the informal foster father to LaTroy put a crimp in Jones's social life. But he and Shaneta found ways.

"Come on, man, I know a Mickey D's right near here," LaTroy made a final protest.

A. L. laughed it off, pushing the boy into the Starbucks, crooning, "Jasmine. Jasmine."

Shaneta flashed a big smile when she spotted them.

The Starbucks was nearly empty on a Saturday afternoon. The workers who filled the surrounding office buildings Monday through Friday rarely ventured downtown on the weekends. So the young woman behind the counter had time to banter with A. L. and LaTroy.

"What can I get you two gentlemen?" Shaneta asked in an exaggerated formal tone. "A latte, perhaps? Cappuccino?"

"Just gimme a coffee," the detective grunted.

"Yes, sir," Shaneta responded brightly. "Would you like Sumatran coffee? Haitian? Kenyan? French roast? Kona? House blend? Hazelnut? Vanilla cr—"

"Come on, Shaneta," A. L. interrupted her recitation. "Don't give me no jive. I need coffee real bad. I don't care what flavor it is. Just give me a damn cup of coffee."

Shaneta laughed at his grumpiness. She really did like this man. He sure was different from most of the dudes who came on to her.

She siphoned strong French roast out of its metal thermos container into a cardboard cup, clamped on a plastic lid, and handed it across the counter.

A. L. immediately sucked the hot liquid through the small hole in the lid, burning his mouth. He didn't care. He needed coffee.

The detective hadn't gotten to bed until 6 A.M. He'd been up all night at the scene of a shooting in the Brookland section near Catholic University. A girl about the same age as LaTroy had been killed while riding her bike through an alley near her home. It could have been a gang thing. Could have been a drug thing. Maybe she had accidentally stumbled into a deal going down, or a deal going bad. Or maybe she'd been shot for no reason at all.

A. L. didn't know. None of the neighbors would acknowledge hearing anything or seeing anything.

Jones put his hand protectively on LaTroy's shoulder.

He was determined to save this boy from the plague that was slaughtering Washington's children. LaTroy had come so close to getting wasted once. A. L. wasn't going to let it happen. They had to get out of this city. But where would they go?

"Tell Shaneta what you want, boy."

"I don't want nothing," the teenager grumbled.

"How about some bottled water, LaTroy?" the young woman coaxed. She understood the boy's attitude. She'd gone through this rebellious stage herself, before she'd decided to make something of her life. Shaneta admired the detective's unofficial adoption of LaTroy. If A. L. could save just one boy . . .

LaTroy had seen Shaq and the other NBA stars guzzling bottled water on TV, so it must be a cool thing.

"Yeah, okay, give me some water," he muttered.

Shaneta rang up their order and told A. L. what he owed.

"Damn, that's a lot of money for one coffee and one water," A. L. complained. "I coulda got them for half that at the 7-Eleven."

"You could," Shaneta replied pertly, "but the person who waited on you wouldn't be half as baaad as me."

The detective's lined brown face crinkled into a grin.

"You right about that," he laughed in his rumbling baritone. "What time you get off?"

"Why, sir, we're not allowed to date the customers," Shaneta told him, reverting to her mock-formal tone.

"Come on, girl, don't be fooling with me," A. L. scolded. "What time you get off? Me and LaTroy take you to dinner if it ain't too late."

"Five o'clock."

"Okay. We going to buy LaTroy some clothes and then we pick you up back here."

"Oh, man," the boy protested. "I don't want no clothes."

"Don't give me that 'Oh, man' business," A. L. instructed. "I want you to wear something better to school than them damn baggy shorts."

"Oh, man."

The detective put his arm around the boy's shoulder and steered him out the door.

When they got outside, they found the right rear tire of the detective car was flat.

"Shit," A. L. pronounced.

They jacked up the car, wrestled the tire off, and replaced it with a spare from the trunk. The replacement was just as bare of tread as the flat.

A. L. drove from the Starbucks to a lot on New York Avenue. The yard, surrounded by a high chain-link fence topped with razor wire, held dozens of out-of-commission police cars. The D.C. government didn't have enough money to repair them.

The guard at the gate waved Jones through. He knew why the detective was there.

A. L. stomped through the lot, inspecting the tires on broken-down cop cars.

He eventually found a tire that had a little more tread than the flat. A. L. and LaTroy undid the lug nuts and threw the tire into the trunk of the detective's car. A. L.'s new spare. They disposed of the flat by rolling it down the lane of dead police vehicles until it toppled over.

"The nation's capital," Jones announced sarcastically as they drove out of the yard. "Makes you proud, don't it?"

CHAPTER FIFTEEN

Sunday night. The Kennedy Center Honors gala show. The hot ticket of the year for Washington's VIPs. *The* place to see and be seen. Anyone in the capital's political, lobbying, legal, or journalistic worlds who didn't attend was immediately suspected of being on the skids or terminally ill.

The high-price seats in the orchestra went for $5,000, and sold out months in advance. Even the cheap seats, up in the second balcony of the crimson opera house, at nosebleed altitude, cost $175.

Jerry Knight had insisted on picking up Jane Day at her Adams Morgan apartment in his Cadillac and driving her to the mammoth cultural center as if she were his date. In fact, they were both working, Jane as one of the *Post* reporters covering the event and Jerry as presenter of one of the award winners, legendary jazz guitarist Jose Sequeros.

"You look nice," Jerry offered when she opened her apartment door. From him, it was a lavish compliment.

Reporters and the usually scruffy photographers and TV minicam operators were required to wear formal garb for the Kennedy Center Honors event.

Jane had managed, after all, to squeeze into her black knit dress. She topped it off with a slightly worn black velvet evening cape, complete with hood, which she'd bought at Second Hand Rose, a bargain shop on the second floor of a Georgetown town house that specialized in the cast-offs of Washington's rich and fashion-conscious women.

Snow was falling and traffic was a mess.

"Damn wimps," Jerry cursed the other drivers crawling along nervously.

The snowfall was light, barely a dusting, which melted as soon as it hit the streets. But Washington panicked at even the rumor of snow. On the car radio, a hysterical newscaster announced that suburban schools would be closed the next day and government workers would be granted liberal leave if they were too frightened to drive.

"You know why people here can't drive in the snow?" Jerry asked rhetorically. "Because a lot of them come here from the South, where they've never seen the stuff."

Jane held up two fingers sarcastically. This was the second winter she had heard him expound his theory. Second winter? She had known him for more than two years, Jane realized. Longer than she had known almost any other man in her life.

"Take a taxi!" Jerry shouted at a woman clutching her steering wheel tightly and creeping along K Street at about ten miles an hour. He swerved around her.

"I read your piece on Carla Caldwell in the Style section this morning," Jerry informed Jane, blaring the horn at a driver spinning his wheels ineffectively on an icy patch in Washington Circle. "You should have been tougher on that old bitch. What she did to the President at the White House was a disgrace."

"The only way I could have been tough enough on her to satisfy you," Jane fired back, "would have been to reveal that she personally helped the Rosenbergs steal the atom bomb secrets."

"That *would* have satisfied me," Jerry agreed. "I hate to admit it, but you *did* dig out a lot of information about Carla."

"I dug out a lot of information," Jane replied. "But I have the feeling there's a lot more information I didn't dig out, that Carla didn't want me to dig out."

They parked in the cavernous cement garage beneath the Kennedy Center and agreed to try to hook up after the ceremony.

Jane's first stop was the long driveway on the east side of the Kennedy Center, where a line of black Lincolns, Cadillacs, and Mercedes disgorged the tuxedoed and gowned celebrities of politics and show business, along with the less recognizable captains of industry and entertainment who financed them. The arrivals were illuminated by bobbing lights attached to TV minicams and by the flashbulbs of news photographers and delirious tourists.

In her reporter's notebook, Jane scribbled the names of celebrities sliding out of the limos.

A couple of second-string senators. A cabinet member. An ambassador in colorful robes. Senator Oscar O'Malley. Warren Beatty. Angela Lansbury. A limo-load of well-fed men she didn't recognize accompanied by impossibly thin women with suspiciously smooth faces. Dan Rather. Sally Fields. Another senator, with a much younger woman. Could be his daughter. Yeah, but could be his girlfriend. Jane made a note to find out. Elizabeth Taylor, with an AIDS ribbon pinned to her tent-sized gown. Jane silently promised herself to stick to her diet. Al Franken doing shtick for the cameras. Ethel Kennedy.

The reporter's attention was attracted by chanting from the far side of the driveway. Dodging through the double line of black cars, she arrived at a small park where about a hundred demonstrators marched and shouted, penned in by uniformed policemen and plainclothes security officers.

"Stop the sex! Stop the violence!" the demonstrators yelled, and "Carla must go!"

They waved hand-painted signs reading "Hammond = Decency," "Carla Wins Kennedy Center *Dis*-honor," and "God Will Punish the Wicked."

Their shouts grew louder and their sign waving more militant whenever the television cameras panned them. Softly falling snow sparkled in the TV lights.

Jane picked out the leader of the demonstration, the Reverend Harlow Baskin of the Stamp Out Smut organization, at the center of a semicircle of TV cameras. She tried to wiggle through the press pack to hear what he was saying. But she could catch only snatches of his statement.

". . . poisoning the minds of children, debasing our culture . . . pornography from Hollywood . . . Carla Caldwell and her liberal fellow travelers condone . . . rid our country of this evil woman . . . cast her out like a harlot . . . remove this sinner from the society of decent people . . ."

Jane recognized the same southern-accented rant Baskin had delivered on Jerry Knight's show.

These were Jerry's people, Jane thought.

No, not exactly, she corrected herself.

Jerry was conservative, all right, and agreed with their antismut crusade. But he expounded his views with boisterous charm and considerable good humor.

By contrast, Baskin and his followers seemed filled with hatred and anger, their faces contorted by rage.

If these people could reach Carla, Jane thought with a shudder, they looked like they might really hurt her.

The reporter pondered how to handle the demonstration in her story on the Honors event. Drop a couple of paragraphs into her main piece? Or write a separate sidebar? Better to bury a brief mention of the protesters in the main story. She didn't want to give too much attention to these right-wing kooks.

Jane left the demonstrators, dodged through the arriving limos, and resumed logging in celebrities. She checked her watch. Six-forty-five. Ticket holders were under instructions to be in their seats by seven-thirty, an early start by New York or Hollywood standards. The winter sky was still light. But Washington was an early-to-bed, early-to-rise town.

Jane drifted down the long facade of the Kennedy Center to a quiet spot away from the arriving celebrities. Standing beneath a marble overhang supported by bronze pillars, she withdrew a tiny cellular phone from her black satin evening purse and called in her story for the early edition of the *Post*. Flipping back and forth through her scribbled notes, Jane described who arrived with whom wearing what, ending with a short, bland description of Baskin's demonstration.

She would update her story for the later editions as the event unfolded.

During a break in the celebrity arrivals, Jane ducked through the glass doors into the Hall of States. The flags of the fifty states hung from horizontal staffs near the top of the high walls. A wide red carpet stretched from the entrance to the Grand Foyer at the far end.

Along both sides of the carpet, held back by velvet ropes

strung between gold-colored stanchions, tourists and no-name ticket holders craned to identify the arriving show business and political VIPs. Whenever a particularly well known or popular figure arrived, the spectators applauded and popped their flashbulbs.

At the end of the red carpet, Jane joined the line waiting to pass through the metal detectors. An accepted inconvenience of life in the age of terrorism. With President Hammond in attendance, no gowned Washington grande dame or tuxedoed Hollywood leading man was exempt from the Secret Service's scrutiny.

Cleared, Jane turned left into the Grand Foyer.

No matter how many times she'd been there before, she was always overwhelmed by the scene. The marble-and-gold chamber, twice as long as a football field, crowded with the rich, powerful, and beautiful, was illuminated by eighteen enormous crystal chandeliers hanging from the ceiling three stories above. For the holiday season, the Grand Foyer was decorated with dozens of small Christmas trees festooned with tiny white lights.

A floor-to-ceiling glass wall offered an almost pastoral scene—a gentle curve of the Potomac River and the green refuge of Roosevelt Island on the far shore.

Halfway along the glass wall, facing the opera house, one of the three performing arts halls opening onto the foyer, a colossal bronze sculpted head of John F. Kennedy rested upon a marble column. As always, the impressionistic depiction of the youthful and idealistic president—a saint in her parents' home—brought tears to Jane's eyes.

CHAPTER SIXTEEN

For TWENTY YEARS, the Kennedy Center Honors celebration had followed an unvarying ritual. Since the first five honorees had been presented with their medals by President Carter in 1978 for their lifetime contributions to the performing arts, each season's winners had sat as guests in the President's box and watched their careers celebrated by admiring fellow artists on the stage below.

As soon as Jane entered the opera house, she saw that the ritual had ended. This year, five easy chairs covered in deep red fabric to match the decor of the theater were arrayed on the right side of the stage for the honorees.

Standing against the curving red plush wall, Jane scribbled a description of the new seating arrangements in her reporter's pad. She guessed that Grady Hammond was responsible for the change, her revenge for Carla Caldwell's outburst at the White House.

Jane spotted the First Lady's hard-edged chief of staff, Grace Lindberg, and hurried over to confirm her hunch.

Grace acknowledged that Grady had sent a handwritten note to the Kennedy Center board of trustees the day after the episode declaring that neither she nor the President would attend the gala, and that they would boycott all the Honors events for the rest of Dale's term if Carla Caldwell was seated in the presidential box.

Jane demanded to know if Dale Hammond had approved his wife's threat in advance. Grace Lindberg refused to answer.

The chief of staff did reveal that the board of trustees had held a secret meeting, with Grace representing the First Lady, and had negotiated a compromise. Carla would not sit in the presidential box. But neither would any of the other honorees. They would all sit in special chairs at the side of the stage.

A new tradition was born. An angry First Lady was placated. Another Washington deal was consummated.

For a selfish reason, Jane was glad Carla and the other honorees had been moved out of the presidential box. It corroborated her story that Grady would allow Carla in the box only "over her dead body." Jane would find an opportunity to remind Kirk Scoffield that her anonymous tipster had been right.

The reporter buttonholed every VIP she recognized, seeking comments on the controversy, preferably comments critical of the First Lady and of the President.

Promptly at seven-thirty, a disembodied voice announced over the PA system, "Ladies and gentlemen, the President of the United States and Mrs. Hammond."

The band in the orchestra pit struck up "Hail to the Chief." The audience rose and turned toward the presidential box in the center of the first tier. Dale and Grady Hammond entered, waving to the crowd below. The First Lady, Jane scribbled, had chosen one of her outrageous outfits, a clingy white knit gown, open to her waist in back, with a white feather boa wrapped around her neck.

The applause was tepid, mixed with subdued booing.

"Please welcome," the announcer commanded, "the winners of this year's Kennedy Center Honors. Ludwig Mersch. Aki Omaka. De-Wayne Robinson. Jose Sequeros. And *Carla Caldwell!*"

The elderly winners tottered out from behind the crimson curtain and shuffled toward the chairs set up for them at the edge of the stage. Omaka, a ballet choreographer who'd suffered a stroke two years earlier, leaned heavily on the arm of Robinson, a playwright.

They wore their medals on rainbow ribbons around their necks. Except, conspicuously, for Carla. She was dressed in a plain outfit of silk khaki pants and blouse unadorned by any jewelry except for a ruby-and-diamond ring glinting in the spotlights. Jane remembered the ring from her breakfast with the actress.

The artists were greeted with tumultuous clapping, cheers, and shouts of encouragement, which went on for a long time. If there had been an applause meter, Jane scribbled in her reporter's pad, the score would have been Carla and the other winners ten, Dale and Grady Hammond two.

The orchestra struck up the melodious Kennedy Center Honors theme music, the house lights dimmed, and the announcer introduced the annual master of ceremonies, Walter Cronkite.

Jane slipped out a side door to phone in an update on her story. The unprecedented eviction of the honorees from their customary place in the presidential box, obviously, was the hot news.

Jane returned in time to catch most of the tribute to Ludwig Mersch, a refugee from Nazi Germany who'd become a child prodigy on the cello and later a popularizer of classical music through numerous concerts and recordings.

The Honors program followed a familiar pattern unchanged since the beginning. A short film recounted each honoree's life and career. At the end of the film, the artist rose and received a standing ovation from the audience. That was followed by tributes from friends, colleagues, and protégés in the form of dance, song, instrumental, comedic, or dramatic performances, as appropriate. At the end of the tribute to each winner, the honoree rose and accepted another standing ovation.

At the end of the Mersch segment, there was a pause. Then the announcer's voice boomed, "Ladies and gentlemen, Mr. Jerry Knight."

He walked out from behind the curtains, strolled to a clear Lucite podium, and rested his note cards on top. Jane thought Jerry looked somewhat chubby but rather handsome in his sharply pressed double-breasted tuxedo.

Mixed with the applause, Jane heard some good-natured hissing. She hoped it was good-natured. Jane prayed silently that Jerry would not be too outrageous.

Her prayers were not answered.

"Ladies and gentlemen," he began in his full radio voice, "I am standing before you tonight because of the Kennedy Center's affirmative action program. I am the token middle-aged angry white male conservative."

More hissing. This time Jane was sure it was not good-natured.

"Typical reaction from a bunch of Hollywood and Washington liberals," Jerry sneered. "You people are all in favor of freedom of speech, as long as it's certified politically correct by the liberal thought police."

Jane cringed against the wall. Jerry was being more offensive than she'd expected.

TV cameramen, taping the event for playback on CBS during Christmas week, crept down the aisles on their knees, recording Jerry's reproach and the audience's reaction.

Jane looked up at the presidential box. Dale and Grady Hammond seemed to be the only two people in the opera house who were enjoying Jerry's castigation.

"But I wasn't invited here tonight to tell you what I think of your commitment to the First Amendment," Jerry continued.

"That's for damn sure!" a voice shouted in the darkness.

The heckler received scattered applause and laughter. Jerry ignored the taunt.

"I was invited here tonight to pay honor to a great musician and a great American, a man I am proud to call my friend, Jose Sequeros."

A wizened brown man in an ill-fitting tuxedo rose from his chair among the honorees, pantomimed an *abrazo* to Jerry, and waved to the applauding audience.

"Jose came to America as an immigrant, as my grandfather did, and as the parents and grandparents and great-grandparents of so many of us did. Jose was three years old when his family came from Mexico and settled near San Diego. His father built a pushcart with his own hands, from materials he scrounged. He sold tacos from that cart while Jose's mother cleaned hotel rooms and his older sister sold tickets at a movie theater. They saved their money and opened a restaurant. Jose taught himself to play the guitar to entertain the customers. By the time he was a teenager, Jose Sequeros was one of the finest jazz musicians and composers in the world. And he still is."

Jane found herself moved by Jerry's account.

"My friend Jose is a great American success story," Jerry declared from behind his see-through podium. "His family is a great American success story. And they achieved it without any help from the *government*. No welfare. No handouts. No *programs*. They did it on their own, following their dreams, saving their money, instilling in Jose and his brothers and sisters a commitment to education and to excelling in whatever they did. This family didn't rely on government *help* or government *pity*. And they sure as hell didn't let the government or anyone else convince them that they were *victims*. Ladies and gentlemen, watch and listen—and learn from—the life story of Jose Sequeros!"

The house lights darkened. On a giant screen at the back of the stage the video biography of the jazz musician began with a grainy sepia still of a dirt street in a Mexican town.

Jane let out her breath. Jerry's presentation was over. He hadn't embarrassed himself too badly, she thought. Of course, he wouldn't think he'd embarrassed himself at all.

The Sequeros segment included tribute performances by another great jazz guitarist, Charlie Byrd, by a hot Mexican mariachi band, and by singer Gloria Estefan.

The next tribute, to playwright De-Wayne Robinson, consisted of scenes from his gritty dramas of black urban life acted by well-known Hollywood and Broadway stars.

Then came intermission. Jane dashed to the terrace overlooking the Potomac to file another update from her cellular phone.

Conscious that her editors at the *Post* were wary of her relationship with the conservative talk show host affecting her reporting, Jane went out of her way to depict Jerry's remarks as outrageously over-the-top. She knew she'd have to deal with his hurt feelings when he read her story in the morning.

After the break, the stroke-crippled ballet choreographer Aki Omaka was honored by members of the American Ballet Theater dancing several of his works, Suzanne Farrell and José Limón performing solos.

There was another pause before the final tribute of the long evening.

The voice of the PA announcer proclaimed, "Ladies and gentlemen, Mr. Steven Spielberg."

The producer-director praised Carla Caldwell for devoting her life to fighting on behalf of justice and truth, for resisting efforts to stifle and censor the arts, and for tirelessly supporting the downtrodden, both through her roles and through the causes she championed.

Spielberg was followed at the Lucite podium by Senator Ted Kennedy.

"As you know, Steven has devoted the last few years to exposing the horrors of the Holocaust," Kennedy told the hushed audience. "It's not an exaggeration to say that without the conscience and courage of Carla Caldwell, latter-day Nazis here in Washington might today be imprisoning artists and performers whose soaring imaginations are creating works that are unacceptable to tiny and timid minds."

"Bullshit!" Jane heard a muffled exclamation from backstage. It had to be Jerry!

A movement in the first tier caught the reporter's eye.

Grady Hammond was leaving the presidential box! The First Lady was publicly expressing her indignation at Carla Caldwell by walking out!

Jane scribbled notes at a furious rate.

"Ladies and gentlemen," Kennedy concluded, "tonight we honor our real First Lady, the First Lady of the stage, the First Lady of the screen, the First Lady of a better world we all hope to build."

The aged actress rose slowly from her dark red chair and bowed regally.

The audience went wild, standing and applauding for five minutes, demonstrating its support for Carla.

Jane looked up toward the presidential box. Dale Hammond applauded slowly and methodically, his face deadpan.

The tribute to Carla consisted of excerpts from her most famous films and plays, and from her most famous political speeches, re-created by a chorus of adoring actresses. Her recent outburst at the White House was not included in the recreations.

Instead of the usual rousing finale, the Honors show ended with all the entertainers who had participated—except Jerry Knight—filing onto the stage and facing the audience without speaking as a silent protest against President Hammond's speech condemning popular culture.

After three minutes of silence, the performers turned their backs and walked off while the audience once again applauded madly.

The orchestra struck up the Kennedy Center Honors theme music.

Cronkite intoned his annual accolade to the honorees:

You have graced our stages, you have graced our lives, you have graced our history. Now it's time for you to take another bow for us to show our gratitude.

Jane dashed out to file her final update.

CHAPTER SEVENTEEN

THE CONCLUDING EVENT of the Sunday night Kennedy Center gala each year was a candlelit supper for the high-priced ticket holders in the Grand Foyer beneath the gigantic chandeliers. But by the time the show was over, it was past eleven o'clock, and Monday was a workday for the lobbyists, lawyers, and government officials. So most of them did a little table-hopping, a little schmoozing, and slipped away to their homes in Chevy Chase and McLean without staying for the supper.

Done revising her story for the final edition, Jane decided to seek out Carla Caldwell to congratulate her and, perhaps, to pick up a few more juicy quotes.

A Kennedy Center PR aide directed Jane to Carla's designated table. But the actress wasn't there.

"You know Carla," an old-time actor at the table laughed. "She's probably back in her dressing room fixing her makeup. She'll wait until everyone else is seated and then she'll make her big entrance."

Jane headed backstage.

She would stop in Carla's dressing room briefly, then find Jerry.

The reporter felt remorseful that she'd lampooned his presentation in her story out of concern for retaining the approbation of her colleagues at the newspaper. This was certainly a complicated relationship, she reflected.

The backstage entrance to the opera house was a set of double doors off the Hall of Nations near the driveway entrance. A sign affixed to the door proclaimed OPERA HOUSE STAGE DOOR. PERFORMERS AND STAFF ONLY. But with the President and First Lady gone and the show over, security was loose. Jane's press pass got her through.

An inner set of doors displayed another sign, in red, warning performers to lock their dressing-room doors when leaving. Crime backstage at the nation's cultural palace? Jane wondered. Not likely.

A musician packing away his trumpet directed her to Carla's dressing room.

Stagehands were already noisily dismantling the set.

Jane was amazed at how high the ceiling soared above the stage. She craned her neck like a gawking tourist, peering up into a dark cavern five stories high, crisscrossed with lighting grids, catwalks, hoisted curtains, and suspended scenery.

Jane rapped lightly on Carla's dressing-room door.

No answer.

The door was slightly ajar.

Jane pushed it open a few inches and peeked through the sliver.

She found herself looking at the inside of the door and her own eye, reflected in the mirror above the star's makeup table. The mirror was framed in lightbulbs. Just like in the movies, Jane thought. She'd never been in a theatrical dressing room before.

The wall to the left of Carla's dressing table was covered in corkboard to which were pinned what appeared to be congratulatory notes and telegrams, clippings—including Jane's Sunday Style piece!—and a couple of photographs.

Through the crack in the door, Jane could see clothes hanging from an open rack on the right side of the room, and a sofa covered with a jumble of newspapers.

Aside from the frame of lights around the mirror, the room was brightly illuminated by fluorescent tubes shining coldly through translucent ceiling panels, and by odd hanging light fixtures suspended from chains like upside-down tulips.

Carla was seated in a low-backed chair at the dressing-room mirror, her head resting on the table amid a clutter of makeup paraphernalia.

Poor woman, Jane thought. She must be exhausted from the show and from the week of activities and controversy leading up to it. After all, she was more than eighty years old.

"Miss Caldwell," Jane called softly through the narrow opening. "It's Jane Day, from the *Post*. Can I help you? Are you all right?"

The actress didn't move.

Jane twisted an orange curl nervously.

Something was wrong here.

"Miss Caldwell?" Jane spoke louder, hoping to awaken the actress.

Still no response.

Jane pushed open the door. She walked the few steps to the dressing table and looked down at the actress.

That's when she saw a silver handle sticking out of Carla's right side. And stains darkening the khaki silk of her blouse and pants. And blood coagulating like black Jell-O on the gray carpet.

Before Jane could scream, Carla turned her head to the right. Her blood-encrusted lips moved.

"What?" Jane asked, trembling.

She leaned down and put her ear close to Carla's mouth.

"I hope she will forgive me."

Jane barely made out the breathy whisper.

Carla said no more.

Jane straightened up and looked at the actress. Carla was still. Her eyes were fixed and staring at a tube of theatrical makeup. She was dead.

Jane shrieked and shrieked and shrieked.

The next few minutes were a blur.

Jane was aware of people crowding into the dressing room. Someone yelled, "Doctor! Get a doctor!" A man in a tuxedo appeared, tried to revive Carla, shook his head. No use. Two men and a woman in police uniforms appeared, surveyed the scene, spoke into radios they carried on their belts.

And Jerry Knight arrived.

He had been visiting with Jose Sequeros and Jose's family in a nearby dressing room when he heard the shrieks.

Jerry took Jane in his arms and rocked her.

"What happened?" Jerry asked.

"I came back here to congratulate Carla," Jane sobbed, "and I found her stabbed."

Jerry restrained his inclination to comment that the old bitch deserved it. Instead, he hugged Jane's shaking body and made soothing noises. Meanwhile, more and more people jammed into the dressing room despite the efforts of the overwhelmed police officers to keep them out.

"I've got to file!" Jane suddenly pronounced, pulling back from Jerry's embrace. "I can still make the final!"

"You're not in any shape to file a story," Jerry protested. "Look at you. You're shaking like a leaf. I'll call the *Post* and tell them what happened. They can send another reporter."

"I've got to file!" Jane repeated as if in a delirium. She reached for her cellular phone.

CHAPTER EIGHTEEN

THE CALL ABOUT the Carla Caldwell murder reached A. L. Jones in his dirty white detective car fifteen minutes before his shift ended at midnight. Fifteen minutes later and he would have been off the bubble, no longer the Homicide detective designated to investigate the next murder in Washington, D.C. Fifteen minutes later and he would have been steering the wheezing Ford toward his apartment in LeDroit Park to make sure that LaTroy had survived another day on the city's mean streets.

But instead, at fifteen minutes before midnight, while A. L. was cruising Georgia Avenue, keeping his eye out for a drug boy he wanted to question about a drive-by near Logan Circle, the voice of Michelle, the Homicide dispatcher, crackled over his radio.

"Hey, honey, got something for you."

"Oh, no!"

"Oh, yeah. Kennedy Center. Some actress got stabbed in her dressing room."

"Say again."

"Kennedy Center. You know where that is?"

"Yeah."

"Kennedy Center. That old actress? Carla Caldwell? You know? Officers on the scene say somebody stabbed her. I don't know no more."

"I'm on my way," A. L. informed the dispatcher in a weary baritone.

"Okay, honey. You see any of them stars around, get me Will Smith's autograph, hear?"

The detective made a U-turn on Georgia Avenue and headed south.

"Shit," he cursed aloud.

Jones hated these kinds of cases. A lot of important uptown white dudes with their condescending smugness and their friends in high places. The newsies would be on him. And the mayor, too, probably.

A. L. would much rather deal with a drive-by or some crew member popping a rival crew member. He spoke the language and knew where to look.

But, when you're on the bubble, you take what you're dealt.

A. L. Jones pulled up in front of an all-night carryout on Fourteenth Street. He bought himself a large container of black coffee and a white bag of powdered doughnuts left over from the previous day, or maybe the previous week. The doughnuts showed, white and inviting, through a little cellophane window in the bag.

Driving through the dark, glistening streets to the Kennedy Center, A. L. gulped his coffee and munched his doughnuts. He figured he needed them. It was going to be a long night.

The streets were almost deserted at that hour on a Sunday. Softly falling snow twinkled in his left headlight. The right light was burned out and the police department had no money to replace it.

Jones took New Hampshire Avenue, steered around Washington Circle to Virginia Avenue, zigzagged around the Watergate complex, and headed up a steep grade into the Kennedy Center driveway. The flashing red, white, and blue lights of an ambulance and three police cars, and a small crowd of curiosity seekers, pulling their coats tight around their formal clothes, greeted the detective.

He brushed powdery white sugar from the doughnuts off the front of his wrinkled tweed sport jacket before getting out of the car.

As an amateur student of local landmarks—all that remained of his terminated architectural studies at Howard University—A. L. admired the plain lines and bold size of the performing arts center. He'd read criticism of the building as "the world's largest Kleenex box" and "a beached white whale." But he liked it.

Not as much, however, as he had liked the enormous redbrick fortress it had replaced, the Christian Heurich brewery for more than a half century, then briefly the location of the homegrown Arena Stage Company, before it was demolished in the early 1960s to make way for the Kennedy Center.

A. L. had seen the great brewery on the Potomac many times as a boy when he traveled around the city with his father. He imagined it looked like the castles clinging to the bluffs above the Rhine.

*   *   *

The first people Jones encountered when the uniformed police officer in charge of the crime scene escorted him to Carla Caldwell's dressing room were Jane Day and Jerry Knight.

"Oh, no!" the detective exclaimed. "Not you two again!"

"I was thinking the same thing," Jerry shot back.

This pair, playing amateur detectives, had entangled themselves in two of Jones's cases, once when A. L. was investigating the parking lot murder of a guest leaving Knight's program, and later when he was trying to find out who poisoned a CNN reporter at the White House correspondents banquet.

Both times the loudmouth talk show host and the girl newsie had been pains in the ass, complicating his investigations. But, the detective grudgingly admitted to himself, they *had* helped him navigate through the part of Washington where he felt least comfortable and least knowledgeable.

And here they were again.

"Get these two out of here," A. L. commanded in a deep rumble. "I ain't got no time for no reporters."

"She's a witness," a uniformed officer informed A. L., nodding at Jane. "She discovered the body."

"And him?" the detective asked, indicating Jerry.

"One of the first people to reach the dressing room after the body was discovered," the cop advised Jones.

"Okay, hold them somewhere," Jones instructed the officer. "*Separately.* I'll interview them after I finish examining the crime scene."

Jane protested that she needed to phone additional details to the *Post.*

A. L. waved her away dismissively.

"You better call your studio, Mr. Night Talker," A. L. said

to Jerry. "You ain't going to be doing no talkin' on the radio tonight to them nutcases listen to you."

"No live show on Sunday nights," Jerry replied cheerily. "On Sundays, my loyal fans get recorded highlights from previous programs."

"From what it sounds like to me, more like recorded *low*lights, ain't it?"

The uniformed officer led Jane and Jerry away.

Withdrawing a bent notebook and a chewed-up ballpoint pen from his jacket pocket, A. L. turned his attention to the dressing room.

A crime-scene technician advised him that the evidence gathering had been compromised by the crowd attracted by Jane's shrieks. There was no way of telling what had been moved, trampled, destroyed, or deposited by people who rushed into the dressing room.

"Damn," Jones cursed the corruption of the crime scene. He knew that would make it more difficult to catch the murderer. And to convict him.

Even Carla's corpse had been moved from its original position at the dressing table to the floor by the well-meaning doctor recruited from the Grand Foyer supper to try to resuscitate her.

A. L. turned his attention to the body.

Cause of death seemed obvious, a silver letter opener stuck into the old woman's side below the ribs. But he'd await the medical examiner's report to be sure.

Jones knelt beside the body and looked at the face of the actress, fixed in a slight grimace. Her eyes were half-open, cloudy, staring at nothing. A. L. remembered seeing her in movies a long time ago. But not recently. She must be eighty years old, or more. Her face was waxy yellow now. Still, not bad looking for a woman that old.

The detective straightened up with a grunt. He stared down at the corpse, trying to see whether any puzzle pieces fit together yet.

Every murder case was like a jigsaw puzzle to A. L. Jones. He collected pieces as his investigation unfolded, tried fitting them together in various combinations, and when he'd accumulated enough pieces to make a picture, he had his murderer.

Right now, he didn't have too many pieces.

But he had a few.

One, the likely murder weapon. The letter opener had been withdrawn from the woman's side by the medical examiner's crew. It now nested in a plastic evidence bag. Examining the opener through the plastic, A. L. noticed that something was engraved on the silver handle.

Reserved for my love letters. Affectionately C.B.

A. L. mouthed the words, then wrote them in his notebook.

Puzzle piece number two, the engraved message.

"Check the opener for prints," the detective instructed the evidence gatherers.

Turning his attention back to the corpse, Jones spotted the ring. Diamonds surrounding a deep red ruby on a white gold band, worn on the little finger of the left hand.

Puzzle piece number three. Robbery apparently was not the motive.

Unless the murderer had come to steal something else. Or unless he'd been frightened away before he had a chance to grab the ring.

A. L. removed the ring from the dead woman's finger and dropped it into another evidence bag, using his left hand, which was encased in a protective latex glove.

When he'd gleaned all he could from the corpse, Jones

motioned for the morgue crew to take it away. They zipped the body into a pale green plastic bag and rolled it away on a gurney.

News of the murder had spread, so when the body appeared, TV crews staking out the dressing room switched on their lights and jostled for position.

"Get those goddamn cameras out of here!" A. L. growled. He slammed the dressing-room door on the media pack.

For another half hour, he and the evidence team went over the room, looking for clues. They didn't find many.

But in the dead woman's pocketbook, A. L. discovered puzzle piece number four, a leaf from a memo pad embossed with the Watergate Hotel monogram. On the slip was written in a shaky hand the name Lucinda Caldwell and a room number. Same last name as the actress. A sister? A daughter? A granddaughter? A. L. placed the memo sheet between the pages of his notebook. He would find out.

Leaving the evidence team to go over the scene one more time, the detective decided it was time to question Jane Day and Jerry Knight, and the stagehands and others who had rushed to the dressing room when Jane sounded the alarm.

CHAPTER NINETEEN

In a tiny interrogation room set up in what was normally the stage manager's office, A. L. led Jane through a detailed reiteration of her discovery of the murdered actress, writing down her story in his smudged notebook. Then he went back to the beginning and asked her to tell it again. The story didn't change.

"You see anybody in the dressing room, or leaving the dressing room?" the detective asked.

"No."

"You move anything? Take anything?"

"No!"

"What you getting so excited about? It's a routine question."

"I find one of the most famous actresses in the world murdered. I'm in shock. I'm screaming my head off. And you ask me if I *took* anything! What do you think I am?"

"I know what you are. You're a newsie. You looking for

a scoop to put in your newspaper. You held out on me before, remember? You didn't tell me Dan McLean was messing around with some senator's wife. And you didn't tell me what you found in his notebooks. So don't be acting so put out when I ask you if you took anything from the dressing room."

"I didn't take anything!" Jane insisted.

"You told me everything you know about this case?"

"Yes."

Almost everything, Jane amended to herself.

"Am I going to be surprised when I read your story tomorrow?" Jones persisted.

"I don't know what surprises you," Jane dodged.

When he read about Carla's final, cryptic whisper, "I hope she will forgive me," A. L. *would* be surprised. And furious.

But if she told him about it now, the detective might get ambushed by some blow-dried TV pretty boy camped outside and she'd lose her exclusive before the *Post* could hit the streets.

Besides, reporters were not supposed to help the police. They'd lose their credibility with their sources if they did. That was journalistic ethics.

"Are Harlow Baskin and his army of religious zealots suspects in Carla's murder?" Jane asked, pulling *her* notebook and ballpoint from her evening purse.

A. L. looked disconcerted by this turnabout. How had the interview*er* become the interview*ee*?

"Baskin, the preacher?" Jones asked.

"Baskin, the head of a right-wing hate group," Jane corrected. "He runs an organization called Stamp Out Smut. Baskin led the demonstration against Carla outside the Kennedy Center tonight."

The demonstration had disbanded by the time Jones arrived.

"What was the demonstration all about?" he asked.

"Baskin and his followers are outraged because Carla Caldwell publicly criticized President Hammond for trying to impose censorship on TV and the movies."

A. L. remembered hearing something about a controversy at the White House involving Carla Caldwell a few days earlier.

"Demonstrating against her is a long way from sticking a letter opener in her," Jones told the reporter.

"Baskin and his followers are fanatics," Jane replied. "They're like those militias out in Montana. The demonstrators were shouting 'Carla must go' and waving signs saying 'God Will Punish the Wicked.' "

Yeah. *God will punish the wicked.* A. L. didn't think he could put that in his report as a threat of bodily harm.

Jane saw his skepticism.

"Baskin talked to the TV cameras during the demonstration," the reporter elaborated. "I heard him say something like, 'Decent people should get rid of this sinner,' meaning Carla."

Uh-huh. *Decent people should get rid of this sinner.* The detective didn't think he could put that in his report as a threat of bodily harm either.

"Believe me, Harlow Baskin and his followers hated Carla and what she stood for so much, they were capable of murder," Jane asserted. "So, are you going to investigate them as suspects?"

Her pen was poised over her notebook, ready to capture a killer quote.

But Jones grunted noncommittally.

It might be a puzzle piece. He'd have to check it out.

"So, want to make a deal?" Jane asked the detective.

"What kind of deal?"

"You tell me what you find out and I'll tell you what I find out."

"Seems like I made that deal with you one time on the McLean case," Jones reminded her. "Trouble was, you didn't keep your end of the bargain."

She tried to look offended but couldn't quite pull it off.

"Let's make this deal," the detective suggested. "You tell me what you find out. Period."

"Am I released?" Jane asked, closing her notebook.

"Don't leave town," A. L. ordered.

"Do detectives *really* say that? I thought it was just in grade B movies."

A uniformed policewoman led Jane out and escorted Jerry Knight into the makeshift interrogation room.

"Detective Jones, it's almost two o'clock in the morning," Jerry blustered. "Can we get on with this?"

A. L. Jones leaned back in the stage manager's chair and rubbed a pudgy hand over the white stubble on his chin. He wished he had a cup of coffee.

"Mr. Night Talker, this been a long day for me, too. I got a dead actress here, a famous one. When the sun comes up, a whole lot of dudes in big offices is going to be wanting to know why I ain't caught whoever busted her. You probably going to be one of them dudes. I listen to you on the radio sometime when I'm driving around at night. You big on law and order. Well, that's me. Law and order. That's why I got to keep you around to two o'clock in the morning to ask you what you saw here tonight."

Jerry Knight stood in front of the desk, ignoring the detective's gesture to sit.

"I was visiting my friend Jose Sequeros, one of the Honors winners, in his dressing room after the show."

Jerry waved vaguely in the direction of Sequeros's dressing room.

"Suddenly, I heard someone screaming. I ran out to find out what it was. I found Jane in Carla Caldwell's dressing room, screaming hysterically. Carla was slumped over her dressing table. A lot of other people ran in. Someone in a tuxedo came in, a doctor I guess, and gave Carla CPR. But he couldn't bring her back. That's all I know. Can I go now?"

The detective sighed wearily. He wrote down Jerry's recollections. Then he asked the talk show host to tell it again, in more detail.

"Who do you think did it?" Jerry asked, lapsing into his interviewer's mode, as he often did even off the air.

"Don't know yet," A. L. replied. "I'm just starting to gather the evidence."

Why was it every time he got mixed up with Jerry Knight and Jane Day, he ended up giving more answers than he got?

"You expect to catch anybody?" Jerry asked.

Knight had needled him about his investigation of the Davenport murder and about the McLean killing. Now again.

"You don't think much of me, do you, Mr. Night Talker?" A. L. said.

"Nothing personal, Detective Jones. I don't think much of *any* cops who can't protect me from muggers, car thieves, housebreakers, drug addicts, crazy panhandlers, homeless people peeing in the street, and murderers. Since the D.C. police department can't protect me and other law-abiding citizens from the creeps, no, I don't think much of how you do your job."

"Glad to be of service," A. L. growled sarcastically. "Who do *you* think did it?"

Might as well hear it, Jones figured. Jerry would probably offer his opinion to his listeners soon enough anyhow.

"Carla Caldwell made a lot of enemies in eighty years," Jerry proclaimed in his broadcast voice. "She stabbed a lot of backs in Hollywood. Plus, the feuds in all those left-wing causes she was involved in. Those people are great haters. They have long memories about the most arcane deviations from liberal dogma. And that's not counting irate wives and girlfriends of the men Carla slept with. I'd say you're looking at enough suspects to fill one of the Kennedy Center theaters."

Arcane deviations from liberal dogma. A. L. hated this case already. He wished he were back on Chapin Street trying to persuade the neighbors to tell him what they knew about the dead man in the black-and-red basketball shoes bleeding into the gutter.

"You know anyone with the initials C.B. might have known Miss Caldwell?" the detective asked, trying to decipher the inscription engraved on the handle of the letter opener that had been used to kill the actress.

"C.B.? Maybe Cecil B. DeMille?" Jerry offered.

Was Knight joking with him? Jones wondered. Or could the letter opener really have been a gift from the famous director?

"What about Harlow Baskin?" A. L. proposed. "I hear him and his followers was pretty worked up about Miss Caldwell dissing the President. You pretty much agree with them people, don't you, Mr. Night Talker?"

"I agree with them that Carla Caldwell acted outrageously by insulting the President," Jerry pontificated. "And

I agree with them that Hollywood is producing cultural garbage. But it's a vicious smear to suggest that because Harlow and his followers hold these views, they should be suspects in the stabbing of Carla Caldwell. Am *I* a suspect because I share those views? I was backstage. I could have done it."

"Man, I'd love to make you for dropping her," A. L. told Jerry. "But I don't think you did it. Go on home. But stay around where I can find you."

Jones spent another hour interviewing others who had been backstage when Carla Caldwell was discovered dead. Then he looked around her dressing room one more time. He'd collected a lot of puzzle pieces. Problem was, none of them fit together yet.

Four A.M. There wasn't anything else he could do until morning. A. L. needed sleep.

In the driveway, under the Kennedy Center's marble overhang, his car wouldn't start. Dead battery.

"Shit."

No taxi was going to pick up a black man in that neighborhood at that hour.

A. L. persuaded a squad car cop to drive him to his LeDroit Park apartment. In the morning, he'd swipe a battery from a dead police car at the New York Avenue yard and transplant it into the white Ford.

CHAPTER TWENTY

T HE CLOCK RADIO on the bedside table of Jane's Adams Morgan apartment awoke her at 7 A.M. with *Morning Edition* on National Public Radio. She'd slept only three hours. But she threw back the covers and bounded out of bed.

This startled Jane's cat, Bloomsbury, who had been sleeping at her feet. He hopped off the bed and retreated to safety behind the bedroom door. What had gotten into *her?* he wondered. Jane usually hit the snooze button a couple of times, giving the cat plenty of time to wake up, stretch, and yawn before she reluctantly rolled out of bed.

Well, Bloomsbury was up. He might as well rub against her leg and make those little whimpery nasal sounds to encourage her to give him his tuna. He'd go back to sleep when she departed for the office.

Jane felt muzzy-headed from lack of sleep. But she wanted to start lobbying the editors early to keep her on the Carla Caldwell murder story. It was *her* story! How could the

Post assign it to anybody else? After all, she had conducted probably the last interview the actress ever gave. And she had discovered the body. The story would keep Jane's byline on page one for days.

Besides, it would get her off the White House beat for a while, away from covering the borrrring nonactivities of President Dale Hammond.

Jane peered at herself in the bathroom mirror.

Yuck!

Worse than usual.

Her big green eyes were squeezed into squinty slits. Her skin looked blotchy. And a reddish zit was forming on her chin. And her hair! An impossible tangle of garish orange curls. Another seventy-five dollars to George's hair salon and her hair *still* wasn't straight.

She lifted the T-shirt she slept in to inspect her hips. The ten pounds she'd lost in order to squeeze into her dress for the Kennedy Center gala was really noticeable. It was sort of noticeable. Wasn't it?

Jane usually began her day with a jog north on Eighteenth Street, across Duke Ellington Bridge, and down into Rock Creek Park. But she didn't have the energy for it. She promised herself that she'd work out to an aerobics tape that night. Yeah, sure.

After a shower, Jane felt better.

She poured herself a large glass of orange juice, retrieved that morning's *Post* from the hallway outside her apartment door, and sat down at the tiny kitchen table to study the newspaper. The stabbing of Carla Caldwell backstage at the Kennedy Center Honors ceremony was the lead story, page one, down the right side, with Jane's byline. The subhead proclaimed, "*Post* Reporter Finds Body in Dressing Room."

Yes!

She read the piece, frowning at a couple of edits made on the desk. Someone also had written a three-paragraph insert rehashing the White House confrontation between Carla and the President. A flattering feature story on Carla's movie career and political activism filled three-quarters of the front page of the Style section. It read like a hurried revision of Carla's canned obit, Jane thought.

The page one story prominently quoted Carla's dying words whispered into Jane's ear, "I hope she will forgive me."

Well, she'd be hearing from A. L. Jones about that, the reporter guessed.

Jane decided to beat him to the punch. She'd go to the detective's office in the Municipal Center first thing and apologize, claiming she'd been in such a state of shock during his backstage interrogation that she'd completely blanked out Carla's last words.

Then she'd press Jones to tell her about developments in his investigation for her second-day story.

First, though, she had to call the newspaper before the morning editorial meeting, to stake her claim to the story. She could sweet-talk Russ Williamson. He was her editor and her mentor at the *Post,* and hoped to be her lover. So far, Jane had managed to sidestep his clumsy and persistent pursuit. But her put-downs didn't deter him. Jane had found that men driven by their hormones were not easily deterred.

Jane noticed that the telephone answering machine on the kitchen counter was flashing its red light. She'd been so dazed by the time she got home the night before she'd forgotten to check for messages.

The first was from Jerry.

I looked for you backstage after Detective Jones was finished with me, but you'd left. What an incompetent he is. If Jones is in charge of the investigation, you can forget about finding out who killed the old bitch. Which is fine with me. She's no great loss. You probably don't see it that way. But if you were in Vietnam, like I was, when she was holding peace rallies with Ho Chi Minh in Hanoi, you wouldn't miss her either.

He paused.

I thought you'd be home by now. But I guess you're at the paper working on your story. I'm not going to call you there. Call me when you get up. Okay? I'll talk to you then.

Jerry. What was the attraction? she wondered. Something.

Today was the day he switched back from his weekend sleeping schedule to his Monday through Friday sleeping schedule in preparation for his midnight show. He'd be napping after 3 P.M. She'd call him before then.

The other message was from her mother in Los Angeles.

Hi, honey. It's your mom. Your dad and I just heard the terrible news about Carla. It's awful! We're so upset. What is this country coming to? All these extremists and militia groups and I don't know what. The religious right. Now they've killed Carla. Isn't there any way to stop them? We saw Carla many times at rallies. She was such a marvelous speaker, and she believed in the same things we believe in. Anyhow, your dad and I knew you were going to be at the Kennedy Center and when we heard the news about Carla we wanted to make sure you're all right. Call us when you get in. It's three hours earlier here, so call even if it's late. We'll be up. What did you wear, honey? Did you go with anybody? Did I mention that your cousin Brenda is engaged? Yes, a very nice doctor from—

Jane hit the STOP button. Even on tape, she couldn't handle Mavis at this hour of the morning on three hours sleep.

She needed to get to Starbucks for coffee and a muffin.

Then, to see A. L. Jones.

CHAPTER TWENTY-ONE

T HE DETECTIVE DID not give her a warm welcome.

He'd had less sleep and worse coffee than she had. The storage yard for old police cars had been locked when he'd got there at dawn to swipe a battery, so his cruiser still sat lifeless in the Kennedy Center driveway.

And from her page one story in the *Post* he'd learned that she'd withheld information during his backstage interrogation the night before.

Jones glowered at the newsie when Jonetta, the policewoman assigned to Homicide headquarters, escorted Jane through the chaotic warren of offices on the third floor of the Municipal Center and deposited her at A. L.'s disorderly desk.

"So, you accidentally forgot to tell me something last night, Miss *Washington Post?*" the detective growled.

"I'm sorry, Detective Jones. I was so shaken up, I wasn't thinking straight."

"Uh-huh," Jones rumbled disbelievingly. "You was too

shook up to inform me that Carla Caldwell told you something before she died. But you wasn't shook up no more when you wrote it in the newspaper?"

"What do you think her words meant, 'I hope she will forgive me'?" Jane asked, pulling a reporter's notebook from her oversize tapestry shoulder bag. "Was she trying to tell me who stabbed her?"

"I ain't had no time to figure out what it means yet," A. L. told her, "since I just read about it in your newspaper. Maybe it don't mean nothing."

He sipped cold, bitter coffee from a cardboard cup and glared at her.

"You don't like reporters, do you?"

"You got that right."

"Why?"

"Ain't we had this conversation before? I say, 'Because when I tell you something, you put it in the newspaper.' And you say, 'That's what reporters are supposed to do.' And I say, 'That's why I don't like reporters.' Yeah. We had that conversation before. So, let's skip it. I got too much to do to be talking to you."

"Got any idea who killed her?" Jane persisted.

"Do you?" A. L. shot back. "Last couple of times I come across you, you seem to be doing more detective work than me."

"I told you last night you ought to check out Harlow Baskin," Jane reminded the detective. "Baskin has gone completely around the bend about Carla since she denounced Hammond for advocating censorship. Baskin is consumed by rage. I mean, you should have heard the kinds of threats he made toward Carla during his demonstration outside the Kennedy Center last night. He, or one of his followers, could have slipped inside and killed her. Did anyone see him back-stage after the show?"

A. L. grunted noncommittally. He hadn't checked.

"So, can I quote you as saying you're investigating whether Baskin might be involved?"

"You can't quote me saying nothing," A. L. barked. "This conversation is off the record."

"You can't put a conversation off the record retroactively," Jane protested. "You can't make ground rules—"

"You can't quote me saying nothing," Jones repeated. "Them's *my* ground rules. I make the ground rules here. You don't like 'em, I'll get Jonetta to show you out. And you won't be coming back."

"All right, off the record," Jane agreed grudgingly "So, who else are you interviewing?"

"Everybody," Jones replied testily. He was tired of this cat and mouse game.

"Like who?"

"Like everybody who might know something. People backstage. Her friends. Her enemies. Family. The daughter. Try to find who had motive and opportunity . . ."

The daughter? Carla Caldwell had never married. And Jane could recall no reference to a daughter in the research she'd done on the actress.

"What daughter?" the reporter blurted.

"The dead woman's daughter," the detective responded. "Lucinda Caldwell."

Before heading home early in the morning, A. L. had sent the Chinese woman detective Mai Ling Fung-Berrigan to the Watergate Hotel to check out the name and room number he'd found in Carla Caldwell's pocketbook.

When he'd arrived at Homicide that morning, Jones had

found a typed report from the always reliable Mai Ling on his desk.

He ticked off the highlights to Jane. Lucinda Caldwell was Carla's daughter. Forty-three years old, lived in Beverly Hills with her mother. Occupation, poet. Took the news of her mother's murder remarkably calmly.

"I didn't know Carla had a daughter," Jane said.

"Amazing," A. L. responded sarcastically. "There's something Miss *Washington Post* don't know. That's news right there."

"Carla was never married," Jane informed the detective.

"Being married ain't a requirement for having a kid," the detective retorted. "Ain't you noticed, there's a lot of that goin' on?"

"I mean, I've read a lot about Carla Caldwell and I don't remember any mention of a daughter. She must have wanted to keep—Lucinda?—a secret."

"Maybe she was afraid having a kid would hurt her image as a glamorous movie star," Jones offered.

"And maybe she hid her daughter because she was afraid people would ask who the father was."

"Who *was* the father?" the detective asked. Maybe this was another puzzle piece.

"How would I know?"

"Damn," A. L. exclaimed mockingly. "*Two* things the newsie don't know."

"Where's the daughter now?" Jane asked.

"In her room at the Watergate Hotel, probably."

A. L. realized as soon as the words were out of his mouth that he'd made a mistake by divulging Lucinda Caldwell's whereabouts. The newsie would be banging on her door in thirty minutes. Well, there was nothing he could do to stop her. Freedom of the press. All that shit.

Jane stood up.

"Don't quote me on nothin'," the detective repeated.

"You didn't say anything to quote," Jane replied tartly. "Always a pleasure, Detective Jones."

"The feeling's mutual," A. L. said with equal asperity.

Jane was dialing the *Post* librarian Ravi Bahrami on her cellular phone before she was out the door of the Municipal Center.

"Ravi, do you remember seeing any references in the clips to Carla Caldwell having a daughter?" she asked when the librarian picked up his phone. "A daughter named Lucinda?"

"No, I don't," he replied. "But I've only become an expert on Carla Caldwell since you started writing about her."

"Maybe neither one of us is quite the expert we thought we were," the reporter said. Standing on the sidewalk outside the fortresslike Municipal Center, Jane shivered in the gray December air.

"Pull everything you can find on Carla in the—let's see, the daughter's forty-three—in the mid-fifties," she instructed. "Gossip. Men she was seen with. Romances. Unexplained absences. Illnesses. Rumors about her love life. Everything you can find."

"Okay," Ravi assented.

"I'm on my way to try to talk to Lucinda Caldwell at the Watergate Hotel," Jane advised. "After that, I'll come straight to the paper to see what you've found."

"Remember your lunch with that Hollywood producer about your screenplay," the librarian reminded her. "Noon at Kinkead's."

"Damn! With Carla murdered and everything, I completely forgot about it. I'll call him and cancel."

"You should keep the appointment," Ravi urged her. "It could be your ticket to Hollywood."

"But the story. I've got to—"

"Go have your lunch while I see what I can find on Carla's daughter," the librarian interrupted. "Call me before you go to her hotel. That way, you'll have more background when you see her."

"All right," the reporter agreed. "I guess I should find out what the producer is offering."

"Tell him you'll need a researcher for your screenplay," Ravi suggested hopefully.

CHAPTER TWENTY-TWO

KINKEAD'S WAS A hot restaurant with the legal/government/lobbyist/journalism boomer crowd, as well as visiting show business personages. It was located just off Pennsylvania Avenue halfway between the White House and Georgetown at the edge of George Washington University.

The restaurant was part of a mall built behind the facade of a nineteenth-century block called Red Lion Row, after the pub that once occupied the site. Retention of the handsome redbrick front wall was the price extracted by preservationists for dropping their opposition to building the modern mall and office building above, around, and behind the old facade. Jane had covered that battle in her early days as an environmental reporter for the *Post*.

Jane liked the multilevel, bright and airy restaurant because it was fashionable without being pompous. White tablecloths conveyed a seriousness of purpose without being pretentious. She especially liked the lively works of art decorating the walls of Kinkead's. The current collection came from the Zenith Gallery on Washington's Seventh Street art corridor. Jane visited that gallery occasionally, smiling at the whimsical works and hoping she would soon be able to afford them.

Jane entered the restaurant through the door facing H Street, reached by mounting a restored wrought-iron stairway. At the host's podium, she tried out her Hollywood vocabulary: "I'm doing lunch with Sheldon Berman."

She thought she had it right, *doing* lunch, *taking* a meeting.

The captain bestowed the most welcoming smile she'd ever received at Kinkead's, and waved her up a broad curving staircase with a polished brass railing to the more desirable floor above.

At the top of the staircase, another functionary led her to Sheldon Berman's table, a raised booth along the left wall in the section reserved for celebrities.

The producer did not look like he'd sounded on the phone. He'd sounded tall, suave, and young. He looked short, dumpy, and middle-aged. But not unattractive. Dark hair flecked with gray very expensively coiffed. Pale, twinkly blue eyes. Big chested, like he worked out. Dressed California casual—tailored blue blazer with gold buttons, faded denim jeans, rough-textured flax-colored collarless sport shirt.

When Sheldon Berman turned on a dazzling smile, Jane's anxiety lessened.

By the time he told her, over breadsticks dipped in olive oil, how much he liked her writing, she felt at ease.

"Your article on Carla was tremendous, just *tremendous*," he gushed in a high-pitched voice. "Summed up her whole career—her *life*, really—so *beautifully*."

"I think I had the last interview with her."

"Hard to believe Carla is gone," Berman sighed, shaking his head. "She was an absolute *monument* for so many years."

When the producer had suggested having lunch with Jane while he was in Washington for the Kennedy Center Honors celebrations, it had been for the purpose of discussing his interest in making a movie of her Style section feature about Congressman Revell Gates.

But the day after Carla's murder, the reporter and the producer—like just about everybody else in Washington—found it difficult to talk about anything but Carla's death.

After the waiter had brought her portobello mushrooms with sourdough bread and his seared tuna, and green bottles of Perrier water for both of them, Jane asked Berman if he'd heard any gossip among his Hollywood associates about why someone would kill the actress.

"I haven't a clue who killed Carla Caldwell," Berman replied, sipping Perrier. "But a lot of people in Hollywood breathed a sigh of relief this morning."

"Because?" Jane dug in her tapestry shoulder bag for her notebook and ballpoint.

"Because she was writing her memoirs."

"She told me during my interview," Jane recalled, realizing that less than a week earlier she had been chatting with the living and vibrant Carla Caldwell over breakfast. "But she demanded that I not print it. Why was Carla so insistent that I not divulge she was writing her memoirs? And why are people in Hollywood so relieved she was killed before she finished writing them?"

"There are a lot of secrets Hollywood prefers to keep *secret*," the producer explained.

"Like?" Jane persisted. He might know something she could use to find Carla's murderer.

"Carla was around the studios a long time," Berman

noted. "*Decades*. That's a lot of time for a very smart woman to hear where all the bodies are buried."

Jane looked up from her notebook, startled.

"Not *real* bodies," Berman assured her hastily. "Not necessarily. I'm talking about shady deals, money for making movies coming from some pretty odd places. Weird love affairs that would wreck a lot of reputations if the public knew about them. Kinky sex. I mean kinky even by Hollywood's standards. Some clean-cut leading men who beat their wives, and worse. Some wholesome leading ladies who weren't very wholesome off the screen. And, of course, the political hypocrisy."

"Political hypocrisy?" Jane interjected. "That sounds more like Washington than Hollywood."

Berman flashed her another dazzling smile.

"You'd be amazed how many Hollywood people talk the liberal talk, because that's what the politically correct culture requires of them, while they give money under the table to conservatives because they want their taxes cut. They want to wear their fur coats. They want to develop their beachfront property. They want their tobacco stocks to go up. Et cetera."

Jane liked Sheldon Berman's candor and sardonic insights. Not what she expected from a Hollywood producer.

Hollywood and Washington sounded a lot alike to her. The most famous citizens of both cities loudly proclaimed what they stood for in public while cutting private deals to achieve just the opposite.

"The threat that Carla might reveal political hypocrisy doesn't seem enough of a motive for someone to murder her," Jane offered, swallowing the last of her mushroom.

"Probably not," the producer agreed. "If it were, there'd be a lot more murders in Hollywood."

"In Washington, too," Jane laughed.

"Even if it wasn't politics, Carla kept her eyes and ears open all those years and could have ruined a lot of people if she'd put *half* of what she knew in her book," Berman said.

They sat in silence a moment, scanning the restaurant for well-known faces. The host of a weekly television public affairs shouting match was putting the moves on a young woman producer. The chairman of a Senate committee was being entertained by a former senator, now a lobbyist for the plastics industry. And a comedian who had played a small role in the Kennedy Center Honors production was eating alone, reading *Daily Variety*. Slim pickings. Well, Jane thought, Monday was a slow lunch day in Washington.

"Do you know anything about Lucinda Caldwell?" she asked Sheldon Berman.

The producer put down his fork and stared hard at Jane. She wasn't sure if the look conveyed respect for her reporting skills or disgust at her intrusiveness.

"How did you know about her?"

"Why is Lucinda such a secret?" Jane parried his question with a question. "Why did Carla hide the fact that she had a daughter?"

"She didn't *totally* hide it."

"You mean Carla acknowledged she had a child?"

"No, not really," Berman conceded. "I *did* see them together once at an Academy Awards ceremony. Carla introduced the girl as her niece and Lucinda looked very uncomfortable."

"Who's the father?" Jane asked, more bluntly than she intended.

Berman stared at her with his pale blue eyes as if considering how much to tell her.

"I don't know."

Jane looked skeptical.

"I really don't know. Only a few people know about Lucinda. They speculate about the father. But no one knows for sure."

"What's the speculation?" Jane pressed.

"One of her leading men, maybe." The producer's pale eyes shifted like he wasn't telling everything he knew. "Maybe someone not in show business."

"Like who?"

"Maybe somebody in politics." Berman's squeaky voice dropped almost to a whisper.

Jane sat back to absorb that possibility.

A politician the father of Carla Caldwell's daughter? Someone whose political future might be threatened if Carla revealed his paternity in her memoirs?

What was she thinking? Carla had been in her eighties. Unlikely a politician at that age would be worried about future election prospects. Unless he was Strom Thurmond.

Wait a minute! Who said the father had to be Carla's age? Maybe he was a younger man who'd had an affair with the older actress, Jane speculated. Now he could be in the prime of his political career and anxious to hide their romance and the child that resulted, lest the revelation wreck his election ambitions.

"Let's talk about turning your *wonderful* article on Congressman Gates into a movie," Berman suggested.

They did talk about it, and about his proposal that she come to Hollywood to help write the screenplay.

But her mind was focused on the Carla Caldwell case and the possibility that the father of her secret daughter might be a politician with a motive to keep the affair a secret. Jane, absently twisting and untwisting an orange curl around her finger, barely heard Berman's Hollywood chatter.

The waiter, wearing Kinkead's standard fish-patterned

apron, brought the check. Berman paid with a platinum American Express card.

The producer again beamed the dazzling smile and urged Jane to accept his offer. He needed her answer quickly, before the actors who'd expressed interest in the movie accepted other roles and before the money men who were willing to finance the movie found other deals.

Jane promised Berman her answer by the end of the year, just a couple of weeks away.

That seemed a long way off. Right now, she needed to interview Lucinda Caldwell, and to direct Ravi to comb his files again for the name of a politician who might have had an affair with Carla more than forty years before.

CHAPTER TWENTY-THREE

JANE TROTTED ACROSS the triangular park that separated Kinkead's from Pennsylvania Avenue, dodged through the traffic to the far side of the wide thoroughfare, and hailed a cab heading west. The driver mumbled an uncertain affirmation when Jane instructed him to take her to the Watergate Hotel. As the cab lurched past the George Washington University medical complex and turned toward Virginia Avenue, Jane called Ravi on her cellular phone. She instructed him to focus on politicians in his search for a mid-1950s lover who might have fathered Carla's daughter.

"Her boyfriend was probably younger than Carla," Jane advised the researcher. She calculated in her head. If he was an active politician worried about a scandal ruining his future electoral aspirations, the guy was probably now in his late fifties, early sixties. Lucinda was forty-three, born in 1954 or 1955. So, if her theory was right, that meant the father would have been about twenty when he impregnated Carla.

Twenty! And Carla would have been in her late thirties. An unseemly age differential, especially back in the staid fifties. So, assuming all the ifs were true, that would explain why Carla, and her lover, were so eager to keep their affair a secret.

Ravi twittered excitedly when Jane imparted this new clue. Jane hit the END button, folded the phone, and dropped it back into her tapestry bag.

Maybe she was going down the wrong path, Jane worried, twisting a strand of hair and staring out the window of the cab.

Maybe the man who had fathered Lucinda *wasn't* a politician, much less an inappropriately younger one. Maybe the gossip Sheldon Berman had whispered to her was just that, Hollywood gossip, with no basis in fact. Maybe there was another, perfectly logical explanation for Carla's decision to keep her daughter's existence, and the father's identity, a secret. An explanation that had nothing at all to do with the actress's murder.

In which case Jane had no story.

She shook off that possibility and concentrated on figuring out how she was going to talk her way into Lucinda Caldwell's hotel room.

A doorman in a long green coat with gold buttons and epaulets helped her out of the cab and shepherded her to the door. On tall staffs in the circular courtyard, flags of the countries of origin of hotel guests snapped in the winter wind—Korea, Japan, the British Union Jack, the red Canadian Maple Leaf.

The lobby was quiet and regal, furnished with tasteful antiques. Or good imitation antiques. Jane found the marble floor striking, black triangles on a white background with gray stripes.

Getting Lucinda's room number turned out to be remarkably easy. Jane, who had dressed conservatively in a black suit and gray silk blouse for her lunch with the Hollywood producer, put on a melancholy face and told the woman behind the front desk that she was Lucinda Caldwell's cousin Joyce, just arrived from New York to console her relative and help with arrangements.

The hotel clerk looked skeptical. But she'd heard stranger tales that turned out to be true. And she was reluctant to challenge an obviously grieving relative.

"Miss Caldwell is in twelve seventy-seven," the clerk informed her sympathetically. "The elevator is through there."

Going up on the dark, wood-paneled elevator, Jane fleetingly considered the ongoing journalistic debate about the ethics of lying or pretending to be someone else in order to get a story. She would wrestle with that issue another time.

Jane decided a soft but authoritative knock on the door of Lucinda Caldwell's room was her best strategy. There was no response.

Maybe the daughter was out, Jane thought. Making funeral arrangements, perhaps. Or being consoled by friends. Did she have friends in Washington? Maybe she was in the room, but too despondent to open the door.

Jane was about to knock again, more loudly, when she heard a soft shuffling sound on the other side of the door.

"Who's there?" asked a weak voice.

"A friend of your mother's," Jane replied. She was, sort of.

The door opened about three inches.

"Who are you?" Lucinda Caldwell challenged her visitor.

"My name is Jane Day. I knew your mother." Jane spoke quickly, trying to ingratiate herself before the woman closed the door on her. "I had breakfast with your mother last week. I was at the White House when she spoke out against—"

"You're the one who found her, aren't you?" Lucinda Caldwell asked. "You're the reporter from the *Washington Post.*"

"I am," Jane conceded. Confronted with the obviously distraught daughter, her conscience wouldn't let her carry on the charade.

Lucinda's eyes were wet. No makeup disguised her blotchy face. Her gray-streaked hair was pulled back severely. Wrapped in a white terry-cloth hotel bathrobe, her body looked shapeless.

"I only knew your mother a short time, but I've admired her—"

"I'm sorry," Lucinda interrupted, sounding genuinely apologetic. "I can't talk to you now."

"My father and mother attended many rallies where your mother—"

"I'm sorry."

The door was closing.

"I want to find out who killed your mother," Jane said insistently. "Just give me five minutes. Please. Two minutes."

"I'm sorry."

The door closed on Lucinda Caldwell.

For an instant, Jane thought about pushing against the door before the lock clicked. But the lessons in propriety she'd learned from Mavis overwhelmed her reporter's instincts.

In a tidy lounge off the hotel lobby, Jane sat on an uncomfortable divan and scribbled everything she could remember of the brief encounter in her notebook.

The reporter could see echoes of Carla Caldwell in Lucinda's face.

But some of the woman's features reminded Jane of someone else. Jane couldn't recall whom Lucinda resembled.

CHAPTER TWENTY-FOUR

THE TAXI DRIVER taking Jane from the Watergate Hotel back to the *Post* chose L Street, one-way east and generally less crowded than K or I Streets, which were jammed at all hours ever since the Secret Service had disrupted traffic in the heart of Washington by closing three blocks of Pennsylvania Avenue in front of the White House as a precaution against terrorists.

The driver turned off Washington Circle onto New Hampshire Avenue and then right on L.

The turn onto L was two blocks from the studios of ATN, the All Talk Network, which made Jane think of Jerry Knight, which reminded her that she hadn't returned his voice-mail message from the night before.

She looked at her watch. Three o'clock.

Jerry would be asleep at his apartment across the Potomac in Rosslyn, Virginia, switching his sleep cycle in preparation for another week of midnight to 5 A.M. talk shows. She thought about waking him. But he'd be *extremely* grumpy if she did.

She decided, instead, to leave a message with the desk clerk at Jerry's apartment building, apologizing for not returning his call earlier and promising to get in touch with him before he went on the air that night.

Why was she so solicitous of Jerry's feelings?

He was, no doubt, going to rehash all his grievances against Carla Caldwell on his program that night to the delight of his coterie of rabidly conservative listeners.

Jane admired everything Jerry despised about Carla Caldwell.

They truly were different. She was embarrassed to let her colleagues at the *Post* and her parents know she was friendly with him.

And yet.

And yet, what? Well, she wanted Jerry to tell her he would miss her if she left Washington for Hollywood. She thought she would miss his acerbic wit and self-assuredness. He sure was unlike most Washington men.

The cab swung left on Fifteenth Street, made a U-turn, and deposited her in front of the *Post*. She'd worry about her Jerry dilemma later.

Ravi was waiting on the fourth-floor level of the newspaper's two-story library with large brown envelopes stuffed with clippings about Carla dating back to the 1940s. Jane had only an hour to spend that afternoon on what could be a quixotic search for clues about a politician who *might* have fathered Carla's daughter during a secret affair more than forty years earlier.

After an hour, Jane's editor, Russ Williamson, would start

screaming at her for copy for the follow-up story on Carla's murder for the next morning's paper.

The reporter spread out the yellowed clippings on a table Ravi had reserved for her. She'd never be able to go through all the clips in an hour. And for any stories about Carla printed after 1989, Jane would have to tap into the paper's computer database. Her search could take a long time.

There were clippings about Carla speaking at war bond rallies during World War II and at rallies protesting the Vietnam War two decades later, being harangued by Senator Joe McCarthy during his Reds-in-Hollywood hearings and haranguing other congressional committees about her pet causes, leading "goodwill" delegations to visit Fidel and the Sandinistas.

But there wasn't much gossip about her social life.

In those days, when Style was still referred to as the "women's pages" or the "Society section," details about the private lives of public figures weren't printed as much, Jane knew.

One old photo, dated 1954, caught her attention. It showed an unlikely couple—Republican éminence grise Oscar O'Malley Sr., then Eisenhower's commerce secretary, and Carla, posing at some party. The caption identified the college-age boy grinning in the background as O'Malley's son, Oscar junior.

While Jane was trying to figure out what it was about the old photo that held her interest, Russ Williamson phoned.

"I thought you were covering the investigation of Carla Caldwell's murder."

"I am."

"Well, where the hell's your copy for tomorrow's paper?"

"I'm doing research," Jane explained. "I'm on my way to the newsroom. You'll have my piece in an hour."

"Great," the editor said. "And if it's good, I'll buy you a drink after work."

"I'm *so* sorry, Russ," Jane replied with heavy sarcasm. "Tonight's the monthly meeting of my embroidery group. I'd *hate* to miss it. Maybe another time for that drink."

Before ascending the spiral staircase to her cubicle in the newsroom one floor above, Jane returned to the old photo of Carla with Oscar O'Malley senior and junior.

What was it about the picture that nagged at her?

Maybe it was just the striking resemblance between father and son. The famous wide O'Malley jaw. The tipped-up O'Malley Irish nose. Caricatured in thousands of political cartoons.

No. There was something else that Jane couldn't quite . . .

Oh my God!

Now Jane realized what she saw in the photo.

Lucinda Caldwell had a wide jaw and a tipped-up nose.

Glimpsing the woman through the hotel-room door, Jane had thought she resembled someone familiar.

But one of the O'Malleys? The father of Carla's daughter? Jane found the idea absurd.

The O'Malleys had been a fixture of conservative politics for two generations. A symbol of Irish Catholic rectitude.

It was unthinkable that one of them had been Carla Caldwell's lover.

Yet. The jaw. The nose.

CHAPTER TWENTY-FIVE

JONES WASN'T TURNING up many puzzle pieces.

Sitting at his paper-strewn desk at Homicide headquarters the day after Carla's murder, A.L. reviewed what he knew. Which wasn't much.

The detective had determined that the Reverend Harlow Baskin had been in plain sight of uniformed policemen until he disbanded his anti-Carla demonstration outside the Kennedy Center and departed the scene. So the girl newsie's theory that Baskin was the perp didn't stand up.

Of course, one of Baskin's followers could have sneaked backstage and iced the actress, A. L. noted.

But the head of security for the performing arts center—a former precinct captain with whom A. L. had worked on a couple of cases—had told Jones during an interview earlier in the day that no suspicious-looking person was seen near Carla's dressing room. The security chief acknowledged, however, that it was chaotic backstage after the show, with the TV crew, friends of the honorees, Kennedy Center staff, and assorted hangers-on all milling around.

"Somebody could've slipped into her dressing room and done it without us seeing them," the security chief conceded.

"*Did* slip in," A. L. corrected. "Not *could've. Did.*"

The security chief nodded, looking morose.

The murder of a famous actress whom his staff was supposed to protect was probably going to cost the ex-cop his job, and his reputation, A. L. guessed.

He patted the man on the shoulder consolingly and advised him that detectives were interviewing everyone they could locate who had been backstage at the time of the killing. Maybe something would turn up that would allow Jones to close the case quickly.

Yeah, that would be good. But unlikely.

A. L. had already been summoned by Captain Wheeler, head of Homicide and ass-kissing buddy of the mayor, who was conducting an undisguised campaign to become chief.

There was *pressure*, Captain Wheeler had informed Jones, to nail the perp fast.

Yeah, *pressure.*

There was always *pressure* to nail the perp fast when some white chick or white dude went down on the good side of town, especially some celebrity like Carla Caldwell. There was never any *pressure* to nail the perps who popped the four hundred black nobodies found every year in alleys in Anacostia or apartments in Columbia Heights.

A. L. thought of LaTroy, who had come close to being one of the four hundred.

The boy was now safe in school, the detective hoped.

Jones needed coffee.

Then he needed to talk to Carla Caldwell's daughter.

Thanks to his stupid slip that morning, the detective guessed that Jane Day had already been to see her. He better find out what the daughter knew before he read about it in the next morning's *Post*.

A. L. parked his dirty white detective's cruiser—he had paid a police tow truck driver to haul it away from the Kennedy Center driveway and install a cannibalized battery—next to a fire hydrant near the Nineteenth Street Starbucks where Shaneta worked.

It was on the way to the Watergate Hotel, where Lucinda Caldwell was staying, the detective rationalized.

Downtown office workers apparently were on their afternoon coffee breaks and the place was crowded. Shaneta grinned at A. L. when she spotted him in line.

Although the detective's order was simple—large coffee of the day, nothing in it, to go—the young woman dragged out her preparation to give herself time to flirt with Jones, who was still uncomfortable in the upscale coffee bar.

"You sure I can't offer you a latte or a cappuccino, sir?" Shaneta teased sassily. "They good, warm you up on a cold day like this."

"Girl, I ain't got no time to be messin' with you today. I'm working a case."

"Oh, a *case*," she exclaimed, opening her black eyes wide. "A case of what? A case of Rolling Rock?"

"I'm on that case where the actress was slammed."

"Really!" Shaneta feigned surprise. "You ain't that famous detective A. L. Jones I was reading about in the newspapers, are you?"

"Come on, Shaneta," he growled.

"Come on, Shaneta," she mocked him.

The people in line behind Jones shifted impatiently.

"Come back later, when it ain't so busy," the young

woman told him, taking his money for the coffee. "I get off at six."

"I don't know if I can," A. L. mumbled. "The case . . ."

"Well, *try,*" she instructed, patting her fat braids in place. "Otherwise, call me."

"Yeah, I'll try. Otherwise, I'll call you."

He took his coffee and left.

Shaneta watched the detective go. He sure was different.

Jones showed his credentials to Lucinda Caldwell through the narrow opening in her hotel-room door. She let him in resignedly and led him to the sitting area of the two-room suite.

Lucinda looked nothing like her famous mother, glamorous even in old age, the detective noted. The plump woman huddling in a corner of the sofa, wrapped in a bathrobe, clutching a wad of tissue, looked worn and apprehensive.

After some preliminary explanations, A. L. began his interrogation, his deep voice encouraging and gentle.

"Were you in the theater last night when your mother won her award?"

"Yes. She got me a ticket."

"Did you go backstage afterward?"

"No. I walked back here and waited for her."

"Did anybody see you come back here?"

Her shoulders shrugged in the bathrobe. "I don't know. I didn't talk to anybody."

"Why didn't you go backstage?"

"My mother didn't like me around her in public."

"Why?"

She shrugged again.

"Most people didn't even know your mother had a daughter," A. L. informed her, remembering Jane Day's surprised reaction.

Lucinda didn't reply.

"You know who your daddy was?"

"No," the woman sniffled.

A. L. thought she did know. But he decided not to press her on it for the time being. Lucinda Caldwell looked like she might go mental on him at any moment.

"You know who might want to kill your mother?"

"Could be a lot of people."

"Oh?"

"My mother was not a nice person, Detective. She made a lot of enemies. She always had to do everything *her* way. If you got in her way, she'd walk right over you."

"Including you?"

"*Especially* me."

The detective stared at her, considering the implications of that comment. A puzzle piece, definitely a puzzle piece.

"I didn't kill my mother, Detective Jones," Lucinda said in a stronger voice.

"Sounds like you had reason to."

"I guess it could look that way. She kept me hidden away, out of sight, like there was something wrong with me. Like sometimes you read about crippled children who are kept locked in a closet because the parents think they're a mark of shame, or a punishment. I wasn't locked in a real closet. But I guess you could say I was kept in some pretty expensive metaphorical closets when I was younger. Private schools, registered under an assumed name by her agent. My mother never came to visit."

"And you didn't hate her?"

"She was the only person in the world I've ever loved, Detective Jones. And, in her own way, I think she loved me. As she got older, we became closer. I was her only companion. She was my only companion. In fact, once she accepted that she was going to grow old just like everybody else, she seemed less concerned about keeping me a secret."

A. L. looked puzzled.

"I was born when my mother was approaching forty," Lucinda elaborated. "At that age, she was desperate to hang on to her sex appeal. She thought a child would ruin her glamorous image, not just in the movies but in politics. She believed her glamour was her power. So, she decided to keep my birth, my *existence,* a secret from all but a very few trusted friends."

"And you didn't hate her for that?"

"I have worked out my feelings toward my mother in twenty-five years of therapy and twenty-five years of poetry. I didn't hate my mother."

A. L. looked at her skeptically.

"I didn't kill my mother," Lucinda repeated.

He waited a moment to see if she'd say more. Sometimes suspects can't stand silence and reveal things just to fill the pause. But she didn't.

"Why hasn't your father come forward?"

"He has his reasons."

So she did know who he was.

"Did your father have a motive to kill your mother?"

"I don't think so."

"Who is he?"

"Do I *have* to tell you?"

"I can't make you, at least not without going through a lot of legal procedures."

"Then I'd rather not."

Jones sat silent for a time to see if she'd volunteer more. But she remained huddled in the corner of the sofa.

"You're not planning to leave town, are you?" he asked.

"No. I'm staying for my mother's memorial service."

CHAPTER TWENTY-SIX

T HE PHONE IN Jane's cubicle in the newsroom rang while she was writing her follow-up story about Carla Caldwell's murder. The story was thin. In a frustrating day of reporting, Jane had turned up little usable new information, other than the revelation that the murdered actress had a middle-aged daughter whose existence had been kept largely hidden.

Jane jammed the phone against her shoulder and kept pounding the computer keyboard.

"Yeah?"

"It's Jerry. The desk clerk at my apartment gave me your message. I'm sorry I missed you last night."

She looked around to make sure no one could overhear the conversation. She'd given Jerry strict instructions not to call her at the office, which he regularly ignored.

"I can't talk," she told him curtly. "I'm working."

He ignored her terseness, which he was used to.

"I'm emceeing a fund-raiser at seven o'clock. Meet me

there, then we'll go to dinner afterward. I don't have to be at the studio until eleven."

"Who's the fund-raiser for?" she asked him sarcastically. "The National Rifle Association?"

"Close," he replied. "The Fund to Promote Baby Seal Roundups."

"Really?" She could never tell when Jerry was putting her on.

"No! It's for the Heritage Foundation."

"Conservative nuts," she replied.

"Conservative, but not nuts," he corrected. "Meet me there. Okay?"

"I can't," Jane explained. "I'm writing a second-day story on Carla's murder and it's slow going. I won't be done for another hour and a half, two hours."

"Then meet me for dinner after the fund-raiser."

"All right," Jane agreed.

"Nine o'clock at Sam and Harry's," he instructed.

"No way," she protested. "I'm not going to eat at a place populated by a bunch of two-hundred-sixty-pound carnivore lawyers in thousand-dollar suits."

"They're not *all* lawyers," he replied. "And some of them only weigh two hundred pounds. If you don't like Sam and Harry's, we'll do the Palm."

"That's worse! The steaks at the Palm could feed a family of four for a month."

"Where do *you* want to eat, then?" Jerry demanded exasperatedly.

"I don't know. I don't care. I haven't got time to think about it."

"If you don't care, then let's do the Palm," he suggested again. "I'll ask them for a table in the no-meat section."

"They really have a no-meat section?" Jane asked, again not sure if he was teasing her.

"No! It was a joke," Jerry laughed. "Where's your sense of humor? The Palm at nine?"

"All right," Jane agreed reluctantly. "I haven't got time to fight about it."

She rationalized that she could pump Jerry for information about the O'Malleys, father and son. Jane needed a lot more than an old photo and a Hollywood producer's cryptic remark before her editors would allow her to suggest in print that one of the O'Malleys might be the father of Carla Caldwell's daughter and, therefore, a suspect in her murder. Jerry had been in and around politics for a long time. He'd know things about the O'Malleys that might help her ferret out the truth.

But Jane conceded to herself that she also wanted to meet Jerry for his companionship.

What else was she going to do? Go home and watch TV with Bloomsbury? Fend off Russ Williamson?

The Washington branch of the Palm restaurant chain was located on the ground floor of an office building on Nineteenth Street. Its green canopy led from the sidewalk to the front door of what Jane considered a men-only clubhouse for lawyers and lobbyists and TV talking heads from the surrounding neighborhood.

She didn't avoid the Palm so much because it was a meat-and-potatoes place—*big* portions of meat and potatoes. She avoided it because of its overwhelming maleness. On those rare occasions when Jerry talked her into eating there, Jane saw a scattering of other women customers. And the Palm had even been pressured into hiring a few female servers under threat of bad publicity from feminists.

But they were the rare exceptions that proved the rule. The Palm was a guy's place.

To Jane, it had the loud, swaggering, testosterone-drenched atmosphere of a men's locker room.

The only distinctive feature of the Palm, as far as she was concerned, was the dozens of colorful caricatures on the walls depicting Washington's famous, sort-of-famous, and formerly famous. Of course, almost all the sketches were of men.

Jane deliberately arrived ten minutes late. She wanted to make sure Jerry was there first. She did not intend to sit alone at a Palm table being leered at by a bunch of gluttonous lawyers.

Jerry was halfway through a Sam Adams at his usual spot, one of the "good" tables reserved for celebrities in the back dining room near the bar.

Jane resisted the urge to kiss him on the cheek. In front of this crowd? It would be all over town by morning.

Joe, the most senior waiter, made small talk for while, then went off to fetch her Perrier.

Jerry and Jane exchanged stories about their separate backstage interrogations by Detective Jones the night before.

Jane reported that she had urged Jones to check out Harlow Baskin and his band of antismut demonstrators.

"They hated Carla for publicly criticizing Hammond," the reporter explained.

"So do I!" Jerry snorted. "And for her left-wing idiocies over the years. But I didn't stab her with a letter opener because I thought she was wrongheaded. And neither did Baskin."

"Then who *do* you think did it?" Jane challenged.

"I don't know," Jerry replied. "But I wouldn't be surprised if Carla's murder had something to do with her involvement in all those left-wing causes. The people in those organizations are always feuding with each other—jealousies, rivalries, debates over incomprehensible points of dogma. They're great haters and even greater grudge holders. And, of course, some of those old lefties have never forgiven each other for the way they responded to Joe McCarthy in the fifties. Some of them saved their own skins by turning in their comrades."

"But Carla refused to answer any questions when McCarthy questioned her," Jane recalled from her research.

"Maybe so," Jerry said with a shrug. "But my gut tells me the motive for her murder goes a long way back and involves some obscure old fight with one of her fellow left-wingers."

"You're just saying that because you hate liberals," she chided.

"Just because I hate liberals doesn't mean I'm always wrong," Jerry retorted.

Joe the waiter returned to take their orders. Jerry chose a porterhouse steak, medium rare, and a side order of fried onion rings.

"They ought to have a frequent eater program for people like you," Jane twitted. "For every ten thousand grams of cholesterol you consume, you get a free angioplasty."

"Don't give up your day job yet," Jerry advised. "The stand-up comedy thing may not work out."

She ordered a chopped salad with vinegar dressing on the side, and a plate of spinach, the vegetable of the day. Based on past experience, the plate of spinach would be five times more than she could eat.

Jane noticed that Jerry had been seated so that he faced his own caricature' on the wall. She also spotted another familiar visage sketched above the banquette to her right. The wide jaw and uptipped nose of Senator O'Malley.

"Do you know anything about Oscar O'Malley?" Jane asked Jerry.

"Senior or junior?"

"Both."

"Sure. The old man must be ninety or more. Still lives in Scranton, where he made the family fortune from coal mines. A power behind the throne in the Republican Party for decades. He was in Eisenhower's cabinet—I forget which department—and he wanted to run for president himself in 1960. But old Double O senior didn't have the personality for it. He's a mean son of a bitch, doesn't suffer fools easily. And there are a lot of fools to be suffered in politics, even in the Republican Party. Nixon got the nomination and O'Malley senior shifted his ambition to his sons. Some people think the old man's keeping himself alive by sheer willpower until Oscar junior wins the White House."

"What happened to the other sons?" Jane asked.

"One son was killed in Vietnam. The youngest son was a diplomat who got blown up by a terrorist bomb in Beirut. And another son drowned while sailing his boat. And to top it off, the only daughter killed herself."

"Sounds like the Kennedys," Jane suggested.

"Some people call the O'Malleys the Republican Kennedys. The O'Malleys probably have a little more money than the Kennedys. The Kennedys are probably ahead on ambition. And I guess it's a tie on family tragedy."

Jane nodded. If Oscar senior or Oscar junior was involved in Carla Caldwell's death, it would certainly fit in with the family's larger-than-life history.

"Why the interest in the O'Malleys?" Jerry asked.

Jane told him about the discovery that Carla Caldwell had a forty-three-year-old daughter named Lucinda, about the mystery over the father's identity, about Sheldon Berman's hint that the father might be a politician, about her failed attempt to interview the daughter, about the resemblance between Lucinda and the O'Malley family's distinctive facial features, and about the photo showing Oscar junior and Oscar senior with Carla in 1954, about the time Lucinda would have been conceived.

"Whoa!" Jerry exclaimed so loudly that other diners at the Palm's close-packed tables turned to look. "You're saying Oscar senior or Oscar junior is the father of Carla Caldwell's daughter?"

"I'm saying she looks a lot like the O'Malleys," Jane replied. "It's possible."

"It's *impossible*."

"Why?"

"The O'Malleys have been bedrock conservatives since they came to America during the potato famine. None of them would *ever* sleep with a flaming liberal like Carla Caldwell. It would destroy their reputations."

"Everything with you is politics, liberal versus conservative," Jane responded. "That's the way you look at the world, on the radio and off the radio. But people *are* motivated by other things, you know."

She lowered her voice.

"Look at us. Liberal and conservative. *We've* slept together. So couldn't a conservative O'Malley and the liberal Carla have had a fling?"

"Have you quit the *Post* and gone to work for the *National Enquirer?*" Jerry retorted. "Or are you practicing the Hollywood gossip mode before you move to LaLa Land?"

"If Oscar senior or Oscar junior was the father of Carla's daughter, it could have something to do with her murder."

"Jane!" Jerry exclaimed, raising his voice, again attracting the attention of other diners.

"Shhhhh," she hissed. *"Please* don't talk so loud about this."

"What are you saying?" Jerry continued, speaking more softly. "That a United States senator, or his father, killed Carla Caldwell? Is that what you're saying?"

"I'm not saying that. I'm just suggesting that if one of them is the father of Carla Caldwell's daughter, and if he knew she was writing her memoirs and might expose their affair, then he could be a suspect."

"That's an awful lot of 'ifs,' 'mights,' and 'could bes.' "

"I know."

"How do you know she was writing her memoirs?" Jerry asked. "One of your new Hollywood friends tell you?"

"I know."

"You people are unbelievable. Just because the O'Malleys are conservatives, you automatically assume they are capable of every kind of terrible deed, even murder."

"I'm not 'you people' and I'm not assuming anything," Jane shot back defensively. "But it's something to look into. Two minutes ago you were telling me that the O'Malleys are such staunch conservatives that they would never consider sleeping with a flaming liberal like Carla Caldwell because it would ruin their reputations if it ever became known. Well, suppose one of them *did* sleep with her and what if it *was* about to become known and it *would* ruin their reputations? Oscar junior wants to run for president. And you said the old man is hanging on just to see his son in the White House. Whether the father or the son was Carla's lover, it would destroy Junior's presidential ambitions. Voters are not going to vote for a conservative family-values candidate whose family values include an illegitimate daughter by a well-known liberal activist. Hypocrisy is the one crime voters won't forgive. Isn't that a motive for murder?"

Jerry was uncharacteristically silent, sipping his beer.

"It's got to be Oscar junior," Jane concluded. "You said

the old man's ninety years old or more, probably not physically up to stabbing Carla. And, besides, Junior had an additional motive. The daughter's forty-three, which means Oscar junior would have been twenty and Carla would have been almost forty when they had their affair. The age difference is likely to strike most voters not as just sex, but as inappropriate sex."

"So, what are you going to do?" Jerry's normal bombast was muted.

"Try to find the truth."

"How?"

"I don't know yet."

"Why don't you just ask Junior? Nothing seems to be off-limits to the news media these days."

"Yeah, right. 'Senator, did you father an illegitimate daughter by Carla Caldwell during a youthful affair and then kill Carla so she wouldn't reveal the romance and destroy your presidential ambitions?' I don't think so."

"Some reporters would ask him the question just that way," Jerry sneered.

"I know," Jane acknowledged. "But I can't."

Again, Jane came face-to-face with the fact that she lacked the killer instinct of some of her colleagues.

"So, what are you going to do to pursue your suspicions?"

"Let's team up again, Jerry, and find out who killed Carla," Jane proposed, "like we did on the Davenport and McLean cases."

"You want the story."

"I want the story," she conceded. "But I also want the murderer. I've always admired Carla Caldwell—she was a saint to my parents—and I got to like her even more when I interviewed her last week."

"And you don't think A. L. Jones is going to catch the murderer?" Jerry asked.

Jane let her raised eyebrows serve as her answer.

"So, what do we do to catch Carla's killer?"

"Invite Senator O'Malley to be interviewed on your show," Jane urged. "K. T. can find some pretext—Congress coming back into session in early January, O'Malley's presidential plans, how he thinks Hammond is doing—some pretext. Then you bring up Carla Caldwell's murder and see how he reacts. Please!"

Jerry looked dubious. But he agreed.

"All right, I'll do it. But only because I think it will prove that O'Malley didn't kill Carla Caldwell."

Jane reached across the table, took his hand in hers, and squeezed.

"Jerry, thank you."

She opened her mouth to say more, something affectionate. But she decided not to, on the assumption that Jerry would dismiss her sentiment with a wisecrack.

He surprised her by saying something affectionate to her.

"I'll miss you if you take the Hollywood offer."

She was so surprised by his unexpected declaration that she couldn't reply immediately.

"I've told you how much *you'll* hate being in L.A.," Jerry continued. "I haven't told you how much *I'll* hate being in Washington without you."

At some point Joe the waiter had brought her salad and spinach and his steak. But neither of them had touched the food.

"Jerry . . ."

"Yes?"

Jane wasn't sure what she wanted to say.

"Jerry, I . . . I haven't decided whether to accept the screenwriting deal yet," she offered, promising herself to be absolutely honest with him.

"Didn't you have lunch with the producer at Kinkead's today?"

"How'd you know?"

"Somebody told me he saw you and Sheldon Berman there."

"Mostly I pumped him for information about Carla."

"And he didn't ask you for an answer to his offer?"

"He did," she acknowledged. "I told him I hadn't decided yet. I told him I'd give him my answer by the end of the year."

"I feel like the death row prisoner who's just been given a stay of execution by the governor," Jerry commented.

"Lovely analogy," she shot back.

"It's the best I can do on the spur of the moment."

"You're no Yeats."

"Probably not."

Neither of them spoke for a moment.

"Jerry," Jane said at last, "I don't want to be away from you, either. That's the reason I'm having such a hard time making a decision."

He looked at her skeptically.

"That and my concern about living again in the same city with a domineering mother," she added candidly.

Jerry nodded his appreciation for her honesty.

"But, Jerry, this would be a fabulous opportunity for me," she continued in a plaintive tone, trying to ignite his enthusiasm for the screenwriting adventure. "I'm bored with daily reporting. I want to try something new. *You* moved a lot when *you* were climbing the ladder. You should understand."

"Unfortunately, I do understand," he said. "I want you to

stay because I want to be with you. But I also want you to succeed. I want you to be happy with your work. And it looks
like that means not being with you for a while."

"What's the right answer?" Jane moaned.

"There is no right answer," Jerry sighed.

"Well, we're not going to make the decision tonight,"
she said.

That "we" hung suspended in the air over the table until
he paid the check and they left.

CHAPTER TWENTY-SEVEN

JANE FOUND THE lock had been broken again on the outer door of her apartment building in the Adams Morgan neighborhood. She pushed the door partly open and looked warily around to make sure no one was lurking inside. Stepping into the decaying black-and-white tile lobby, Jane almost gagged on the stench of urine.

Adams Morgan, on the northern edge of downtown, was known as a mixed neighborhood, which meant that muggers, housebreakers, drug dealers, and drug addicts mixed with yuppie professionals who believed they were making an affirmative political statement by living in the diverse urban environment.

Jane tried to avoid the pungent urine fumes by holding her breath until the elevator deposited her at her floor.

The government should be doing more for the homeless, she thought angrily. The least it could do was provide decent and convenient public toilet facilities. But ever since Dale

Hammond and his conservatives had come to power, they had looked out for the rich and made life more unbearable for the less fortunate.

Jane didn't actually approve of street people using her lobby as a bathroom. But what else were they suppose to do? Damn conservatives.

Safely inside her apartment, with all three locks engaged, Jane turned to find her cat Bloomsbury sitting on the hall rug staring at her accusingly.

Where the hell had she been? Leaving him alone all day and half the night in the chilly apartment, with nothing to do. And worst of all, with no fresh food! If he knew how to dial the phone, he would have reported her for cat neglect.

Jane went to the tiny kitchen, opened a can of tuna, emptied it onto a plate, and placed it on the floor for the cat. When he loped to the food, she scratched his head between the ears.

Okay, Bloomsbury thought, he'd forgive her this time. But she better not let it happen again.

Preparing for bed, Jane pondered her next moves in the hunt for Carla Caldwell's murderer. It would take several days, at least, for Jerry to arrange for Senator O'Malley to appear as a guest on his *Night Talker* show. Even then, it was a long shot that O'Malley would blurt out something damaging about his relationship with Carla. If he'd had a relationship with Carla.

Meanwhile, there were other leads to pursue.

Jane replayed in her mind her lunch at Kinkead's with Sheldon Berman. In addition to his vague suggestion that Lucinda Caldwell's father might have been a politician, the producer had hinted that Carla knew other secrets that people in Hollywood wouldn't want publicized.

What had he said? Carla's death had caused a lot of people in Hollywood to breathe a sigh of relief. The producer had alluded to fears in the movie industry that Carla might tell in her memoirs what she knew about shady deals, kinky love affairs, political hypocrisy.

How was Jane going to pursue those leads? She had zero contacts in Hollywood. Except for Berman. Maybe she should try to pump him for more information about who might be anxious to silence Carla before she could publish her memoirs.

And then there was Jerry's idea that Carla's murder could be connected to some Old Left feud dating back to McCarthy and the Hollywood blacklist days. There were still some old reporters around Washington who had covered the anticommunist witch-hunts. She'd try to track one down and pick through his recollections for any enemies Carla might have made in those days.

Jane stood in front of her medicine cabinet mirror studying herself.

"Ugh."

She was in one of her moods again, Bloomsbury concluded. From experience, he knew that food and/or affection were unlikely when she stared at herself in the bathroom and made those noises. He retreated to the bedroom, curled up at the foot of the bed, and dozed off.

Jane eyed her body through the Run for the Cure T-shirt she slept in.

"Ugh," she proclaimed again.

Okay, tomorrow she was starting a *real* diet. No procrastination this time. Grapefruit juice for breakfast. A salad for lunch. And a small piece of plain grilled fish for dinner. No more muffins. No more bread. No more pasta. No more sweets. No more potato chips. And no more wine until she lost twenty-five pounds. Twenty pounds. Make it realistic, so she could really stick to it.

In bed, with Bloomsbury curled against her body for warmth, Jane couldn't sleep. The Carla Caldwell murder was on her mind. She wanted to uncover the murderer, write a brilliant story about it, and leave for her new life as a screenwriter in Hollywood in a blaze of glory.

If she went to Hollywood.

Her thoughts kept returning to the possible involvement of Oscar O'Malley. Jane knew he had been in the audience in the opera house for the Honors show. She had registered his arrival in her notebook, along with the other VIPs.

But had O'Malley gone backstage after the Honors show? If so, she would definitely consider him a suspect.

A. L. Jones would probably know.

Jane sat up in bed and switched on the bedside light, awakening Bloomsbury.

What was it now? the cat wondered. When was she going to bed so he could get some sleep?

Jane decided to phone the detective's office and leave her question about O'Malley's presence backstage on his voice mail to assure herself of an answer first thing in the morning.

She was surprised when the phone at Homicide was answered not by a recording but by A. L. himself.

"Detective Jones," he announced in his rumbling baritone. "How can I help you?"

"It's Jane Day. What are you doing up at this hour?"

"Working."

"On what?"

"Two drug boys was smoked in their car at Tenth and C Southeast."

"That's on Capitol Hill," Jane commented.

"Yeah. What are *you* doing up at this hour?"

"Thinking. Do you know who was backstage at the time Carla Caldwell was murdered?"

"I got a pretty good list," Jones replied, letting his normal reticence slip because he was tired and her call had caught him by surprise. "I don't know if I got everybody. Security was pretty loose."

"Is Senator Oscar O'Malley on your list?"

"O'Malley ain't on the list," Jones replied. "Should he be?"

What the hell was the newsie onto now? O'Malley was a big-time white dude. *Big-time.* TV said he could be the next president. Was the newsie suggesting he had something to do with dropping the actress?

"Why you asking about O'Malley?"

"I'm writing a story about people backstage after the Honors show who might have seen Carla's killer without even knowing it," Jane fibbed. "Somebody told me O'Malley might have been there. I guess it was a bum tip."

"You ain't playing amateur detective again, are you?" Jones demanded.

"Detective Jones, your job is catching murderers," Jane said with forced sincerity. "My job is writing stories for the newspaper."

Yeah, bullshit, A. L. thought.

After turning off the light and burrowing under the covers, Jane still couldn't sleep.

She decided to listen to Jerry's *Night Talker* program to take her mind off the murder case.

". . . if they were working for a corporation, all the people you represent would have been fired for incompetence a long time ago," Jerry's voice pontificated from the speaker of Jane's clock radio.

"The people I represent do not work for a corporation," the guest sputtered in response to the host's attack. "They are schoolteachers, endowed with the most important duty in our society—almost a priestly duty—of educating our nation's young people for the twenty-first century."

"And doing a damn poor job of it," Jerry shot back.

From his voice, Jane recognized the guest as the president of the National Education Association.

"After being subjected to the 'priestly duty' of your teachers union for twelve years, most students arrive at college unable to read, unable to write, unable to speak except in unintelligible monosyllables, ranking right down there with Burma in math and science skills, knowing nothing about history except that a bunch of dead white guys did everything wrong. So, that's what you call 'educating our nation's young people for the twenty-first century'?"

"Now just a minute, Mr. Knight, let me correct your facts," the guest protested.

"My facts *are* correct," Jerry proclaimed. "Since the teachers you represent aren't teaching, or can't teach, shouldn't they be fired for incompetence? Yes or no? Just answer my question."

"Let me explain—"

"Yes or no? Teachers whose students don't learn should be fired for incompetence, right?"

"If you will permit me—"

"Your refusal to answer my question is a yes, as far as I'm concerned," Jerry concluded triumphantly. "We're going to take a break here for commercials, and when we come back, I'm going to ask my guest for his views on distributing condoms to fourth graders."

Jane changed the station to NPR.

Better to be lulled to sleep by a soporific discussion of the rural economies of central Africa than to be kept awake by Jerry's Neanderthal rantings.

CHAPTER TWENTY-EIGHT

F RIDAY NIGHT. COMING up on one week since Carla Caldwell's murder, and A. L. Jones hadn't been able to fit many puzzle pieces together.

No fingerprints on the letter opener. Nothing traceable left in the star's dressing room. No one remembered seeing anything or anyone suspicious backstage. The Reverend Harlow Baskin seemed to be in the clear. And the daughter had been mostly noncommunicative.

Of course, Captain Wheeler had summoned A. L. again, to say he was under pressure to show progress on the case.

The detective phoned Dr. Willie Wu, one of the medical examiners at the D.C. morgue. Jones wanted to find out if the body provided any leads.

"Hello," the Chinese doctor answered in a high-pitched voice.

"Hey, Willie. It's A. L. How you doing, man? You working late tonight."

"Oh, yes, very busy here," the doctor explained. "Lots of people dying to get in."

A near-hysterical cackle came from the phone.

Willie used the same line every time they talked. It had long since stopped being amusing to Jones.

"You got a report yet on Caldwell?"

"Caldwell? We've got so many. . . ."

"That old actress," A. L. elaborated. "Slammed last Sunday at the Kennedy Center."

"Oh, yeah, her," the morgue examiner recalled. "Examination's done. Did it myself. But no time to write report yet. Computer's broken. Typewriter is ripped off. And we've run out of forms. In other words, everything the same as usual."

"I'll drive on over there and you can tell me what you found," Jones suggested.

"Don't rush," the morgue doctor said. "I ain't goin' anywhere. And neither are my guests."

A. L. hung up on Wu's maniacal laugh.

The detective headed the dirty white Ford first toward his apartment in LeDroit Park, off Florida Avenue near Howard University.

He wanted to check on LaTroy.

Friday night. With no school the next morning, the temptations of the streets and the gangs might be overwhelmingly alluring for the teenager, Jones worried.

He assumed the boy still yearned to avenge his mother's murder by drug boys. LaTroy had almost been wasted himself the first time he went after the crew he suspected of popping his mother. The boy was still recovering from his wounds. And he would try again, Jones guessed.

But that night he found LaTroy and his friend Ernie sprawled on the floor of the apartment, surrounded by Mc-

Donald's wrappers and empty Coke cans, laughing at a movie on the VCR in which Michael Jordan consorted with cartoon characters.

A. L. had replaced the VCR stolen from his apartment. He'd attached a metal loop to the bottom of the new machine, screwed another metal ring into the floor, and secured the tape player with a chain and padlock.

Let's see the mothers rip off that one.

Jones rubbed his hand over LaTroy's tightly coiled black hair and tugged playfully at the gold ring in his left ear.

"You stay in, hear?" A. L. growled. "I'll be back in a couple of hours."

"We ain't going nowhere," the boy assured him.

Jones wanted to believe that.

The boy had changed under his care. Six months ago, LaTroy's reply to his admonition would have been, "Fuck you, man. I go wherever I damn please. You ain't my daddy."

A. L. was the closest thing to a daddy LaTroy would ever have.

The detective thought about his ex-wife, living in New Jersey and married to a doctor. Before they'd split up—because she never thought A. L. would amount to anything—his wife had wanted to have children.

LaTroy was probably not what she had in mind.

Jones turned left on Florida Avenue and right on North Capitol Street. The dome of the United States Capitol building gleamed white in its spotlights at the end of the street a mile to the south.

The radio was quiet, especially for a Friday. A. L. was on the bubble again, so the next homicide in D.C. would be his case. He hoped to go off duty before he was called.

In earlier days, A. L. had relished the calls. He was like

a hound, always eager for the hunt. But that was years ago, when he first came home from Vietnam, when he still believed he could maintain law and order in his hometown. That was before the avalanche of crack, before the easy availability of Glocks and 9-millimeters, before the epidemic of killings overwhelmed the ability of the police and the courts to catch and confine the shooters.

A. L. felt old and tired.

Nowadays he cringed at the crackle of the radio, hoping it would not call his name for another drive-by, another execution-style killing. The dead children, innocents caught in the crossfire, were the worst.

Jones shook the picture out of his mind.

He swung left onto Massachusetts Avenue at Union Station and headed east on the empty night streets, toward the morgue.

Massachusetts Avenue, which began so fashionably in the comfortable Maryland suburbs, dead-ended abruptly ten miles away near the banks of the Anacostia River in a decidedly unfashionable part of town.

Dead-ended was right, A. L. mused. Lot of people dead-ended here. He knew from his aborted architectural studies that the Washington poorhouse had stood on the very site in the late nineteenth century. Well, not much had changed. It was now the site of the D.C. morgue, the D.C. jail, and the D.C. General Hospital.

For as long as A. L. had been on the police force, the morgue had been a vile place. But in the past few years, as a result of the murder epidemic and the city government's financial crisis—or the city government's incompetence, take your choice—the morgue had become unspeakable.

The cooling and ventilation system failed frequently and

the drains in the autopsy room often backed up. In summer, the stench was unbearable.

The refrigerator room was built with shelves for twenty-five bodies. Often the place was crammed with three times that many. The overflow corpses were stored on the floor or on rusting gurneys, covered with bloody sheets because body bags were in short supply.

The overcrowding problem was exacerbated by the periodic breakdown of the morgue's crematorium, used to dispose of unclaimed bodies.

Wu's complaint on the phone about missing report forms and nonworking computers was common. He'd once told Jones that he'd been forced to beg for basic supplies from funeral homes to keep the place running.

Under those conditions, it wasn't surprising that Jones couldn't remember the last time he'd gotten information from an autopsy report that helped him on a case. Maybe the Caldwell case would be different.

Jones parked his car in the lot and went inside. No grieving family members in the lobby for a change. It *was* a slow Friday. A lidded plastic bucket had been placed inexplicably in a corner. The word SKULL and a code number had been written on the bucket with a felt-tip pen.

A. L. inhaled cautiously. Not too bad. Thank God for cold weather.

The smell would be worse in the autopsy room. A. L. had stopped going in there a long time ago. He peered through the window in the door, rapped on the glass, and motioned to Wu to come out.

"Detective Jones," the morgue doctor greeted him enthusiastically. "Welcome."

Wu extended his right hand, encased in a latex glove covered with bloody goo.

A. L. recoiled.

"Don't be so afraid!" the doctor cackled. "My guests are completely harmless."

Jones didn't find it funny.

"So, you want to talk about the Caldwell killing," Wu continued. He led the detective to a tiny office off the lobby, peeling off the bloody gloves as he walked. "Nice and quiet to talk. Quiet as a tomb here."

The doctor's high-pitched laugh rose toward hysteria.

Willie's humor was wearing thin.

Jones tugged a bent notebook and a ballpoint pen from his jacket pocket.

"So, what'd you find out about her?"

The doctor rummaged through the disorderly mess of papers on his desk until he found a yellow legal pad on which he kept his scrawled notes from examinations while he awaited the arrival of official report forms.

Wu squinted at the notes to refresh his memory.

"She was in pretty good health for an old lady," he recited. "Little scarring on her heart. Probably had a mild heart attack, maybe twenty years ago, might not even have known it. Small benign cyst on her left lung. Not uncommon. Had her gallbladder removed at some—"

"And she had a letter opener stuck in her side," A. L. prompted.

"Yes, the letter opener. It entered her right side just below the ribs from slightly behind and at an angle perpendicular to the floor. Almost no bruising on the outside. Just a little from the handle."

"And inside?" the detective asked.

"Ah, inside. A lot of damage. The blade pierced or nicked parts of her liver, intestine, pancreas, and lung."

"She died of . . . ?" A. L. prodded.

"Shock and internal bleeding. The shock of such a wound would have killed someone her age almost immediately."

"Can you tell anything about who stuck her?"

"Not much," Wu replied. "From the position of internal organs, I'd say Mrs. Caldwell was seated at the time she was stabbed. I'd guess the perp was standing behind her right shoulder, with his right arm hanging at his side, clutching the opener in his right hand. He probably swung his arm back and then forward. Zip. She dead."

The morgue examiner giggled.

"How much force did it take?" Jones persisted.

"Not much," Wu responded. "Mrs. Caldwell was wearing a light silk blouse. No strength needed to penetrate that. And her skin and muscle, of course. But the opener encountered no bone. Not much strength needed."

"Did she struggle with the perp?"

"No sign of it. No cuts on her hands. No skin under her fingernails."

"So, she must have known the perp. She let him into her dressing room. She let him stand close behind her. And she didn't try to ward off his attack."

"I don't know," the little Chinese doctor replied with a shrug. "That's your job. I just cut 'em up. You figure out who popped 'em."

Again, the high-pitched giggle.

"Anything else?" Jones asked. He was ready to get out of there.

"She'd had a couple of face-lifts," Wu grinned.

"How do you know *that?*"

"Scars under the hairline, where the plastic surgeon pulled back the skin and cut off the excess."

"Yeah, well. I don't think that's going to help me catch the perp."

A. L. put away his notebook and moved toward the door.

"Come back and visit again soon, A. L.," Wu called after him. "I never have a single complaint from my guests."

His crazed laugh bounced off the tile walls as the detective pushed open the outside door and sucked in fresh night air.

The detective was sure the morgue stink had permeated his skin and his clothes. So he drove back toward his apartment with the windows open despite the icy temperature.

Almost 2 A.M. The streets were deserted. But menace seemed to lurk in every doorway and alley. Even the gun in his holster didn't make A. L. feel safe.

He turned on the radio for company. See who Mr. Night Talker was roasting.

". . . final hour with our guest, Senator Oscar O'Malley, son of a great Republican family, a leader of the conservative movement, and a possible future presidential candidate."

Jerry Knight's familiar voice blared out of the cruiser's speaker.

O'Malley?

The name refocused the detective's attention.

First that *Post* newsie with the weird orange hair calls him in the middle of the night and asks him a lot of questions about whether O'Malley was backstage when the actress was popped. Now, a few nights later, her boyfriend is interviewing the senator on his radio program.

That was too much to be a coincidence. What was going on? A. L. thought he knew. The two of them were playing amateur detective again.

Instead of turning right on North Capitol toward his

apartment, Jones steered his vanilla-colored detective's car west on Mass Avenue, past the beautiful but bedraggled Carnegie Library at Mount Vernon Square, past the convention center, toward the studios of the All Talk Network.

CHAPTER TWENTY-NINE

JANE DAY WATCHED Jerry's interview with Oscar O'Malley from the control room through the big glass window.

She was disappointed. The questions she had written for the host, hoping they would fluster the senator into disclosing an affair with Carla Caldwell, were getting nowhere.

Nervously twisting and untwisting a curl, Jane stood anxiously beside Jerry's diminutive producer, K. T. Zorn. K. T. wore her usual black leotards, lace-up black boots, and bulky black sweater. A black beret perched on her gray crew cut.

Jane kept up an anxious running commentary on Jerry's interview with O'Malley, trying to will the senator into saying something revealing. But it wasn't working.

When Jerry brought up Carla Caldwell's death per Jane's prompt sheet, O'Malley smoothly shifted the conversation to President Hammond's attack on sex and violence in popular entertainment and Carla's denunciation of the President. The senator voiced support for Hammond and criticism for the actress.

Through the control-room window, Jane stared at O'Malley's profile as he faced Jerry across the baize-covered interview table. The famous Irish pug nose, the famous wide jaw that so resembled the face Jane had glimpsed through the door of Lucinda Caldwell's hotel room.

The reporter peered intently at the senator, hoping to catch some nervous tic, some twitch that might suggest his smooth answers about the dead actress were hiding an inner emotional turmoil.

But O'Malley gave no such sign. Maybe Jane was following a false lead. Maybe Oscar O'Malley wasn't Lucinda's father. Maybe he had nothing to do with Carla's death.

Jerry gamely repeated her suggested questions until K. T. signaled it was time for the next commercial break.

"We'll be back with Senator Oscar O'Malley, a leading candidate for the Republican presidential nomination, right after these messages."

Jerry shrugged at Jane through the window. It was no use.

For the rest of the hour, the host chatted with his guest on other topics.

Jane was disappointed, but not quite ready to give up.

At 3 A.M., Jerry bid farewell to the senator and opened the phones for two hours of "Talk Back, America"—airing the most paranoid fantasies and outrageous accusations of his far-out listeners.

Jane followed O'Malley to the elevators.

She introduced herself, explaining that she was writing an appreciation of Carla Caldwell for the Style section.

"Did you know her?" Jane asked innocently.

"I met her a few times at various Washington events,"

O'Malley replied, pushing the elevator button repeatedly, even though the down arrow light was already on. "I didn't care much for her politics or her causes."

"In doing my research, I came across an old photo of you and your father posing with Carla at some function back in the mid-fifties." Jane spoke hurriedly, afraid the elevator would arrive and cut short her last shot at O'Malley. "Do you remember that?"

"Mid-fifties?" he laughed. "That's more than forty years ago. Afraid I don't have any recollection of such a photo."

There was no laughter in his slate gray eyes, Jane noticed. Well, she couldn't make a story out of that. Insincere laughter was not exactly a rare occurrence among politicians.

"Were you friends with Carla in those days?" Jane was going for broke now.

"Friends with Carla?" The senator laughed again. "In the mid-fifties I was still in college. Unlikely a college boy would be friends with a famous movie actress."

O'Malley hadn't actually denied he was friendly with Carla, Jane noticed. He had carefully used a lawyerly formulation to say only that it was *unlikely* a college boy would be friends with a famous actress.

In Washington, cover-ups of gigantic scandals had been constructed on smaller nondenial denials than that.

But before she could ask O'Malley another question, the elevator came. He bowed slightly to her, got in, and was gone.

"Damn!" Jane cursed aloud in the network's empty lobby.

Why hadn't she been able to ask O'Malley straight out, *Did you have an affair with Carla Caldwell? Are you the father of her child?*

But she hadn't. She couldn't.

Damn Mavis for teaching her manners!

Jane slammed her palm against the wall in frustration at her own unreporterlike tact.

Then the elevator door opened again and out rolled the stumpy figure of A. L. Jones.

"Detective Jones. What are you doing here?" Jane asked in surprise.

"What are *you* doing here?" the detective growled. "You and your boyfriend, Mr. Night Talker, are playing amateur detectives again, ain't you? First, you're asking me questions about Senator O'Malley being backstage when the actress is busted. And next thing, Mr. Night Talker is asking O'Malley questions about the actress on the radio. So, you tell me what's going on. You know something about the case, you tell me so I can investigate. I don't need no newsies doing their own investigation. We been through that before."

Jane made a quick calculation. She couldn't force O'Malley to answer her questions honestly. But Jones could.

"If I tell you what I know, will you give me the story first when you solve the case?" Jane bargained.

"I ain't making no deals with you, Miss *Washington Post*," A. L. rumbled. "You tell me what you think you know, or we go find a magistrate to make you tell me what you think you know."

Jane decided to take the chance that A. L. would give her a break on the story, if there was a story. She had no choice.

Standing in the silent lobby, Jane related to the detective what she knew and what she suspected about O'Malley, the actress, and Lucinda, about Carla's memoirs and about the senator's presidential ambitions.

Halfway through her recitation, Jones pulled out his pad and started making notes.

Jane explained that the revelation of an affair between a liberal and liberated older actress and the college-age son of

America's most famous conservative family could wreck the White House dreams of Oscar junior and his father. A motive for killing Carla.

"Yeah," A. L. Jones grunted, rubbing the white stubble on his chin. "Anything else?"

"You know everything I know," Jane insisted.

"All right, you stay out of it now, hear?" Jones instructed, stabbing the elevator button with his stubby paw. "I'll do the investigating."

"So, I can write that you're investigating O'Malley's possible role in Carla's murder?" Jane asked.

"You cannot!" A. L. shot back. "I ain't even talked to the man yet."

And he sure was not looking forward to that. Asking a United States senator and future presidential candidate about his sex life. Asking him if he had stuck a blade into some famous actress.

A. L. wished he was working a drive-by in Anacostia instead of this mother.

The elevator arrived.

"What time is it?" Jane asked.

"About twenty after three."

"Can you help me find a cab?" She was afraid to be alone on the streets at this hour, even in the relatively safe West End around the ATN studios.

"You still live in Adams Morgan?" the detective asked, remembering the time he had surreptitiously followed her home when she and Knight were playing amateur detectives on the Davenport case.

She nodded.

"Come on. I give you a ride home," Jones offered.

He scooped a roll of shirts he'd meant to drop at the laundry, several empty 7-Eleven coffee cups, an empty KFC box, old newspapers, and some tape cassette boxes off the passenger seat and tossed them in the back.

"Sorry about the mess. Been too busy to clean up."

Jane nodded, listening with fascination to the chatter on the police radio.

"Ever been in a cop car before?" he asked as they drove up deserted New Hampshire Avenue toward Dupont Circle.

She shook her head.

"Never covered the police beat?"

She shook her head again.

"Until now," he said.

It took Jane a second to catch his dig.

"Thanks for the ride, Detective Jones," she said sincerely as the car navigated the circle and turned north on Connecticut. "I'm sorry to take you out of your way."

"Well, to tell the truth, my battery is getting kinda weak, so I wanted somebody with me to help with the pushing in case it died."

CHAPTER THIRTY

T HE NEXT MORNING, Saturday, Jane was awakened by sirens on Florida Avenue outside her apartment.

She peered at the clock radio.

Oh my God! Nearly 11 A.M.

Fatigue had finally caught up with her. She hadn't dropped into bed until shortly before 4 A.M. after an exhausting and emotional week.

Jane wanted to burrow under the blankets and go back to asleep. But she couldn't. Bloomsbury was sitting on the bed, glaring at her and making accusatory mews.

A fine parent she was, the cat scolded. Sleeping half the day while he was on the verge of starvation from lack of feeding.

Jane got his message. She rolled out of bed and padded across the cold floor to the kitchen, to the tuna and the can opener.

Bloomsbury smiled victoriously.

Jane yearned to return to the warm bed. But she had too much to do. The President and Grady Hammond were at Camp David for the weekend, so she didn't have to cover the White House. Barring a big new development, the Sunday paper wasn't interested in another story about the unsolved mystery of Carla's death.

So Jane planned to spend the day catching up on errands and doing her Christmas shopping.

Jerry had invited her to attend a performance of Handel's *Messiah* at the National Cathedral in late afternoon, followed by dinner.

Jane was often appalled by Jerry's particularly outrageous right-wing rants—on the air or in private. On those occasions she wondered what she found attractive about this insensitive and uncouth loudmouth. Then he would do something incredibly thoughtful, like invite her to the Christmas concert, and she was forced to reappraise him.

After reading the *Post* over a late breakfast of coffee and sugar doughnuts—she'd decided to postpone her diet until New Year's Day, after the culinary and alcoholic excesses of the holiday season—Jane changed the sheets on her bed, washed a week's worth of dishes, tidied up the small apartment, carted ten pounds of old newspapers to the recycling bin, scooped Bloomsbury's litter box, washed and dried her laundry in the coin-operated machines in the basement of the apartment building, and called her mother in Los Angeles. Mavis wanted to hear all about the Carla Caldwell case.

Then Jane hiked to the Metro stop near Dupont Circle and caught a Red Line train going north. The tunnel ran beneath Connecticut Avenue to just past the Uptown Theater, then veered left, beneath ritzy Cleveland Park, to Wisconsin Avenue, where it turned north again.

Jane got off at the Friendship Heights stop, at the boundary between D.C. and Maryland, and rode the escalator up to street level.

The fifteen-minute subway ride had taken her not just from one part of town to another, but from one world to another. The short journey had transported her from the grungy, edgy, ethnically and sexually diverse Generation X urban midtown world to the upscale, polite, clean, polished, moneyed, and mostly white suburban world of cars and shopping.

And what a shopper's paradise greeted Jane when she emerged from the subway entrance at the intersection of Wisconsin and Western Avenues.

On one corner squatted the massive marble fortress of Mazza Gallerie, housing a three-story Neiman Marcus and many pricey specialty stores. Across the street, dozens of even pricier shops surrounded the atrium of Chevy Chase Pavilion. A shopper who still couldn't find what she sought had only to walk a short distance to Saks Fifth Avenue, passing on the way such establishments as Tiffany and Brooks Brothers.

Mavis had taught her daughter to excel and to strive to succeed. She had also taught Jane to shop. The lessons had been arduous during childhood—long hours examining the outfits on the third floor at the old Saks on Wiltshire Boulevard, trying on every one in her size before selecting the one that radiated quality, individuality, and good taste.

Jane would have preferred grabbing a cute dress in the fad of the moment, one that looked just like the dresses all her classmates were wearing, so she could get to the Saks coffee shop more quickly for an order of the outrageous apple pie with sour cream crumb topping.

Mavis had taught her well. Now, as an adult, Jane could tell fashionable quality from trendy schlock, even expensive trendy schlock, from twenty paces.

For two hours, Jane followed her mother's lessons, joyfully filling four shopping bags.

She was unsure what to buy Jerry for Christmas. She wanted to get him a dark Italian shirt with matching tie. But she knew he would likely scoff at both the foreign label and the chicness, and would never wear them.

So she settled for a Jhana Barnes sweater in muted tones of charcoal and taupe that went with his graying hair. She wondered momentarily whether the gift was too expensive, whether Jerry would appreciate—or even recognize—the designer label.

But one of her mother's lessons prevailed: Always buy the best, even when you can't afford it.

By prearrangement, Jerry picked her up at the entrance to Saks at 3:30 P.M. in his black Cadillac. She hated the ostentation of that car. But, she had to admit, it was comfortable. And the trunk held all her shopping bags.

Jerry steered the big car south toward the National Cathedral, scene of the *Messiah* performance. The Gothic church—sixth largest cathedral in the world—and its attendant buildings sprawled across Mount Saint Albans where Wisconsin Avenue intersected with Massachusetts Avenue.

"This is the highest point in Washington," Jerry commented, turning into the grounds. "Symbolic. God set above the petty temporal affairs of men."

"Lyrical," Jane commented sarcastically. "Where'd you read that?"

"I didn't *read* it," Jerry protested, sounding hurt by her disdain. "I made it up."

He did surprise her sometimes.

The central sanctuary of the cathedral was already crowded when Jerry and Jane entered. They found two empty chairs near the back. The chairs were low-backed, and hard.

While no congregation held regular services beneath the soaring and ornately carved stone arches, Washington's WASPs gathered at the cathedral at important moments of their lives—christenings, marriages, burials, celebrations, remembrances.

Jerry scanned the audience while waiting for the performance to begin. Grandparents, parents, and children of wealth, privilege, and power. Taking time from busy lives for a couple of hours of inspiration and reflection. Teaching the next generation to enjoy beauty, to partake of the life of the mind and the spirit.

"If the rest of America was like this," Jerry whispered to Jane, "it would be a hell of a lot better place to live."

"Don't swear in a church," she admonished.

The audience quieted when the musicians entered and took their places on folding chairs at the front of the enormous chapel. Several choirs of adults and children, dressed variously in red, black, and white robes, shuffled into the facing rows of the choir loft behind the great stone pulpit. The late-afternoon sun slanted through the stained-glass windows along the right wall.

The concert began.

Handel's glorious music and the voices of the singers reverberated off the marble and stone, filling the huge space, bombarding the listeners with intense sound.

"You know Handel wrote this for Easter, not Christmas," Jerry whispered into Jane's ear. "It's about death and resurrection, not about birth."

His treasure of facts amazed her.

After a while, Jane's mind began to wander, as it usually did when she listened to serious music. Carla's murder floated into her consciousness. And Oscar O'Malley's possible involvement. Jane was frustrated that her questions, and Jerry's, had failed to dent the senator's smooth facade the night before.

She had to find out if he was Lucinda Caldwell's father, and if he was involved in stabbing Carla.

Jane had an idea.

"Do you know any reporters who covered Washington in the fifties?" Jane hissed into Jerry's ear. "Somebody who might remember Carla Caldwell's activities here in those days?"

"That was a long time ago," Jerry said out of the corner of his mouth.

"*Somebody* must still be around," she whispered.

A sixtyish woman sitting in front of Jane looked back with a disapproving expression.

Jerry frowned in concentration.

"Ned Chasen," he whispered.

"What?" Jane asked over the singing.

"Ned Chasen. Covered the Hill for the old *New York Herald Tribune*," Jerry elaborated, sotto voce. "He's still around and he still has most of his marbles."

Jane slipped her reporter's notebook out of her shoulder bag and wrote down the name.

"Where can I find him?" she hissed.

A man in the row behind shushed them.

"National Press Club bar, Monday through Friday, four o'clock sharp, ordering his first martini."

The deafening "Hallelujah!" chorus drowned out their conversation and all other sound. Many in the audience sang along with the massed choirs.

On the way out, Jerry suggested they stop at the tomb of Helen Keller.

"I didn't know she was buried here," Jane said in surprise. "I thought only government leaders were allowed."

"Nope. Helen Keller's buried here. And so is her teacher, Anne Sullivan."

"Why do you want to visit Helen Keller's tomb?" Jane asked.

"Because I admire her. She overcame her handicap and made something of her life, without whining, without blaming somebody else, and without a government handout."

"Really?" Jane shot back. "And I suppose you admire her life-long dedication to radical socialism, her frequent writings promoting socialism, and her support for the Industrial Workers of the World?"

Jerry made a grunting sound.

"Have you seen the extensive files J. Edgar Hoover kept on Helen Keller?" Jane twitted him.

Jerry grunted again.

Gotcha! Jane exulted.

Light snow was drifting down when they came out of the cathedral. They decided to let the traffic thin out before braving the streets.

"About an eighth of inch of snow and Washington drivers panic," Jerry huffed. "If the Soviets had figured out how to make artificial snow, they could have walked in and taken over this city without firing a shot."

They strolled a short distance up Wisconsin Avenue in the snow and had dinner at Cafe Deluxe.

Later, Jerry double-parked the Cadillac in front of her apartment building while Jane retrieved her shopping bags from the trunk.

There was no question of him parking and coming up to her apartment. At that hour on a Saturday night during the holiday season, a parking place was not to be found in Adams Morgan. Especially for a car that size. Driving around and around the neighborhood in search of a spot, Jane knew, would put him in such a sputtering mood that she was better off going home alone.

Of course, he could have invited her to come to his penthouse apartment in Rosslyn, where he had an assigned parking place in the garage. Sometimes he did. But not tonight.

Why! What was the matter with her?

Probably he held back from making any deeper emotional commitment because he knew she might soon be breaking it off to move to Hollywood.

Sure. That must be it.

Jerry slammed the trunk shut. Jane stood in the street, behind the car, two shopping bags in each hand, crafting a farewell wisecrack.

Jerry took a step toward her, wrapped his arms around her, and kissed her on the lips.

It was a hard kiss, pressing her head back. She felt cold snowflakes landing on her face.

Jane opened her mouth slightly. To protest? To make a joke? To encourage him? She didn't know.

Jerry's tongue slipped between her lips.

A passing car honked its horn.

"Go for it, man!" yelled a raucous voice. "Go for it!"

They kissed for a long time.

Finally, Jerry squeezed her against his chest and stepped back.

He mumbled that he would call her the next day, got into the Cadillac, and drove off down Florida Avenue.

Jane stood in the street, watching the car recede, happy, sad, confused, wishing he'd invited her to come home with him.

CHAPTER THIRTY-ONE

MONDAY MORNING. A. L. chose his one suit that didn't need pressing for his trip to the office of Senator Oscar O'Malley Jr. A gray wool Hart Schaffner & Marx with a fine chalk stripe. He'd bought it at the Woodies going-out-of-business sale.

The detective dreaded the appointment. He killed some time by driving LaTroy to his classes at Eastern High School. Then he killed some more time lingering over a cardboard cup of coffee and chatting with the ancient Korean proprietress of a carryout near Lincoln Park.

A. L. dreaded his visit to the senator's office because he didn't know exactly what he was going to ask the white dude. And he further dreaded it because he expected to get the runaround and the brush-off and the I'm-too-busy-to-see-people-like-you treatment, which he usually got when he was required to interview the big shots.

What did he actually know about any involvement by O'Malley in the Caldwell case? Not much.

O'Malley might have screwed around with Caldwell when he was just a kid and might have knocked her up. That whacked-out woman Jones had interviewed at the Watergate Hotel might be O'Malley's daughter. And if O'Malley was running for president, like they said on TV, he'd probably want to keep all that shit quiet.

So there could be a motive.

Of course, the detective's only source for that theory was the crazy orange-haired newsie from the *Post,* Knight's girlfriend.

Lame for confronting a United States senator.

A. L. poured himself a fresh cup of coffee to kill a little more time.

But, finally, he knew he couldn't put it off any longer.

Jones parked his car in a bus zone beside the Dirksen Building. It was the oldest of the three offices housing senators and their ever-expanding staffs. To the detective's eye, it had the most character.

He thought the building was ornate and rococo, courtly and charming, old-fashioned. Just like Everett Dirksen, the former Senate Republican leader for whom it was named.

Inside, A. L. found endless dark corridors, high ceilings, marble staircases, gold leaf, carved wood, statues, and a lot of people scurrying past him trying to look important.

Because of his seniority and his high profile, O'Malley occupied a corner suite of interconnected, richly decorated offices on the top floor. On one side, the windows offered a view of the Capitol. On the other side, the windows looked down Pennsylvania Avenue, toward the White House, which the senator and his staff hoped to occupy one day.

"May I help you?" the receptionist asked coolly.

"Senator O'Malley, please."

"Do you have an appointment?" she asked even more coolly.

"No appointment," he replied testily, showing her his badge and ID card.

"Just a moment."

Soon a young man in shirtsleeves and very wide suspenders appeared, clutching a handful of documents and looking harried.

"Detective? What's up?"

"Nothing's up. I need to see Senator O'Malley."

"About?"

"I'll tell *him* what it's about."

A. L. hated dealing with these self-important people.

"The senator is having an awfully busy day," the young man explained in a patronizing tone. "Give me your business card. I'll call you when we can work an appointment into his schedule. Okay?"

"It *ain't* okay," the detective retorted. "I need to talk to O'Malley. Now."

"Hold on," the young man said, sounding flustered. "Just wait here a minute. I'll get someone."

Soon another aide approached, a wizened, impish man with a bald head, wearing a bow tie and a perpetual grin.

"Hi!" he greeted the detective, sticking out his right hand. "I'm Kevin Casey, the senator's general counsel. What can I do for you?"

"You can get me in to talk to the senator, like I been asking for fifteen minutes."

A. L. showed his badge and ID again.

"Homicide?"

The detective nodded.

"What case?"

"Carla Caldwell."

The imp kept grinning, but his eyes looked hard.

"You think the senator might have seen something at the Kennedy Center that could help you?" the man asked. "Or that he might know someone involved? What's the exact nature of your interest in talking to the senator at this time?"

"You his lawyer on this?"

"Not necessarily," the little man responded warily.

They stared at each other a moment.

A. L. got the idea that Kevin Casey had a lot of experience handling difficult situations for Oscar O'Malley.

"Look, Detective," the lawyer said, "Senator O'Malley can't see you today. He's chairing an important committee hearing right now. And he's catching a plane at noon to fly to a speech on the West Coast. I'll set up a meeting in an appropriate forum with the appropriate legal representation present, and I'll let you know where and when."

"You want me to get a magistrate to sign an order?"

"Keep your voice down," Casey instructed, speaking in a cold whisper, but still grinning. "I doubt if you could. And if you tried, we'd tie you up in legal knots well past your normal retirement age. You can do it my way or the hard way, Detective. Your choice."

Jones turned and stalked out.

Uppity receptionist, tight-ass flunky, goddamn lawyer. All of them dissin' him.

At least when the drug boys busted each other, he didn't have to put up with that shit.

A. L. needed coffee and the Starbucks on Nineteenth wasn't that far away. Messin' with Shaneta awhile would put him in a better mood.

* * *

When the detective got back to his desk at Third and Indiana, he found a yellow stick 'em pasted to his computer screen. It was from Captain Wheeler: "See me."

The Homicide commander, a light-skinned black man with a pencil-thin mustache and oiled hair, tilted back in his desk chair.

"I got a complaint from Senator O'Malley's office," the captain informed his detective. "General counsel called me to say you barged in, talked loud, threw your weight around, demanded to see the senator, and wouldn't say why."

"Bullshit," Jones replied simply.

Wheeler was dressed in a double-breasted blue blazer with gold buttons, a white shirt with wide red stripes, and a satiny gold tie. Natty son a bitch, A. L. thought, unconsciously smoothing his own cheap gray suit. Running *hard* to be chief. And got his nose buried so far up the mayor's ass he can't see where he's going.

"We've got to walk the fine line here, A. L.," Wheeler lectured. "On the one hand, we're getting pressure to close this case. Our enemies in Congress, the ones who control our budget, are pointing to your failure to arrest anyone yet as a further example of incompetence by the D.C. police force."

"*My* failure?"

"On the other hand, there's a lot of big toes we don't want to step on," the captain continued. "You know what I mean?"

"Yeah," Jones grunted. O'Malley was big toes.

"You got leads, right?" Wheeler asked.

"Oh, yeah, I'm following a lot of leads," A. L. lied.

"Good, good," Wheeler cooed. "And O'Malley looks like a lead?"

"Not a real strong lead," the detective acknowledged,

getting the captain's drift. "I got stronger ones I probably ought to follow first."

"Sounds good!" Wheeler beamed. "You follow the strong leads first and leave O'Malley until later."

"Gotcha," Jones concurred. He didn't mind postponing another dose of the contemptuousness he'd encountered on his visit to O'Malley's office.

"When you going to ice this one?" Wheeler asked.

"Soon," Jones assured him.

The detective took advantage of the captain's silence to stand up and head for the door.

"One other thing, A. L."

Jones turned back toward Wheeler.

"I just got word," the captain informed him, "because of the budget crunch, we're cutting out paid vacations."

"What's a vacation?"

CHAPTER THIRTY-TWO

P ROMPTLY AT 4 P.M., Jane was in the bar on the top floor of the National Press Building awaiting the promised arrival of Ned Chasen, the old reporter Jerry had said might be able to provide firsthand recollections of Carla Caldwell in Washington in the fifties. She ordered a Perrier to sip while she waited.

Jane rarely came to the Press Club, except to cover news conferences. Even though the place had been modernized, it still reminded her of a stuffy, slightly seedy men's club from another era.

For the first half century of the Press Club's existence, it had accepted only male reporters for membership. Women had been barred from even covering newsmaker speeches in the club's ornate ballroom. After years of protests from a new generation of more assertive women reporters and columnists, the club grudgingly allowed women to cover the speeches, but segregated them in the balcony.

Women had been granted full membership in the Press

Club only in 1971 after a long struggle for equality with their male colleagues.

Waiting for Ned Chasen in the Reliable Source bar—previously called the Men's Bar—Jane couldn't see what all the fuss had been about. It was just a small, unassuming wood-paneled barroom decorated with brass plaques on which were engraved supposedly weighty quotations about the press.

Jane noted two women at another table, presumably reporters, drinking beers and smoking cigars. Maybe it was a milestone on the road to women's equality after all, she thought.

An old man shuffled in and Jane knew right away he was Ned Chasen. Tall, but slightly stooped, with wavy yellowish white hair, he was dressed in an overly bright plaid sport jacket, a clashing plaid shirt with an old-fashioned silk paisley cravat knotted around his neck, brown slacks, and thick-soled brown brogans.

Chasen headed straight for a stool at the bar, which Jane guessed was his regular spot, and lit an unfiltered Camel. The bartender reached over the bar and shook hands, then without instructions began mixing his drink, a Bombay gin martini on the rocks with minimal vermouth and two tiny white onions instead of an olive.

After Chasen had taken his first swallow, and smacked his lips appreciatively, Jane slid over to the stool next to him.

"Mr. Chasen?"

"The one and only," he confirmed. "Still alive and kicking."

His face was a map of deep creases and crevices, wrinkles and gullies, pocked with brown liver spots. Bushy white eyebrows nearly obscured his watery blue eyes. Up close, Jane saw that the cravat was an effort to hide the wattles hanging from his neck.

"And you are?" he asked in an ancient, raspy voice.

"Jane Day. I'm a reporter for the *Washington Post.*"

"Nice to meet you."

He extended his bony, liver-spotted hand. She shook it.

"It's been a long time since I was picked up at the bar," he rasped. "At least by such a pretty girl. Buy you a drink?"

They never grow too old to hustle women, Jane thought. They must come on to the nurses in the terminal care unit.

She let him order her another Perrier.

"Jerry Knight told me I could find you here," she explained.

"Jerry Knight. That right-wing son of a bitch," Chasen commented good naturedly. "I remember him when he was a halfway decent reporter. By radio standards, anyhow. Then he got mixed up in that talk show crap."

"Jerry thought you might be able to tell me about Carla Caldwell when she used to come to Washington back in the fifties."

"Jane Day. Okay, now I place you. You're writing about Carla's murder in the *Post,* aren't you? You usually cover the White House."

Jane nodded.

"Didn't you write that profile about Carla in the Style section just before she was killed?" Chasen asked.

Jane nodded again.

"Damn Style sections," the old man croaked. "They ruined journalism. When I first started in this business, we reported *facts.* Who. What. Where. When. How. Inverted pyramid. Names spelled right. Middle initials. Now, I can't *find* a damn fact in half the stories. It's all the reporter's *opin-*

ions. What she *thinks*. How it *feels*. Real journalism was destroyed by Style sections. And by the faggots on television, of course. Can you imagine if I had to put on makeup and hair spray before I wrote my pieces for the *Trib*? Christ, the other reporters would have thought I was a queer!"

Chasen was off on a long, discursive, and very politically incorrect denunciation of modern reporting and a glorification of the good old days, before television and Style, when he and his sainted journalistic contemporaries reigned in the bar and in the newspapers.

At one point he waggled a skinny finger at the bartender, who delivered another Bombay gin martini with onions. Chasen lit a second Camel.

"I'm eighty-six years old and the doctor says if I don't stop drinking and smoking, it's going to kill me."

The ancient reporter cackled until he was overcome by phlegmy hacking.

Jane took advantage of the coughing spell to steer him back to the topic she was interested in.

"So, you remember Carla in the fifties?"

"Goddamn, she was a beautiful woman," Chasen reminisced. "But by then she was a lot more interested in politics than acting."

"Was she also interested in *politicians?*" Jane pressed, now that she had him focused. "Like boyfriends? Did she go out with politicians?"

"She liked men, all creeds, colors, and places of national origin," the old man chuckled huskily. "I remember one time there was a party in somebody's suite right over there at the old Willard."

He waved at the venerable hotel across Fourteenth Street visible through the window.

"I forget what the occasion was. Maybe it was a New

Year's party. I can't remember. Anyhow, somebody brought Carla. After a while, I'm looking around for the bathroom. I stumble into the bedroom by mistake, and there she is in the sack with the goddamn waiter!"

He cackled again. He sipped his martini to suppress the wheezing.

"A friend of mine, he's gone now, used to work for the *Washington Star,* told me he ran into Carla one time at a Democratic convention. I think it was 1956. Maybe 1960. There was a long line outside the ladies' room in the convention center. So Carla marches into the men's room and uses one of the stalls in there. I hope you're not offended?"

Jane shook her head.

"A photographer I know, he died about two years ago, worked for *Time* magazine, said he was covering one of those civil rights marches in Alabama, Mississippi, somewhere down there, about 1963, and Carla showed up. She was always marching in those things."

Ned Chasen lit another cigarette and was off on a rambling account of Carla's purported outrageous behavior.

But none of it involved Oscar O'Malley.

When the old man paused to sip his martini, Jane jumped in.

"Did you ever hear any stories about her sleeping with politicians? Like senators?"

"We didn't pay much attention to the sex lives of politicians in those days," Chasen rasped. "What was it somebody said? 'As long as they don't do it in the middle of the street and frighten the horses, I don't give a damn.' Even the *New York Daily News* and the *New York Mirror* didn't print much of that crap. It's this new generation of reporters—no offense—and the TV fags that are so damn interested in who's sleeping with who. If I'd ever asked a presidential candidate if he'd committed adultery or if I'd ever asked a press secretary if the president had a case of the clap, the *Trib* would have cleaned out my desk and put my stuff in the hallway before I ever got back to the paper. In my time, we didn't do that tabloid junk."

This was not working, Jane realized with disappointment. He was not going to reveal to her an affair between Carla Caldwell and Oscar O'Malley.

"Buy you another drink?" Chasen asked, the old roué twinkle still there in his watery eyes.

Jane shook her head.

"Two's my limit. I've got to write."

He laughed appreciatively.

"I like you, Jane Day."

He reached over and squeezed her thigh with a shaky hand.

They never outgrow it, she thought.

"Did Jerry tell you I covered Carla's testimony before Joe McCarthy's committee?" Chasen asked. And he was off on another trip down memory lane.

But this time Jane paid close attention. Something Jerry said came back to her. He had suggested that Carla's death might involve some feud among Old Left activists that dated back to those terrible days of blacklists and ruined reputations. Maybe the old man would remember something to support Jerry's theory.

"I can see it just like it was yesterday," Chasen said, speaking as if in a reverie. "The hearing room was packed. You couldn't move. You couldn't breathe. And it was hot as hell. It was before air-conditioning, you know. Cameramen stumbling over my feet. Everybody wanted to see the movie stars. Carla shows up in a red outfit. Shirt with gold buttons and pants, like a military uniform. I mean *bright* red. Red was the color of communism, socialism, you know. It was her way of thumbing her nose at McCarthy. It was ten o'clock in the morning and he was already drunk. I was sitting ten feet from him and I could smell his breath from there. It was his usual crap. 'I hold here in my hand a list of thirty-five known communist subversives working in the movie industry, spreading their insidious Red poison through motion pictures. Miss Caldwell, are you now or have you ever been a member of the Communist Party?' "

Chasen imitated the interrogator's menacing growl.

Jane sat riveted by his account.

" 'My name is Carla Caldwell. I am an actress and a loyal American. That, Senator McCarthy, is all I intend to tell you.' She wouldn't even dignify his authority by taking the Fifth Amendment, like a lot of them did. He kept pounding her and she kept repeating her name and that she was an actress and a loyal American. Then McCarthy asked her about other people in the movie industry, and whether they were members of the Communist Party, whether she had seen them at meetings of communist front organizations, whether she was aware of any subversive acts they had committed, all that crap. And she just kept repeating, in answer to every question, 'My name is Carla Caldwell. I am an actress and a loyal American.' Finally, Joe lost his temper and told her she ought to move to Russia if she loved communism so much. She puts her mouth up close to the microphone and in that low, sexy voice of hers, she tells him, 'Sir, you are a bully, without one shred of human decency.' And she gets up and leaves. The audience is applauding and Joe is pounding his gavel, all red in the face, threatening to have her subpoenaed. He never did, of course. She showed him up, in public, and he didn't want any more of it."

Jane was enthralled, overwhelmed by the vividness of his recollection.

Chasen lit another Camel and continued as if she weren't there.

"McCarthy took out his anger at Carla on the rest of the Hollywood witnesses that day. He outdid himself, sneering at them and browbeating them, accusing them of being communists, not fit to live in the United States of America. He told them they all ought to be blacklisted from ever working in the movies again."

"Who were the other witnesses?" Jane asked, eager for him to continue the fascinating recitation.

"I can't remember them all. Dalton Trumbo, the writer, I know was one of them. Another writer—I don't remember his name. Alexander Knox, the actor who played Woodrow Wilson in the movie. Orson Welles, I think. Fran Turner, Carla's great rival in those days. One of the Marx Brothers. I forget which one. None of them were as feisty on the stand as Carla. But when Alexander Knox was asked if . . ."

Fran Turner.

Jane had heard that name recently. Hadn't someone suggested she get in touch with Fran Turner when she was researching her profile of Carla? But the actress was using a different name now. What was it? Jane would check her notes later.

"Those must have been great days to be a reporter in Washington," Jane commented when Chasen stopped to puff his cigarette.

"Those were the worst days I ever spent as a reporter," the old man croaked, his wrinkled face collapsing into a melancholy frown.

"Why?"

"McCarthy used us, goddamn him," Chasen spat. "We were trapped. I told you, in those days we reported what happened. Who said what. No opinion. No comment. No analysis. McCarthy knew the rules, and he took advantage of them. When he stood up on the Senate floor and said so-and-so's a communist, the rules required us to report quote Senator Joseph R. McCarthy today accused so-and-so of being a communist end quote. And somewhere down in the story we'd say so-and-so denied it. I spent a lot of nights in this bar, with my colleagues who were covering McCarthy, drinking ourselves into a stupor because he was using us to ruin people and under the rules, there wasn't a goddamn thing we could do about it. We agonized about it for a lot of years after McCarthy was gone. And the few of us who are alive and kicking are still agonizing about it."

Jane wanted to tell him that modern journalism, which he had denounced so vehemently earlier, would prevent another McCarthy by allowing reporters to raise doubts about the validity of his accusations. Aspiring demagogues were cut down all the time by skeptical comments from journalists who no longer were bound by rules of reporting only *he said, the other guy said.*

But the old man looked so distraught by his memories of being used by McCarthy that she decided not to speak.

"One more, Harry!" Chasen called to the bartender. "If my wife calls tell her I left a half hour ago!"

CHAPTER THIRTY-THREE

JANE CAUGHT A cab in the driveway of the J. W. Marriott Hotel next to the Press Club building and rode north to the *Post*.

She went straight to her cubicle and rummaged through the jumble of filled notebooks in the bottom desk drawer. She was anxious to find out why Ned Chasen's mention of Fran Turner had triggered a recollection of some connection with her Carla Caldwell coverage.

In the notes for her profile of Carla, which had run just before the murder, Jane found what she was looking for.

Jessie Bell, the *Post*'s pudgy gossip columnist, had suggested she contact Fran Turner, a movie star from Carla's era. Jane's notes recorded that Fran's Hollywood career ended abruptly after her appearance before McCarthy. She'd gone home to Covington, Kentucky, and taught drama at the community college under her real name, Francis Anklum. Jane had scribbled in her pad that a former student, Traci Andrews, now a TV star, had paid for Fran to come to Washington to see Carla honored at the Kennedy Center.

Jane's notes showed that Traci had put up her former drama coach at the Watergate Hotel. But the reporter recalled that she had been unsuccessful trying to reach Fran Turner before writing the profile.

Jane remembered Jerry's theory that Carla's murder might date back to some Old Left feud from the McCarthy days.

She wanted to talk to Fran.

The operator at the Watergate Hotel reported no Fran Turner registered there. No Francis Anklum, either. Further prodding by Jane produced the information that a Fran Turner had been registered, but had checked out the previous Monday.

The day after Carla's murder.

The reporter checked with Traci Andrews's publicist in Los Angeles. The TV star didn't know where her mentor had gone after checking out of the Watergate.

Jane phoned other hotels where celebrities stayed. The Bristol. Willard. Ritz-Carlton. Hay-Adams. No Fran.

Wait a minute. Why would Fran stick around Washington after the Honors show? She was probably back in Kentucky.

In her notebook, Jane found a name and phone number Jessie Bell had given her. Terry Pike, editor of the *Covington Weekly Gazette*. Jane remembered she'd called him when she was trying to locate Fran for the profile.

She called Pike again. As far as he knew, Fran had not returned to Covington after her trip to Washington.

Fran had taught at a small-town community college, so she probably didn't have a lot of money, Jane reasoned. If she was still in Washington, she could be registered at any of dozens of cut-rate hotels. As a long shot, the reporter picked a few at random from the yellow pages.

Fran was not listed at any of them.

Dead end.

She had struck out trying to connect Oscar O'Malley to Carla's death.

Fran Turner could not be found.

And Carla's daughter, Lucinda, wouldn't talk to her.

With no new leads to follow, no story to write for the next morning's paper, and nothing to do for the rest of the evening, Jane decided to kill time with mundane office chores.

First, she checked the E-mail on her computer. Ten messages. Nothing important. She read each one, then clicked DELETE. Except one from her editor, Russ Williamson.

Drink at ten? Talk about your career. And other stuff.

Jane clicked on the message and slid its little envelope icon into a PERSONAL file. If he was persistent much longer, she was going to complain to management about sexual harassment. She was saving up the evidence.

Jane typed a reply; *Sorry. Not tonight. Meeting George Clooney. Maybe another time, when your wife can join us.*

She hit the SEND button.

When all the E-mails had been disposed of, Jane turned to her voice mail.

Most were messages from PR flacks cajoling her to write favorably about their clients or their client's pet issues. She hit the 2 button to erase each one without even listening all the way through. One message was from an underling at the White House, spinning her on the benefits of an environmental bill President Hammond would send to Congress soon. She contemptuously zapped that one, too.

The last voice message in the queue was from Sheldon Berman in Hollywood.

I know it's not the end of the year, so you don't owe me your answer yet. But I want you to know how much I really, really want you to accept my offer to write the script for "A Child Is Lost." That's the working title. Did I tell you? William Hurt is definite for the Congressman Gates part. And Annette Bening is this close to signing for his wife. Jane, after our lunch, I'm convinced you'll be great in Hollywood. Look, just in case your hesitation is caused by money, I'm FedExing you a check for fifty K today, half your fee as cowriter. You'll have it tomorrow. And I've reserved an office for you on the Paramount lot. In the Maurice Chevalier Building. It'll be ready February first. Please, please call me and say yes. Okay?

Jane hit the 5 button to save that one.

A mile away, at his desk at Homicide headquarters, A. L. Jones stared at the yellow stick 'em he'd found in the center of his computer screen.

"CALDWELL CASE. WHEN?"

In Captain Wheeler's prissy handwriting.

At least the computer was good for *something*. It was broken for the umpteenth time. And slapping it on the side with the palm of his hand didn't fix it anymore. A. L. typed his reports on an old black Royal manual. The V key was broken. So Jones tried to use only words that didn't contain a V. He usually got by, except for the case of Vincent Volkman, who was smoked while trying to steal a vehicle on Volta Place.

Jones stared at the stick 'em message and sipped the dregs of cold coffee he'd found in the bottom of the office pot. Almost undrinkable, even for him.

A. L. reviewed the puzzle pieces he'd collected in the Caldwell killing.

Nothing helpful from the murder weapon, the dressing room, witnesses, or the autopsy.

The preacher leading the protest against the actress, Baskin, was in the clear.

Jones would have to go through a lot of lawyer bullshit before he'd be able to question Senator O'Malley. Anyhow, the newsie's theory on that connection seemed pretty far-fetched.

Which left?

The daughter.

Jones flipped through his bent pad to the notes he'd scribbled during his interview with Lucinda Caldwell.

They spelled out a weird family situation in which the daughter had a lot of reasons to bust her mother. Her mother had tried to hide the fact she had a daughter. Had kept her hidden away.

My mother was not a nice person, Lucinda Caldwell had told the detective in her hotel suite. *She always had to do everything her way. If you got in her way, she'd walk right over you.*

Didn't she hate her mother? Jones had asked.

No, Lucinda had insisted.

She was the only person in the world I've ever loved.

A. L. would never understand white folks.

Lucinda Caldwell had denied flat out that she'd busted her mother.

What was it she said?

I have worked out my feelings toward my mother in twenty-five years of therapy and twenty-five years of poetry.

Maybe so. But, to the detective, Lucinda Caldwell was emerging as his primary suspect. His only suspect, actually.

He needed to go back and talk some more to that woman.

"Hey, A. L."

The voice of Michelle, the Homicide dispatcher, carried to his desk.

"Yeah?"

"You on the bubble, ain't you?"

"Yeah," Jones acknowledged in a weary baritone.

"Got a nasty one for you, honey. Little girl was dropped in that playground on Stanton Road just off Suitland Parkway. Somebody used a blade on her real bad."

"On the way," A. L. grunted, heading for his car.

Lucinda Caldwell would have to wait.

CHAPTER THIRTY-FOUR

NED CHASEN PHONED Jane the next afternoon. His call came to the *Post's* booth in the White House pressroom. With nothing new to write on the Caldwell investigation, and the paper's more senior White House correspondents slipping away for early Christmas vacations, Jane had drawn Hammond duty.

"Jane Day? It's Ned Chasen. Still alive and kicking."

She recognized the old man's voice.

"You still interested in Carla Caldwell's testimony to Joe McCarthy? On the Hollywood blacklist?"

"Sure," she replied enthusiastically. Maybe a breakthrough, Jane hoped.

"When I got home last night, I remembered a friend of mine—he's gone now, he was a cameraman for the old Fox-Movietone—one time gave me a bunch of sixteen-millimeter newsfilm from stories he covered in the forties and fifties, as a memento. Truman, Eisenhower, Alger Hiss and Whittaker Chambers, and McCarthy's hearings. My son made me transfer them to VHS tapes. He said the film would deteriorate otherwise. Want to see the tape of McCarthy and Carla?"

"Absolutely."

Jane wasn't sure what the tape could reveal. But nothing else was panning out.

"Meet me at the Press Club bar at four o'clock. We'll have a drink. I'll lend you the tape."

"I can't," she replied. "I'm covering the White House and we won't get a lid until six o'clock, at the earliest."

"Oh," Chasen rasped.

He sounded disappointed. Jane wondered whether the real purpose of his call was to invite her to see the tape, or to invite her to see him.

They never get too old.

"I'll send a messenger to pick up the tape," Jane advised. "After I look at it, I'll meet you at the Press Club, maybe later this week, to return it. We'll have a drink then."

"Great!" Chasen exclaimed in what Jane envisioned was a cloud of cigarette smoke. "You make an old man feel frisky again."

How come she never made *young* men feel that way? Jane wondered.

She actually looked forward to hearing more of Chasen's stories from his heyday.

Jerry phoned late in the afternoon, ignoring yet again her instructions not to call her at work. He'd just awakened. When she told him about Ned Chasen's videotape, he insisted they watch it together on the big-screen TV at his apartment.

Jane guessed he was less interested in seeing her than he was in savoring the sight of Carla squirming in the witness chair.

She should take a cab to Rosslyn when she was finished for the day in the pressroom, Jerry directed. They'd watch the tape, discuss it over dinner; then he'd drop her at her apartment before going on to the studio for his midnight program.

She accepted.

He greeted her with an awkward hug and a peck on the cheek.

The first time Jerry had invited Jane to his place, the apartment had not been what she'd expected, which was a cross between a garishly overfurnished Las Vegas hotel suite and a dorm room at an all-men's college without maid service.

Instead, the apartment was sparely and tastefully furnished with what appeared to be very expensive contemporary European furniture. Subdued paintings hung here and there. Two welded metal sculptures rested on the high-gloss wooden floor in the living room.

The colors were all grays and muted taupes.

She had inadvertently insulted him on that first visit by exclaiming, "Jerry, it's beautiful! Who furnished it for you?"

He had looked hurt.

"*I* furnished it."

"*You* furnished it?"

"I furnished it. Are you hung up on the stereotype that middle-aged white conservative guys have no taste?"

"Sorry," she apologized sincerely.

On the subsequent, infrequent occasions when he invited her to his place, Jane had been careful to compliment him on his good taste. Indeed, with each visit, Jane's admiration grew for the quiet and soothing refuge he had created. It was so much better than her place. Thirty-five years old and still living in a postcollege efficiency with hand-me-down furniture and framed posters, she lamented to herself.

"How about a drink while we watch the video?" Jerry asked.

Jane requested white wine, and Jerry went to the gray-and-black tiled kitchen to fetch it.

One wall of the long living room–dining room was all glass and provided a spectacular view of Washington, D.C., across the Potomac.

It was too cold to admire the view from Jerry's wide balcony. But while he was pouring her a glass of wine from a bottle of very respectable California chardonnay he kept inside the refrigerator door, Jane pressed her nose against the glass.

She took in a panorama that included the Christmas lights decorating Key Bridge and Georgetown, the illuminated memorials to Lincoln and Washington on the far bank of the river, and the white wedding-cake dome of the Capitol in the distance. Off to the right, in the darkness, were the gray shapes of row upon row of grave markers in Arlington Cemetery.

"Wow," she breathed, as she did every time she looked out at his view.

Jerry came back with her wine and a frosted mug of Sam Adams lager for himself.

Would he ever ask her to share his wonderful apartment? Jane wondered. Would she accept?

Jerry slid open two smoked-glass doors concealing an electronic entertainment center: a TV screen six feet across, four huge speakers, a compact disc player, a VCR, assorted amplifiers and control panels, and shelves holding CDs and VHS tapes.

He popped Ned Chasen's tape into the VCR. He waved Jane to be seated on a sofa, covered in a rough-textured gray fabric, facing the TV screen. Jerry dropped down beside her, punching buttons on a remote-control device that looked slightly more complicated than Sammy's console at the All Talk Network.

At first the screen was filled only with shimmering dots. Then a picture emerged, a black-and-white scene she could barely make out. Periodically it faded to white nothingness. Black lines, apparently scratches on the original film, wavered from the top of the screen to the bottom. Eventually, Jane's eyes adjusted to the decayed newsreel footage, nearly fifty years old. The camera panned back and forth between a long table at which indistinct shapes of men in dark suits sat and a smaller table at which a lone woman could be seen over a forest of microphones.

Jane recognized the woman as a young Carla Caldwell.

Jerry punched buttons on the remote controller and gradually the muffled, scratchy sound track increased in volume. He tinkered with the bass and treble adjustments, trying to improve the sound quality.

". . . ever been a member of the Communist Party?"

Oh my God. Jane recognized McCarthy's sinister voice from a dozen TV documentaries.

The camera panned jerkily to Carla.

"My name is Carla Caldwell. My profession is acting. My loyalty is to the United States of America. And my mission is to make the United States of America a better place to live for all its citizens. Senator McCarthy, I detest your methods and I shall answer none of your questions."

The camera panned back to the men in the dark suits. But McCarthy's next words were obliterated by a burst of static on the old film.

Jane watched the screen transfixed. It was like being transported back in time. She'd heard her parents bitterly denounce Joe McCarthy so many times. She had often wished she had been around in those days, when America's liberals were united in their common hatred for the scowling demagogue.

Jane had expected Jerry to cheer for McCarthy. But he watched the tape in silence.

The only time he returned to his normal bluster was when she referred to McCarthy as a conservative.

"Typical," Jerry exclaimed. "That's how you people deal with conservative ideas you disagree with. You smear the advocates as the modern offspring of Joe McCarthy."

"You're *defending* Joe McCarthy?" Jane asked.

"Of course not," Jerry retorted. "But just because he was a bad egg doesn't mean there weren't communists in the movie industry and in the government in those days."

But for the most part they watched the tape without speaking.

Unable to browbeat Carla into pleading the Fifth Amendment or discussing her attendance at meetings of various obscure communist "front" organizations, McCarthy pressed her on the videotape to implicate others in Hollywood.

He went through a list of names—including Fran Turner, Jane noted.

In response, Carla reiterated her profession, her loyalty to America, and her mission to make it a better place.

"You realize, Miss Caldwell," McCarthy's voice growled through the speakers, "that by refusing to answer my questions you are leaving the implication that the fellow travelers I have named were, in fact, communist dupes. Is that the implication you intend to leave?"

Carla responded by reciting her litany again.

Finally, an obviously exasperated McCarthy dismissed the actress, waggling a stubby finger and telling her she ought to move to the Soviet Union if she loved communism so much.

"I understand you are Stalin's favorite movie star," the senator sneered.

"Sir, I believe you are a bully, without a single shred of human decency," Carla said on the sound track. The camera tracked her out of the hearing room.

Jane was amazed at how faithful Ned Chasen's memories had been of the scene he had witnessed almost a half century before.

The screen went black with a line of white dots down the edges, the sprocket holes of the old film.

Jerry raised his remote controller to click off the tape. Before he could, another scene flickered onto the screen. Apparently a second newsreel had been transferred to the same tape.

"Let's see what it is," Jane requested.

The second segment apparently had been filmed during a later portion of the hearing.

McCarthy's voice announced that the witness was Fran Turner.

The quality of the footage was so bad that Jane couldn't make out clearly what the then young actress looked like, except that she combed her dark hair in a great swirl that covered the right side of her face. She was dressed in a demure suit buttoned to the neck.

On the scratchy sound track, McCarthy grilled her about her membership in the Communist Party, her associates, and her attendance at subversive meetings.

Jane was surprised to hear Fran Turner's quivery voice deny every accusation. She didn't take the Fifth. She didn't question McCarthy's right to interrogate her. She flatly denied all his accusations.

"If you're so innocent, Miss Turner," McCarthy sneered,

"then why did your good friend and fellow traveler Carla Caldwell refuse to clear you when I asked her if she'd ever seen you at meetings of communist front organizations."

"I don't know why she didn't," Fran whimpered.

"I know why and you know why," McCarthy's voice thundered through the speakers. "Because you *were* at those meetings with your fellow communists. Carla Caldwell saw you there and she knows better than to lie to a committee of the United States Senate. That's why she wouldn't clear your name when she had the chance. That's right, isn't it?"

"No! It isn't! I never went to those kinds of meetings. I never belonged to any organizations. Carla knows that. I don't know why she won't say so. I don't . . ."

The woman on the screen dropped her head, apparently weeping.

The picture flared into a fuzzy white blob. They waited for the hearing to resume. But the tape was over.

Jane and Jerry stared at the blank screen, trying to understand what they'd seen.

"Fran's career was destroyed because Carla refused to say she'd never seen her at a meeting," Jane said softly.

"Maybe McCarthy was right for once," Jerry suggested. "Maybe Fran was involved with left-wingers in Hollywood and Carla knew better than to lie on the stand."

"Did Fran Turner look to you like a woman who was hiding her associations?"

"She was an actress."

"You think she was acting?" Jane asked.

"Probably not," Jerry conceded.

"Fran Turner was ruined because Carla wanted to be a heroine in Hollywood by giving her little speech and not answering any questions from McCarthy," Jane said. "Carla could have cleared Fran, but she wouldn't."

"Carla saved her own career from the blacklist and sank Fran Turner's career," Jerry added.

After a lifetime of hearing Carla Caldwell virtually deified by her parents, Jane now began to see a different aspect of the actress.

And she began to see some other things as well.

"Fran Turner was in Washington for the Honors ceremony," Jane told Jerry.

"Really? How do you know that?"

"A TV actress she once taught paid for her trip," Jane explained. "I tried to interview her for my profile of Carla, but I couldn't reach her. After the murder, I called her again. She'd checked out of her hotel. But the editor of her hometown paper says he thinks she's still in Washington."

"And from the film we just saw, Fran may have harbored a grudge against Carla," Jerry verbalized her speculation. "A long, festering grudge."

Jane nodded.

"If you say 'I told you so,' I'm out of here," she declared.

He suppressed the urge.

"I've got to find her!" Jane exclaimed. "Have you got the yellow pages?"

They agreed to skip dinner out.

While Jerry cooked them a simple meal of pasta with pesto sauce and a tomato salad, Jane sat in the black leather chair at his glass-topped trestle desk and relentlessly dialed one hotel after the other.

By the time Jerry uncorked a bottle of cabernet sauvignon and announced that dinner was served, she had phoned three dozen hotels. Neither Fran Turner nor Francis Anklum was registered at any of them.

When it was time for Jerry to take her home so he could

get to the radio studio on time, he nuzzled her head against his chest.

Jane liked that.

"You'll find her," he assured her.

CHAPTER THIRTY-FIVE

F RAN TURNER WAS registered at the Premier Hotel on Virginia Avenue under the name Annie Muldoon. She had played a character by that name in a 1940s movie whose plot she had long since forgotten. She had always liked the name.

After what happened to Carla, Fran was upset and unsure what to do. She couldn't impose on Traci's generosity by remaining in the expensive Watergate Hotel. She couldn't see any particular reason to go back to Kentucky. But she didn't know anyone in Washington. She didn't even know her way around anymore.

So the morning after Carla's death, Fran packed her bag and walked out of the Watergate without any real plan in mind. At the bottom of the hotel driveway, she spotted the Premier Hotel directly across the street. She ambled across and checked in. She didn't know exactly why she decided to register under a fictitious name.

Fran had money. She'd brought more than a thousand

dollars to Washington, some of it in her purse but most of it wrapped in a hankie and pinned inside her bra. She hadn't had any real plan when she'd left Kentucky, either. But she thought she might need money. So she brought the bills she had accumulated little by little over the years and kept hidden inside an old pair of boots in her closet back in Covington.

She hadn't strayed far from the Premier during the week, taking her meals in the hotel coffee shop and strolling along the Potomac in the direction of the Teddy Roosevelt Bridge when it wasn't too cold. Mostly, though, she stayed in her room and watched old movies on TV.

Now it was Saturday, the day before the memorial service for Carla at the Kennedy Center.

And Fran was still trying to decide what to do. She would go, of course. After all, she had probably known Carla longer than almost anyone else in the world. They had met more than sixty years ago. They had been friends when they first came to Hollywood. Or *friendly rivals,* as the movie magazines and gossip columnists liked to portray them back then.

Before this trip, Fran had not seen Carla in person for almost fifty years, since the day of the hearing.

The day Fran's career ended.

Over the decades, she had followed Carla's exploits in both the movies and politics. She had even cut out stories about Carla. And then, two weeks ago, thanks to Traci, she had been at the Kennedy Center to see Carla receive the highest award an entertainer could get.

Of course Fran would attend the memorial service.

First, she had to decide what to wear. And what to say.

"You cannot go to the memorial service tomorrow!" Grady Hammond advised her husband, the President, in their private living quarters on the third floor of the White House.

"Now, Grady."

" 'Now Grady.' That's what you always say when you intend to ignore me, Dale," the First Lady said exasperatedly. "You cannot go. Barely two weeks ago, that woman stood right in this house"—she pointed downward, in the direction of the East Room—"and insulted you. She called you a fascist here in your own house!"

"Grady, the woman was brutally murdered," the President tried to reason with his wife. "Whether you agree with her politics or whether she agreed with my politics, she was a national treasure. That's what the Kennedy Center Medal certified. She was honored for her lifetime achievement as an entertainer. One ill-considered outburst can't wipe that out."

" 'One ill-considered outburst'? She spent her lifetime crusading against every principle you stand for, Dale. I didn't wish her ill. I'm sorry she was killed. But you shouldn't sanction her beliefs and her insult by your presence at the memorial service."

"A president is supposed to heal, Grady. He's supposed to bring people together."

"I guarantee you, Dale, if you attend the service for that woman, you're going to turn off the conservatives in this country. You're not going to bring people together. You're going to divide people."

"What do you think, Garvin?" the President asked his press secretary, who had been watching uncomfortably while Dale and Grady argued.

"I'm sure he agrees with *me*," the First Lady said.

"Well," Garvin Dillon began, stalling for time. He hated it when they asked him to be referee. "Let's split the difference. I don't think you should go—"

"See!" Grady said triumphantly.

"—because there will be a lot of Carla's friends there

and, frankly, sir, they might boo you. We don't want to give the TV nets that sound bite."

"Hmmm," the President commented noncommittally.

"You can issue a written statement, expressing regret at the untimely death of a great actress," the press secretary proposed, "and challenging Hollywood to honor her memory by producing more quality, family films. That way, you get the last word."

"Yes!" the First Lady exclaimed. "I like it!"

"All right," the President agreed. "That's what we'll do."

Garvin Dillon descended in the wood-paneled private elevator to the ground floor, walked through the glass-enclosed corridor bordering the Rose Garden to his office, and began writing the President's statement.

When he became burned out as press secretary, Garvin thought he might ask the President to appoint him as a diplomatic negotiator. He had the experience.

Senator Oscar O'Malley never had any doubts about attending Carla's memorial service the next day.

For one thing, he was one of the congressional members of the Kennedy Center's board of trustees. It would be perfectly natural for him to be there, sitting in the trustees box.

His election consultant, Richard Morrisey, had conducted a public opinion poll and found that Carla's criticism of the President for trying to impose censorship on movies and TV was viewed favorably by 56 percent of the public and unfavorably by 34 percent, with the rest undecided.

Therefore, Morrisey recommended, it would be good politics for O'Malley to be seen at the memorial service, but not to speak. It would soften his image, keep voters from perceiving him as hard right, but without alienating conservatives.

And his finance director had gleefully advised the senator that attending Carla's memorial service would encourage Hollywood contributors to write checks for his presidential campaign fund when the time came.

More worrisome was his general counsel's report of fending off a D.C. homicide detective who had barged into O'Malley's office demanding to talk to the senator about Carla's murder. And that *Washington Post* reporter's eerie question about a photo with Carla forty years before.

Were they onto his secret?

O'Malley swiveled in his chair and stared through the tall windows of his private hideaway office in the Capitol at the sparse Saturday night traffic on the Mall.

Beyond the Washington Monument, beyond the Lincoln Memorial, he could make out the faintly illuminated Lee-Custis mansion atop a hill in Arlington National Cemetery. Nearby was buried his brother, the martyred peace negotiator.

The senator could not see the White House from here, at the other end of Pennsylvania Avenue. The White House, where that weakling Hammond now resided. Where Oscar O'Malley would soon reside.

The real reason he was going to the memorial service, the senator acknowledged to himself in the dark private office, was his bittersweet memory of that summer when he, the Princeton student, and Carla Caldwell, the famous movie actress, had made love so passionately in her suite at the Hay-Adams.

He had been bewildered at first when she did not contact him at the end of the summer, as she promised she would. Bewildered and then brokenhearted.

And later angry.

And finally, accepting.

And, eventually, eager to keep their affair a secret lest it hurt his presidential aspirations.

Now Carla was dead. Murdered. Their secret had died with her.

He could go to the memorial service and no one would make any connection.

Lucinda Caldwell, in her suite at the Watergate Hotel, was struggling over what to say at her mother's memorial service.

Really, she was struggling over how she felt about her mother's death.

She already had talked twice by phone with her therapist in Beverly Hills.

Now she dialed the therapist's home number a third time.

"It's okay for you to feel angry at your mother," the therapist said soothingly.

"I don't feel angry anymore," Lucinda told her. "I feel . . ."

She didn't know how to finish the sentence.

"Guilty?" the therapist prompted.

"Well . . . ?"

"Why do you feel guilty?" the therapist asked.

"I *don't* feel guilty."

"What do you feel?"

"Afraid."

"Why afraid?"

"She took care of me all my life. Who's going to take care of me now?"

"You're going to take care of yourself."

"Oh," Lucinda said uncertainly.

"Does that frighten you?" the therapist asked.

"A little."

"Why?"

"I miss my mother," Lucinda said simply.

"Your mother wasn't always good to you."

"I know."

"She didn't even acknowledge your existence for a long time."

"I know."

"She kept you hidden. She sent you away to school. She gave you a made-up name. She never let you see your father."

"I know."

"How does that make you feel?"

Silence.

"A little bit like *Mommie Dearest?*" the Beverly Hills shrink prodded. "A little bit like *Places in the Heart?*"

"I never meant to hurt her."

"Hurt her how?"

"By, you know, by . . ." Lucinda's voice trailed off.

"By just being? By complicating her life? By reminding her of someone she might want to forget? Or by secretly hating her? Is that how you think you hurt her?"

"I guess."

They talked for another hour, and when she hung up, Lucinda Caldwell still didn't know how she felt about her mother's death or what she was going to say at the memorial service.

A. L. Jones heard about the memorial service on the 6 P.M. news Saturday.

He knew he should be there.

Sometimes murderers showed up at the funerals or memorial services of their victims. Sick, but it happened.

He'd attend and keep his eyes open.

But this evening, on a rare Saturday off, he, LaTroy, and Shaneta were heading out for Christmas shopping and pizza.

Afterward, A. L. dropped the boy off at a friend's house to spend the night.

"You stay out of trouble, hear?" he admonished LaTroy.

"I *hear,*" the boy replied.

"You ain't going nowhere?" A. L. asked.

"No, man, we ain't going nowhere," LaTroy assured him. "We going to watch basketball on TV. Shaq's my man!"

"Michael going to whip his ass!" LaTroy's friend exclaimed. The two boys wrestled good-naturedly.

A. L. and Shaneta headed for Kaffa House, on U Street, for some jazz.

At 3 A.M., back in his apartment, Jones turned on the TV for company while he got ready for bed.

The title of an old movie starring Carla Caldwell rolled across the screen. The detective sat down to watch. They must be running it to cash in on all the publicity about her death, he figured.

After about thirty minutes, A. L. heard something on the sound track that confirmed his hunch that he might be able to ice this case at the memorial service the next day.

CHAPTER THIRTY-SIX

THE MEMORIAL SERVICE for Carla Caldwell was staged in the Kennedy Center Opera House, the same red-walled theater where the Honors show had taken place exactly two weeks before. Backstage, the dressing room where the actress had been stabbed to death was still locked and sealed with yellow police tape.

On the stage, while the audience for the service filed in, a quintet consisting of Peter, Paul and Mary, Joan Baez, and Pete Seeger sang and strummed antiwar songs and civil rights songs from the sixties and union organizing songs from the thirties.

Jane scurried back and forth between the foyer and the theater, scribbling furiously in her reporter's notebook.

Jerry sat morosely in the last seat of the last row of the orchestra. He hadn't wanted to come, protesting that people might see him there and assume—wrongly—that he had softened his disapproval of Carla and her causes.

But Jane had insisted that he attend to provide her with moral support. It was going to be an emotional day for her. She still shuddered whenever she recalled pushing open Carla's dressing-room door and finding the actress slumped over her makeup table, gasping her last breaths.

Jerry scooted down in the red plush seat and hoped no one would notice him.

A. L. was backstage, peeking through the curtains. The crowd filled most of the orchestra, he noted.

The detective spotted Lucinda Caldwell in the center of the front row, dressed in a simple black dress. She stared straight ahead, no expression on her face. She did not speak to the people around her. A. L. guessed they didn't even know who she was.

Jones took no notice of Fran Anklum sitting in an aisle seat in the front row, dressed in a plain gray suit. The old woman bore no resemblance to the young movie actress Fran Turner he'd seen costarring with Carla Caldwell in the 3 A.M. TV movie.

Ducking under the lenses of network TV cameras, Jane sidled down the curving red wall to the front of the theater so she could write down the names of the VIPs who were sitting in the boxes.

She saw that Dale and Grady Hammond were not in the presidential box in the center of the curving balcony. No surprise. Instead, the President had sent some middle-level White House aides and a woman Jane recognized as his liaison to the arts community, whatever that meant, as well as Charlton Heston.

Was he the only conservative in show business? It seemed that way to Jane. He was always trotted out by the Hammonds on occasions like this. He and Arnold Schwarzenegger.

The reporter scanned the box next to the presidential box. Senator O'Malley was there in his capacity as a trustee, along with several corporate CEOs and wives of corporate CEOs. They had been appointed to the Kennedy Center board by the President as their reward for generous campaign contributions, Jane noted in her pad.

The lights dimmed, hushing the audience. A screen unrolled from above the stage.

Carla was the star of her own memorial service, as she would have wanted it.

On the screen flashed a collection of film clips of Carla's most famous scenes, dating all the way back to her role as the young Maud Jones in *A Child Shall Lead Them* during the depression.

Jane was entranced by the clips.

One of the scenes jerked her to attention.

It was from an old black-and-white movie, *Forgive Her Trespasses,* in which Carla played a secretary having an adulterous affair with her boss. In the scene, another actress, playing the wife, stabbed the secretary in a fit of jealous rage. As Carla's character bled to death, the camera zoomed in to catch her last, murmured words, "I hope she will forgive me."

Those were the same words the real Carla had whispered to Jane in the dressing room just before she died!

What did it mean? Had the actress been trying to tell Jane the identity of her murderer?

Before the reporter could figure it out, another scene from Carla's movie career appeared on the screen.

A. L. Jones, now leaning against the chest-high railing at the back of the opera house, had also heard and recognized the words Carla spoke on the screen. They were the same words the dying actress had whispered to Jane Day in the dressing room. And the detective had heard those words uttered again the night before in the late movie on TV, *Forgive Her Trespasses.*

The puzzle pieces were going together now.

After the video retrospective of Carla's career, Lena Horne walked on stage with the choir from Zion AME Church.

They sang "Amazing Grace" without accompaniment.

Jane heard sobs from the audience. She was crying herself.

Jerry, in the last row, snorted. Using the old hymn to generate a cheap emotional response. That really was too much. Most of the people seated in this theater, he fumed, devoted their professional lives to cranking out movies and TV shows that denigrated Americans who genuinely believed in the message of hymns.

Jerry burrowed deeper into his chair. He hadn't been surrounded by so many liberals since NOW picketed his radio show.

The rest of the service consisted of eulogies from a parade of Carla's friends from show business and politics.

Jesse Jackson. Eugene McCarthy. Katharine Hepburn. Arthur Miller. Jimmy Carter. Paul Newman.

One by one, they rose from their places in the audience, mounted the stage, and told stories about Carla Caldwell. Some were funny, some were touching, some were self-serving.

After Paul Newman, Lucinda uncertainly climbed the steps to the stage.

"I'm Lucinda Caldwell, Carla's daughter," she said nervously, leaning too close to the microphone.

The audience grew still.

"Uh . . . I want to thank you all so much for coming.

Uh . . . my mother would have enjoyed being the center of so much attention."

Some attendees chuckled.

"Uh . . . all I want to say is that my mother lived a long and productive life. Sometimes she did things that . . . uh . . . she shouldn't have done, and some people didn't like her for those things, including myself, sometimes."

Oscar O'Malley leaned forward against the railing of his box and stared down at Lucinda. He hadn't known that Carla's daughter existed until the *Post* story after the murder. The memorial service was the first time he'd seen her. It was like looking at the face of his dead sister Beth. The resemblance was uncanny.

The daughter looked so much like . . .

O'Malley suddenly felt dizzy. He grasped the rail.

The newspaper said Lucinda Caldwell was forty-three years old. That meant she was born in '54 or '55. His and Carla's summer romance had been in '54.

Was Lucinda his daughter?

The senator flopped back in his crimson plush chair. He emitted a moan.

The woman sitting next to him patted him consolingly on the shoulder. She thought O'Malley was overcome by grief for Carla.

He was not thinking of Carla. He was thinking of his presidential hopes. If Lucinda was his daughter . . . how could she *not* be . . . the press would find out. How *would* they find out? They found out *everything*. He couldn't run now, could he? But he *had* to . . . the old man . . . No, it was too much of a risk. The press . . .

"No matter what she did that wasn't always nice, I will miss my mother," Lucinda concluded her tribute. "I know you all will miss her, too. Uh . . . I guess that's all I have to say."

She returned to her seat, shaking slightly after her un-accustomed public appearance.

Taking notes, Jane recorded that Lucinda's halting re-marks had produced tears throughout the audience.

Jack Valenti, the dapper old LBJ aide who had been the movie industry's chief lobbyist in Washington for decades, was scheduled to be the concluding speaker.

But after Valenti, a woman on the aisle in the front row in a plain gray suit stood and walked onto the stage.

"My name is Francis Anklum and at one time I was a very good friend of Carla Caldwell," she announced in a surprisingly strong voice for such an old woman. "Some of you may remember me from the movies. My name then was Fran Turner."

There was a buzz in the audience.

"I didn't even know she was still alive," A. L. heard someone whisper.

Backstage, a woman who was in charge of the memorial service studied the program. No Francis Anklum or Fran Turner was listed among the eulogizers.

"That was me in the movie scene with Carla," Fran explained, "where she was stabbed by the jealous wife. I played the wife."

The audience stirred. Something seemed a little off in this unscheduled eulogy.

A. L. edged down the side wall toward the stage.

"Carla and I were rivals off the screen, too," Fran recalled. "Rivals for the best parts, for the handsomest men—and the richest—for the most favorable reviews and the most flattering photos in the fan magazines. Carla was more famous, but I do believe I was the better actress."

Jane scribbled, trying to get every word. Something was happening. She didn't know yet what it was.

"My career as an actress ended on February twenty-third, 1952," Fran said, her voice dropping. "That was the day Carla and I testified before Senator Joseph McCarthy about what he called communist subversives in the movies. He accused me of attending meetings of communist organizations and of associating with people who were communists."

She paused and stared out at the audience.

"I never attended those meetings!" she declared forcefully. "I never was a communist or a communist sympathizer or anything like that! Carla knew that. She knew I was just a country girl from Covington, Kentucky. I barely understood what a communist was. When we were waiting to shoot a scene sometimes, I would ask Carla what all the fuss was about."

She took a deep breath and continued.

"McCarthy didn't believe my denials. He didn't believe them because when he asked Carla about me, she wouldn't tell him that I had never participated in that stuff. She wouldn't answer *any* of his questions because she wanted to make her little speech about him having no legitimate right to question her. When he asked her about me, she had the chance to clear my name. But she wouldn't answer. To make her point, she wouldn't answer. To make her point, she let me go down."

A producer in the third row turned to his actress wife and raised an eyebrow quizzically. What was going on here?

"I never got another movie role after that day," Fran continued in a low voice. "They called it the blacklist."

Some in the audience nodded. They knew about the blacklist. A few had been on it.

"Friends were afraid to be seen with me. I tried to call Carla. But she never returned my calls. After a while, I went home to Covington and I've been there ever since. I taught drama at the community college until I retired. Maybe some of you out there were my students."

Fran shielded her eyes against the spotlights.

There was a nervous titter in the audience. Something was definitely off here.

"I never saw Carla in person again. Until two weeks ago today, at the Kennedy Center gala. I saw Carla being honored for her achievements. I don't know what happened. I was overwhelmed. By forty-five years of anger and hate. That could have been me. For my achievements. Only I didn't have any achievements. Because Carla wouldn't tell McCarthy I never went to those meetings. To make her point."

She was speaking faster and faster, more incoherently.

A. L. was at the front of the theater, next to the stage.

"I went back to her dressing room after the show. I don't know why. I didn't . . . She was nasty. Worse than she used to be. She told me to leave. She said she had to get ready for the dinner. She wouldn't listen to me. She wouldn't even look at me. She kept staring at herself in the mirror. I hated her! A letter opener. It was there. And then somehow I was holding it. In my mind, it seemed like we were back on the movie set. *Forgive Her Trespasses*. I stabbed her. I killed her. Like in the movie."

The audience gasped.

A. L. climbed the steps to the stage.

"I hated her!" Fran cried. "She took my life from me! Now we're even!"

A. L. put his arm around her waist and gently pulled her away.

"I hope she will forgive me."

Fran Turner delivered the curtain line of her greatest scene, and disappeared into the wings.

CHAPTER THIRTY-SEVEN

T WO HOURS LATER, A. L. Jones returned to the Kennedy Center to clean up the loose ends.

Getting out of his dirty vanilla car in the driveway, Jones encountered Jerry Knight.

"You just getting here?" the detective inquired.

"No, I saw it all," Jerry replied. "I'm just getting back. I walked to the hotel for a drink while I waited for Jane to file her copy."

"Big story for your girlfriend," A. L. commented.

"That's what she lives for," Jerry said, nodding.

"She don't live for *you?*" the detective chuckled.

"Sometimes she doesn't even live on the same *planet* with me," Jerry joked.

They went inside and found Jane sitting in the last row of the opera house, just closing her cellular phone.

"Did you charge Fran Turner?" Jane demanded of A. L.

"Not yet," he replied in his deep voice. "Sent her over to St. E's for psychiatric evaluation."

"How long?" Jane asked, writing it all down in her notebook.

"Maybe forever. Her age, they might never let her out. She's nutty as a fruitcake."

"No wonder," Jerry chimed in. "To make herself look good to her Hollywood buddies, Carla let Joe McCarthy destroy Fran. Fran saw Carla getting that big award, she flipped out."

"When did you know it was Fran?" Jane asked A. L.

"They ran that movie the two of them made together last night, and when I heard that line, 'I hope she will forgive me,' I started thinking maybe Carla was trying to tell you something before she died. Then, when Fran Turner walked out there on the stage and started talking all that stuff about Carla hanging her out to dry, I put it together."

"So you think Carla was trying to let me know Fran was the one who stabbed her when she whispered that line from the movie?" Jane asked.

"We won't never know," A. L. answered. "But seems like she was trying to tell you the same person popped her in real life as popped her in the movie."

"I never picked up on it," Jane said.

Miracle. The newsie admitted she didn't know something.

"Why didn't anybody see Fran backstage after the gala?" Jane asked.

"Who knows?" A. L. shrugged. "Mousy-looking old lady. Nobody paid any attention to her, I guess. Some people look right through old folks like they ain't there."

"Did you have any other suspects?" Jerry asked.

"About the same ones as you two, I guess."

"Lucinda?"

"Yeah, that was one."

"What's going to happen to her?" Jane asked.

"If she didn't pop her mama, she ain't my problem," the detective answered. "She'll go home, live her life, I guess."

"She doesn't seem very well prepared for life," Jane commented.

"Who the hell is?" Jones rumbled.

"O'Malley?" Jerry asked.

"For a while, seemed like he had the motive. But he didn't do it."

"Is he Lucinda's father?" Jerry asked.

"Who knows? Who cares? You had him on your program, Mr. Night Talker. Why didn't you ask him if he was?"

A. L. stood up and shambled toward the exit.

"See you soon, Detective Jones," Jane called after him.

"I hope not," A. L. growled.

Jerry and Jane sat in silence for a time, spent by the emotion of the day and of the last two weeks.

"What are you going to do now?" Jerry asked finally.

"I've got to go to the paper and do some rewriting."

"Then?"

"No plans."

"When you're done, come over. I've got no show tonight. I'll make you dinner at my place."

She accepted.

CHAPTER THIRTY-EIGHT

AT THE *POST*, Jane rewrote the story she had dictated by phone, smoothing it out, adding additional details, including her personal involvement.

Then she went home to her apartment in Adams Morgan. She showered, changed into a full skirt and bulky sweater that she believed hid her ample hips, fed Bloomsbury a can of tuna, and listened to her voice-mail messages.

One was from her mother, Mavis, expressing satisfaction over the news that the police had caught the person who murdered Carla Caldwell.

The other message was from Sheldon Berman, the Hollywood producer.

Jane! I just saw the news on CNN about Fran Turner confessing to killing Carla! Unbelievable!

He sounded breathless.

Listen, forget about "The Cancer Conversion." I'm postponing that project. The hottest thing going is "The Carla Cald-

well Story." I want to make that movie! And I want you to write it. You were part of it. God, the promotional opportunities are fantastic. I'm already talking to Shirley MacLaine's people about her playing Carla. And I've got a call in to Glenn Close's agent for the Fran Turner part. This has Academy Award written all over it, Jane. I know you're going to want more money because this is such a hot property. How's three hundred thousand for the script? You keep the fifty K I sent you and I'll FedEx you another hundred today. And another one hundred fifty K when the script is finished. I'll pay a screenwriter to work with you. Okay? We've got to move fast, Jane. There'll be five Carla Caldwell projects in development by tomorrow. I want to start shooting in six weeks. Call me!

But Jane went out and caught a cab on Eighteenth Street without returning the producer's call.

She wanted to tell Jerry her decision first.

CHAPTER THIRTY-NINE

He handed her a glass of chilled chardonnay when she came through the door of his apartment.

Jerry had set the slate dining table with gray place mats, smoky glass dishes, and black-handled stainless-steel cutlery.

Dinner was, again, pasta with pesto sauce and a tomato salad.

"I don't know how to make anything else," Jerry confessed.

She laughed and squeezed his hand.

"It's just what I was in the mood for."

He had set the table so she faced the great glass wall with the breathtaking view of Washington on a clear winter night.

During dinner they rehashed the events of the past two weeks, bickering over whether Carla deserved what she got because of her long-ago refusal to clear Fran of McCarthy's accusations.

"Carla's life demonstrated that a little bit of acting talent, a lot of money, a huge ego, and good intentions didn't make her immune to misguided political ideas," Jerry asserted. "Didn't make her immune to a weak moral compass, either."

"I still think, overall, she did more good in her life than harm," Jane protested.

"Tell that to Fran Turner."

Jerry kidded Jane good-naturedly about her failure to understand the clue Carla had whispered to her with her dying breath.

"Some investigative reporter you are," he twitted.

He cleared the dishes and carried them to the kitchen.

They decided to wait awhile for dessert, mango sorbet.

Jane signaled him to pour her another glass of the white wine.

The time had come. She had to tell him.

"I had a call on my voice mail tonight from Sheldon Berman," Jane began.

"Yeah?" Jerry replied warily.

He unwrapped the one cigar a day his doctor allowed him, opening the sliding glass door to the balcony a crack to let the smoke out.

"He doesn't want me to write that movie now," she informed him.

"I told you so!" Jerry exulted. "They're flakes out there. You can't trust them."

"He wants me to write *another* movie, about Carla and Fran. For twice as much money. Three hundred thousand dollars for the script."

"That's real money," Jerry acknowledged.

"I'm not going for the money," Jane insisted.

"But you're going."

"I'm going for the challenge. I'm bored with daily journalism. I can write. And if I write for the movies, serious topics, I can reach a much larger audience with my ideas than I can at the *Post.*"

"You mean your *liberal* ideas?"

It was his same old shtick. But it sounded halfhearted.

"Maybe I won't like it," she suggested unconvincingly. "Maybe I'll be back in three months."

"You'll fit in perfectly in Hollywood," Jerry said with more bitterness than she had anticipated. "You and all the other naive liberals out there."

"You've been trying to convert me without success for two years," Jane reminded him. "Probably too late now."

"And I was going to win a certificate from the Heritage Foundation if I brought you around," he joked to hide his dejection.

"You originate your show from L.A. two weeks a year," Jane reminded him. "I'll see you then."

"Yeah, right," he replied sarcastically. "You don't want your *Washington Post* friends to know you know me. You're going to want your Hollywood friends to know you know me?"

Jerry went to the kitchen for the sorbet.

Life had taught him that the moment had arrived when he must accept the fact that he had lost the long argument to keep Jane from going to Hollywood. He had learned to be a gracious loser at such moments.

"I'll miss our discussions," Jerry said resignedly when he returned with the dessert, "even though you are incredibly wrongheaded in your thinking."

"I'll miss our discussions, too," Jane said, "even though your views date from the Hoover administration."

"You'll listen to my show every night, won't you, to keep in touch with the real world?"

"Well, maybe every *other* night. At least once a month, for sure. And you'll see my movie, right?"

"I'll probably wait for it to come out on tape."

"You're a nasty man."

"I try."

They picked at their sorbet.

"I'll miss you," Jerry said simply.

"I'm waiting for the joke."

"No joke."

"I'll miss you, too. Jerry . . ."

She had promised herself she wouldn't cry. But she couldn't help it. The tears flooded out of the corners of her big green eyes, rolled down her cheeks, and splashed on the slate tabletop, leaving dark stains.

"Three hundred thousand dollars, a chance to break out of daily journalism and into screenwriting, a famous producer courting me, movie stars reading my lines," Jane sniffled, "and I *still* almost told him no because I want to be with you."

"I'm flattered," Jerry replied, the acerbity barely discernible. "The worst part is, if I were you, I would say yes, too. When I was younger, I was burning up with ambition. Plenty of times I left friends behind, wonderful colleagues, generous employers, just walked away from them to jump to the next rung up the ladder. So I understand."

"I'm *not* walking away from you!" she wailed. "I don't want this to be the end of us!"

"I know."

Jerry got up, came around behind her chair, bent down, and hugged her.

"I know."

"Can't you originate your show from L.A. more often?" Jane wept. "One week a month? One week every two months?"

"Yes."

"Will you?"

"Yes. A week every two months. Even to see you, that's as often as I can stand the place."

"What do you mean?" she choked, crying and laughing at the same time now. "You'll *love* the chance to demolish those Hollywood liberals."

"Yeah!"

Gradually she stopped crying.

"Want to spend the night here?" Jerry asked.

"Yes."

He rose, gathered up the wine bottle and two glasses, and guided her to the bedroom.

There, another glass wall presented the spectacular Washington panorama.

With the lights out, Jane felt like she was floating in the air above the city.

"You think that by being great in bed tonight you can persuade me not to go to Hollywood, right?" she wisecracked to relieve her nervousness.

"Right."

"Well?" Jerry asked her later.

"Hmmmmmm," Jane sighed contentedly.

"Did I change your mind?" he persisted.

"Not yet," she murmured, nuzzling against his chest. "But I'm going to give you another chance."

"Yeah?"

"Yeah. Three weeks from tonight. My cottage. Beverly Hills Hotel. Be there."

"Okay."

She sat up in bed.

"You will?"

"Sure. But if I'm going to visit you in Hollywood, don't you think I ought to rehearse my performance?"

"Practice makes perfect!" Jane giggled.

They clutched each other and completely ignored the fabulous view.